LONE HUNTER

a novel by

D. F. BAILEY

COPYRIGHT NOTICE

ACKNOWLEDGEMENTS

I am extremely grateful to Lawrence Russell and Rick Gibbs for reading the early versions of *Lone Hunter.* Their insights, wisdom and advice were invaluable to me as I worked through several drafts of the novel. — DFB

For more information about D. F. Bailey and to subscribe to his free newsletter, "Digital Words," visit dfbailey.com.

One billion dollars.

Two killers.

Three ways to die.

※

Inspired by true events.

LONE HUNTER

CHAPTER ONE

APRIL HAD COME and gone, yet winter still held young Alexei Malinin in its grip. He leaned against a denuded birch tree, the bark stripped up to the lowest limbs by ravenous deer. The snow rose over the tops of his leather boots, and his wool mittens, a Christmas gift from his Baba Tatiana, were clotted with ice above his knuckles. He tugged the parka hood over his hat and shivered.

Along the trapline stood the first of six snares he'd set with his grandfather, Ded Vitaly. The wire contraption consisted of a thin strand of steel tied to the base of a birch tree, then buried under the snow up to the fist-sized noose that Ded Vitaly had twisted into shape and set against two twigs peeled from a limb of the tree. They'd baited the front and back of the trap with raw carrot shavings.

"Don't touch the bait with your bare hands," Ded Vitaly had warned him, his breath spiraling from his mouth in long scrolls. "If the rabbits, or any other creatures can smell you, they'll high-tail it out of here. Then we all go hungry."

"They can smell people, Ded?"

"Their mothers teach them. Just like Mat teaches you,

yes?"

Alexei thought about the lessons that parents can teach their children. Before he'd died, Alexei's father had taught him what he called the most important rule of the hunter: "When you kill an animal, do it quickly and in one blow. Never add to its suffering."

All fine and good, Alexei thought as he curled his freezing fingers into the palms of his hands. But now that he stood here alone, stood here watching the white hare struggling in the wire noose, how was he to do it? How to bring this swift and merciful death to the animal twitching in utter exhaustion before him?

But he knew the answer. When enough time had passed, when he understood the terror in the animal's eyes — and after he realized that if he released this wounded creature from the snare he would condemn it to a horrible death in the teeth of a fox or wolf — then Alexei unbuttoned his parka and from the holster on his belt he drew the Nagant pistol that Ded Vitaly had given him that morning after breakfast. His feet rose and fell through the heavy snowpack as he approached the hare. He counted the eleven steps that carried him within inches of the animal. He pointed the barrel of the pistol at the creature's soaking head. He saw the thin sheen of ice that coated the whiskers stemming from the hare's snout. The animal was already half frozen to death. Then Alexei paused, cocked the weapon and murmured a brief prayer.

"You have been given to me and it is right that I should take you."

He fired the Nagant and the recoil snapped his hand backward. Immediately a second — accidental — round discharged into the gray winter sky. He felt the air compress as the stray bullet passed his cheek. In the hills above the open field behind him he heard both shots echo twice: *CRACK-crack, CRACK-crack.*

"That could have been you!" He brushed his cheek with his mitten and checked it for blood. Nothing. "Lucky." He admonished himself and swore to be more careful next time.

Then he drew the game bag from his backpack, leaned over and extracted the hare from the wire snare. He took a few seconds to inspect where the bullet had penetrated the skull and then set the carcass in the hopsack. He took another moment to consider how he felt. His first kill on his own; it should seem special he thought. But since he couldn't feel much more than the cold in his hands and feet, he reset the trap, set fresh bait on both sides of the wire noose and moved up the trap line to the next snare.

An hour later he'd taken three rabbits from the snares. He moved along the forest edge keeping the snow-covered pasture on his left. The cold had numbed his arms and legs now and he knew enough not to let the chill enter his chest and belly. Another ten minutes, he decided, and he would turn back to the dacha.

As he approached the fourth trap he hesitated. Was someone ahead of him? A poacher pulling something from the snare? He stood at the side of a fir tree and studied the thief from the distance. He could make out someone in a dark coat leaning over his prey, tugging hungrily at the dead creature. Alexei gripped the pistol in his hand and wondered what to do.

3

Rather than shoot first, he should call out to the poacher. Maybe he could explain himself, explain this brazen theft.

"Hey, you! That's my trap you're messing with!"

The figure stood, turned to face him with a brief snarl.

A bear.

Alexei felt his heart stop, then beat in double-time as a burst of adrenalin pulsed through his body. He stood his ground and leveled the pistol at the beast. A moment of silence passed between them, a hesitation in which Alexei tried to guess the distance to the bear and wondered if the three shots left in the Nagant could save him if the bear attacked. More important, could he steady his hand and wait for the bear to charge within a meter of his shaking body — and then fire all three shots into the beast's snarling mouth?

The bear lifted his nose to the wind. His nostrils flared, his long tongue licked a spittle of blood from his snout. He appeared to be considering a decision. After some hesitation he returned his attention to the raw feast laying in the snow at his feet.

Alexei took a backward step. Then another. When he'd retraced his path to the big fir tree near the third trap, he turned and began to plod forward through the snow, setting his feet into the foot holes he'd created during the trek out to the forest. After twenty minutes he felt his body relax and the fear subside. The encounter now seemed more like a dream than a threat. Had it really happened? Yes. If the bear had charged him could he have killed it? Yes, he could do that, he assured himself. He knew how to kill now and could do it whenever the need arose.

※

Three rabbits weighed down his pack as he made his way back to the dacha. The stone house had been in the family for generations going back to the czars. After the revolution it had been expropriated by the local Soviet, abandoned two years after Lenin's death, then re-occupied by Ded Vitaly's father. Ded Vitaly had drilled this saga into Alexei whenever they drove up to the dacha from Moscow. A four-hour trip. Plenty of time to recount the family chapters in the thick book of Russian history.

Dusk had fallen by the time he swung open the back door to the dacha and tugged off his boots, mittens and parka. He hung his hat and parka on the peg nearest the little door that led down to the root cellar, pulled on his fur slippers and climbed the stone staircase to the kitchen. The oil stove glowed with a radiant heat and he leaned over the cast iron surface and inhaled the scent of roasting onions and boiled potatoes. His mother and grandfather sat at the oak table, a half-gone bottle of vodka positioned between them.

"Where were you?" Mat swung around to examine the rugged, youthful face of her son. "I was getting worried."

"Out hunting." He slung the hopsack from his shoulder onto the floor and set the palm of his right hand on the Nagant revolver strapped into the holster on his belt.

His grandfather smiled at the twelve-year-old as if he might be remembering something of his own childhood.

"Look." Alexei opened the drawstring on the game bag to display his catch.

Ded Vitaly stood up and peered at the bounty before them.

"Alexei is a true hunter now, Mat. Now we have some meat to add to the broth."

He smiled at his daughter with a grin that suggested a new man had arrived in the house, a home which had nourished generations of Malinins.

"Someone we can be proud of. A lone hunter."

CHAPTER TWO

FIONA PAGE PRESSED her thumbnail into the tight groove of the wood screw and turned her hand until the nail split and ripped away from her flesh.

"Damn," she whimpered, her voice tucked into the back of her throat. Keep quiet, she whispered to herself. Just in case *the worm* is listening through the walls. She glanced at the door to her cell. A sheet of inch-thick foam core had been glued to the door's surface and a sheet of plywood nailed over it. The door had no handle and no inside hinges. A keyed deadbolt provided the only way to open the door, and the worm always wore the key on a retractable steel cable attached to his belt.

She turned her attention back to the rack of iron bars that blocked her escape into the alley. Where could she possibly be? Somewhere downtown, maybe in the Tenderloin District. Maybe in Oakland. Emeryville?

She pressed the heel of her hand to her forehead as the wedge of another headache began its descent through her skull. Justin Whitelaw — the worm — had drugged her, she was certain of that. The drugs he added to her food and wine caused painful, star-burst headaches that immobilized her for hours at a time. You have to give up eating and drinking, she told herself. Go on hunger strike if you can bear it. When you're too weak to go on, then he might release you. Maybe.

She slumped onto the army cot and clamped both hands to her face until the pain of her fingers pressing into her flesh overwhelmed the pain of the migraine. After ten minutes the tension seemed to balance, and then turn ever so slightly away from the heavy throbbing. An hour later she felt some relief and leaned against the wall beside the cot and studied her cell once more.

Apart from the door and barred window, her cubicle consisted of four brick walls, a chipped concrete floor and a panel ceiling. A worn shag rug filled half the space of the eight-by-ten foot floor. Other amenities: a porcelain sink with a cold water tap, a dented metal cup that might have been salvaged from Alcatraz, a worn wash cloth and threadbare towel, an always-on florescent light suspended from the ten-foot high ceiling. And last but not least, a squat-on "Jonny-B-Kwik" port-a-potty that the worm dumped somewhere (a flush toilet down a hallway?) every evening after he brought her meal. Or *presented her meal,* would be more accurate.

The fact that Justin Whitelaw seemed to think he was courting her, worried Fiona almost as much as her confinement. If some kind of deviance governed his affections for her, she had no idea where his perversions might lead. Nor did she want to find out. Maybe she should ask him to boost the measure of her medication. Whatever he'd been dosing her with had effectively blocked her memory. She shook her head at the bleak irony. Which dose offered greater relief? More drugs, or less?

A brief rattling in the alley drew her attention back to the barred windows. Something out there? She gripped the bars in both hands and tried to yank them sideways. Not a budge. Then in the distance she saw three crows in pitched battle over a torn sheet of newspaper, a fish-and-chip wrapper dripping with catsup. That meant restaurants nearby. Fast food. *People.*

Once again she studied the four wood screws that held the rack of bars in place. Setting her teeth, she fit her left thumbnail into the groove on the top of the screw and tried to turn it. "Damn it!" she cried and shoved the broken nail into her mouth. She nursed it a moment and then examined the damage. The nail had torn away into the pink. "Fuck!"

As she sat on the bed she felt tears brimming in her eyes. She hated this weakness. All her life she'd been considered weak by someone. Her mother. Her dismissive father. By Leona, her best friend in high school. James Stinson, her two-timing boyfriend at SF State. Only when her son, Alexander, had come along and she'd had to defend her baby from the obsessive-compulsive madness of her husband — only then had she found the inner strength to stand up for herself. That's what she needed now. Do-or-die determination.

She shifted her weight on the cot and heard the springs groan. Then a tight *snap.* She reached under the frame and felt a steel coil dangling from the frame. Settling on her knees beside the cot she examined the coil and then tugged it free. The spring was about an inch in diameter and two inches long with flat loops that extended from both ends. The loops were meant to hold the spring to the bed frame, but one end had stretched away from the coil and extended into an open arc.

A burst of energy surged in her body as she stood next to the barred windows and tried to fit the flat end of the coil into the screw slot. Damn. Too thick. Maybe she could adapt it somehow. She went back to the bed and lifted one leg of the cot and set the arced end of the spring on the concrete floor. Then she lifted the bed six inches into the air and hammered the leg onto the tip of the coil. Then again. And again. She looked at the coil and in the light cast from the alley she examined the effects of her work. Could she see a few abrasions there? Tiny scars cut into the metal?

She tried to press the open end of the spring into the slot of the wood screw. Still too thick. But convinced now that she'd made some progress, she knelt at the side of the cot and began to hammer the coil under the leg of the cot. *Bang. Bang. Bang.*

Twenty minutes, maybe thirty minutes later, when the sound of the steel leg pounding on the coil replaced the pounding in her head, she realized that the coil tip was a little longer. A little wider. And flatter where it had to fit into the screws.

※

Whenever Fiona heard the key slip into the lock she knew she had about five seconds before the door swung open. The process seemed to require three steps: key in, then a delayed churn followed by the leaden sound of the deadbolt as it unlocked the door. Just enough time to hide her newly-fashioned screwdriver under the far corner of the mattress and prop herself on the edge of the cot to face her captor.

Today Justin Whitelaw appeared in a three-piece suit, the sort of attire Fiona assumed he wore to the corporate offices of Whitelaw, Whitelaw & Joss. The company took its name from

10

Justin's father, Senator Franklin Whitelaw, and his step-brother, Dean Whitelaw — who'd been murdered a few weeks earlier in a bizarre shoot-out in a North Beach parkade. And Joss? As a reporter for the *San Francisco eXpress,* she'd made it her business to learn everything about the organization and the people who ran it. Fiona's research revealed that Joss had started the firm with the Whitelaw brothers in the late 1970s, left the company within two years and died penniless in Venezuela under dubious circumstances.

"Good evening, Fiona." Justin shuffled into the room, a pizza box clutched in his left hand and two glasses of wine balanced in the fingers of his right. He heeled the door closed, listened for the deadbolt to click into place, set his load on the floor and smiled. "Long day."

Fiona tried to decode his cheery banter, to sense how dangerous he might be under the veneer of his slick good looks. She'd decided that tonight she'd try to engage him in a conversation, something that might access his sense of empathy. If she could find that part of him, maybe he would … what? Release her? She could barely imagine the circumstances that would lead to her freedom. Still, she had to try.

"Wearing a suit today. Back in the office? Must be a Monday."

He blinked. Had her casual tone caught him by surprise?

"I got vegetarian." He paused to smile again. "I assumed you're vegetarian. Am I right?"

"I am," she lied. "How did you know that?"

He took a step toward the cot, the smile widening on his face. "Male intuition I guess."

"Male intuition?" She shifted to the right side of the bed, closer to the make-shift screw driver. "Well. I suppose that must be some kind of gender-bender." She immediately regretted this and bit into the side of her cheek. *Concentrate.*

His lips pressed together with a look of dismissal. "I'm not so sure about that." He sat on the edge of the cot. "I brought you some Pouilly-Fumé today. I know you like whites. This one's from France. Three years old. Contrary to common misunderstanding, white wines shouldn't sit too long." He set his glass on the floor and passed the white to her.

She looked at his face and waited until he turned his eyes away. "What are you drinking, Justin?"

"A local barolo. King of wines."

"Maybe we could trade today. Just for a change."

"No, Fiona." His head tilted to one side as he held his glass up to toast her. "You always drink white wines. Best to stick with what you know."

She clinked her glass against his and then set it on the floor. "You think so?"

"Absolutely." A look of mock assurance crossed his face. "Wait until you see what I have for us. *Then* you'll want your wine." He lifted the lid on the pizza box. "They're still hot. From wood-fired clay ovens."

She glanced at the street address printed on the boxes. EXTREME PIZZA. "All the way from the Marina district?"

He frowned. "Fiona — *don't.*"

She tried to hold his eyes but he glanced away again and lifted a slice from the box and handed it to her. She took a bite and chewed hungrily. As soon as the rich flavors hit her tongue,

12

she took another mouthful, then another. She knew it would be her only meal of the day.

"So I've been thinking about what you'd like to talk about after dinner." His tongue swept a smudge of cheese into his mouth.

"How about we go out for coffee. I haven't had any decent java in days."

"Now, Fiona." He smiled and dipped his head to one side. His expression suggested that unless she behaved she might never leave her cell. "Let's talk about you. Tell me about what it's like to work at a newspaper."

She swallowed the last bite of her pizza and took a second slice into her hand. "Maybe we could talk about what it's like to be a kidnapper." Despite her intentions to develop some rapport with him, her voice hardened. "About the fact that you're holding me against my will."

"I don't think so." His eyes narrowed. "Let's talk about how your newspaper slandered my family. About how you've destroyed my life!" He clamped his mouth shut and sneered. A moment passed as he appeared to adjust his mood. "Hey. I'm sorry." His voice dropped a half tone. He took a long slug of the red wine, wiped his lips and set the glass on the floor. "I know this is as hard on you as it is on me."

She looked at him with disgust. "You've got to be kidding me. I've got a three-year-old son who doesn't know where his mother is. An employer who has no idea...." She glanced away, unsure how to continue. "Look," she said and turned back to him, tried to hold his eyes. "Look, I know what you're thinking. Every night it's the same. First you drug me. And then when you *think* I can't remember anything, then you … touch me."

His mouth swung open and he turned away with an expression of disgust.

"I do. *I remember everything,* Justin. Every. Thing. You've. Done."

He began to sip small draughts of air through his nostrils. In-out, in-out. When he regained control of his breathing he turned to her. "Fiona. Do *not* say another word."

"All right. I'm sorry," she offered. Finally she made eye contact with him. Maybe she could spin this thin connection into something more durable. "Look, I know you're like everyone else. Wanting love. Recognition. It just doesn't work when you try to *take* it."

His head dipped slightly, but he still held her eyes.

"Justin," her voice fell to a near whisper as she inched beside him. "Imagine another way. First, just let me go."

His tongue darted between his lips, tiny, indecisive movements that suggested impending crisis. Then he drew away, flexed his hand — once, twice — and smashed his fist against the side of her head.

CHAPTER THREE

WILL FINCH AND Eve Noon stepped through the doors of Café Claude just before the noon-hour rush flooded into the bistro. A few early birds had taken the best tables next to the front window, the tiny space transformed into a stage each night for the jazz acts that played through the evenings. Over the past five years Will had spent hours at the bar talking to patrons, tourists and the staff of waiters and bartenders, most of them loyal employees who took pride in working at one of the city's hippest cafés.

When he spotted Jean-Paul Boisvert at the far end of the bar, Will waved a hand.

"Will Finch! Long time, no see." Jean-Paul's Parisian accent seemed to kiss every word he spoke.

"Bon soir, J-P. Trop longtemps, mon ami." Will extended a hand over over the polished counter top.

Jean-Paul smiled and shook his hand. "Your accent still makes you sound like a Québécois poutine chef."

Will laughed and turned to Eve. "Jean-Paul, let me introduce Eve Noon."

Jean-Paul lifted her hand to his lips and kissed it with a

theatrical flare. "Enchanté." He turned back to Finch. "I see your life has improved since we last met."

"More than you can imagine, my friend."

"Can I get you a drink?"

"Another time, maybe." Finch settled onto a stool and propped his elbows on the bar. "Actually we're looking for someone you might know."

"Justin Whitelaw," Eve said and set her hands on the counter. "I was telling Will that I think he likes to hang at Café Claude and Will said he knew you. So ... one plus one."

"Is just two." Jean-Paul pinched his lips together, a hint of discretion. "You know Justin?"

"Yeah. One of those I-knew-you-whens. I met him at a Missy Elliott concert last year." She waved a hand in the air. "But when Will and I started to talk about him, I thought, why not? Be good to catch up." Eve leaned forward and the gap in her blouse fluttered open to reveal the warmth of her cleavage.

"Maybe you've seen him?" Finch smiled again. "Apparently Café Claude is part of his crawl."

"Sometimes." Jean-Paul's eyes drifted across Eve's chest. He turned back to Finch. "He's usually in here every week or two. So happens you're sitting on his favorite stool."

"Really?" A look of surprise crossed Finch's face. "Maybe I should keep it warm for him."

"Doubt it." He paused. "You heard about all the trouble in his family?"

"Read about it." Finch looked away and tried to recall if he'd ever told Jean-Paul that he worked for the *SF eXpress.* Probably.

"With all that going on," Jean-Paul said, "maybe he's feeling depressed."

"That's why I thought this might be a good time to see him," Eve pressed on. "Cheer him up."

Jean-Paul studied her again, as if he now needed to make a decision about her. Could she be trusted? Then he leaned toward Finch and whispered, "Have you checked across the alley?"

"The alley?" His eyebrows rose a quarter inch.

"Oui. He keeps a bachelor apartment there."

"That one?" Eve pointed through the window to the building on the far side of Claude Lane.

"Down four or five doors." He tipped his head to the right. "White brick building with steel fire escape on the outside. Third floor on the right. With the dormer window facing into the lane."

※

Finch tried to distribute his weight between his feet and left hand as he balanced on the third-floor fire escape. Below his perch Claude Lane now bore the flood of foot traffic from the lunch-hour crowds wandering through the ten-foot wide alley. He didn't like high-wire acts, but better him than Eve, he decided, especially since she was wearing three-inch heels.

To the curious passersby glancing at him from the lane he feigned the look of a forlorn renter who'd lost his keys and locked himself out of his own apartment. When a burly twenty-year-old dressed in army camouflage called up to him — "You all right?" — Finch simply shrugged and said, "Had better days, but I'm okay."

As he inched forward he could see that the window was ajar. He drew his multitool from his courier bag, opened the needle-nose pliers and wedged the tip under the sash. Pressing down on the tool, he tried to lever the window upwards. No give. Then he bunched his fingers into a fist and hammered the multi-tool handle with the butt of his hand. The sash jumped an inch. Finch put the tool away, inserted his fingers under the sash and lifted the glass window. Seconds later he stood in Justin Whitelaw's love nest.

It wasn't fancy. He quickly assessed what appeared to be a standard bachelor pad: a minimalist space with a queen-size bed, surround-sound audio gear, a fifty-inch TV mounted to the wall above a closed-off fireplace that had been retro-fitted with an electric spot-heater. A dozen scented candles adorned the mantle. Just the mood-making atmosphere required to stoke the heat with his latest pick-up from the bistro. And a solitary get-away from the dreary weight of his life. Like his deceased half-sister Gianna, Justin probably needed a variety of escape mechanisms. A place to blow off the excesses of inherited fame and money and reclaim a personal life of his own.

He quickly scanned the room for anything that might belong to Fiona: clothing, her purse, a tube of lip gloss. Nothing. As he crossed the synthetic carpet he tugged on his rubber gloves. He opened the front door and Eve Noon breezed past him into the apartment.

"None too soon, darling. I think there's a drug deal about to go down at the end of the hall."

Finch heard a neighboring apartment door swing open and shut. Footsteps trod along the hall and clomped down the wooden stairs. The building had to be a hundred years old, part of the hasty urban reconstruction following the 1906 earthquake.

He closed the door and turned to Eve. He was about to ask, did they notice you? — and immediately dismissed the thought. Anyone who sees Eve remembers her. A blessing and a curse.

"What do you think?" He waved a hand in the air. "I haven't seen anything that belongs to Fiona."

As she pulled on her latex gloves she studied the place with the apprehension of a biologist considering a sleeping wolf. She sniffed the air. Ran a finger over the fireplace mantle, then assessed the smudge of dust on her glove. She lifted the newspaper lying on the coffee table beside the love seat. "Friday's *LA Times*. Your competitor," she said with a smile.

"So he was here four days ago."

"Maybe." She put the paper down and lifted one of two brandy glasses by the stem. She inhaled the residue of alcohol still alive in the bowl of one snifter. "These we confiscate," she said and slipped each into separate baggies and stowed them in her shoulder bag. "Let's see what other nastiness we can uncover."

She led him to the bed and pointed to the far side. "Let's lift the duvet. We might find some trace residues."

Each of them took a top corner of the duvet and folded it back to reveal the bedsheets.

"Silk." Even through his gloves Finch could feel the sleek material slip under his fingers.

"I love up-market bedding. Maybe we should try that one

day." She smiled at him and then turned her attention to a stain in the middle of bed. "So. There we go. A little leakage from Mr. or Ms. Maybe both. I wonder who?" She applied the tip of a steel blade to the dried fluid and slipped the sample into a glass vial and sealed it. After they folded the duvet back in place, she swept a hand over the cover. "Does that look like how we found it?"

"Close." Finch nodded, impressed by Eve's unhurried, thorough approach. Although she'd left the SFPD years ago, she'd maintained her investigative expertise."What's next?"

"You check the garbage, I'll take the bathroom."

The garbage pail had been emptied and the bag replaced, but the dish rack held a set of plates, utensils and glasses for two. In the refrigerator he found little more than standard fare: orange juice, a rack of canned diet colas, two bottles of high-end French wine: Pouilly-Fumé. He sniffed the cheese, bacon strips, eggs and turned his nose away. In the vegetable tray a head of lettuce had shriveled into a musty lump and a cluster of mushrooms had shrunk to gnarly stumps.

The cupboards revealed a well-organized store of china plates, cups, glasses. A collection of food staples filled half of a shelf in the pantry: canned tuna, pasta, vegetable oil, a jar of salsa, a can of tomato sauce. In a pinch, he decided, Justin Whitelaw could hold out here for two or three days without starving. After that, he'd be forced to eat the china and drink dish soap.

"Look at this, Will." Eve emerged from the bathroom. She held a medicinal bottle between a thumb and index finger.

"Some kind of medication?"

"Maybe. There's no prescription label. Just small white pills with an X scored across the face. I've seen this sort of thing before. Roofies, the date rape drug."

"You mean Rohypnol?"

"Could be." She dropped one of the pills into another vial and sealed it.

"Anything else?"

"We've got a good start." She checked her watch. "Time to push on. But leave the window open a crack. I'd hate to watch you fall into the lane next time we have to break in here."

As they made their way down the stairs to the building entrance another possibility occurred to Finch.

"Let's check the basement, Eve. Some of these bachelor rentals come with a storage room. Maybe there's something beneath." He pointed to the flight of stairs that descended below street level.

He clicked on the light switch and led her down the staircase. The walls, rough-cut rocks and stones that had probably been recovered from the rubble of the 1906 quake, formed a narrow passage that extended the length of the building. Two naked light bulbs, one at each end of the corridor, hung suspended by their wires from the ceiling. The air felt dry and fetid. Unlikely the space had been vented in the past decade or two. They tiptoed along the cracked concrete floor. Every four or five feet they encountered a closed wooden door, each one locked with a keyed deadbolt. Finch tapped on the surface of the second door to test its heft. No echo meant it was solid core construction. Probably an original, he figured and leaned a shoulder into it. No give at all.

He looked at Eve. She shrugged, unsure what to suggest.

"Fiona," he called out. Then he yelled as loud as he could: "Fiona Page! Fiona, it's Will. Are you in here?"

"What's going on?" a heavy voice called from somewhere behind them.

Finch turned to see a large silhouette fill the space where the staircase opened into the corridor. As the stranger stepped forward the backlight from the distant light bulb enlarged his profile.

"Just looking for a friend." Finch decided to improvise. "We heard she was visiting, and somehow wandered down here."

"Who's the friend?" The stranger pulled closer, less than ten feet away.

"My girlfriend," Eve offered. "Fiona Page. Do you know her?"

Silence. Then another step forward. "Fiona? Who's she visiting?"

"Justin Whitelaw," Finch pointed to the ceiling. "Up on the third floor."

After another step, Finch could recognize the face of the young man standing before him. It was the burly twenty-year-old dressed in camo who'd called out to Finch on the fire escape as he tampered with the apartment window.

"Do you happen to know him, by any chance?" Finch asked. His voice carried an easy, casual tone.

As the stranger considered this, he shrugged, obviously unsure how to respond. "If he lives here, my father will know him. He's the manager."

"Your father's the building manager?" Eve stepped past Finch and stood in front of the young man. She smiled. "That's good to know, because I was wondering about this building. By the way, my name's Betty Smith. This is Jim." She pointed to Finch and then extended her hand.

"I'm Arnold." His eyes settled on Eve. A slight shudder rippled through him as he shook her hand.

"I can tell, I mean it's obvious," she continued, "that this building was put up sometime after the big quake in oh-six. And I've got a girlfriend researching reconstruction in the French quarter. I'm just wondering" — she set a hand on Arnold's arm and guided him back to the staircase — "could I get your number and arrange for you to meet with her?"

"Meet with her? M-m-me?" His voice trembled with a hesitant stutter.

"Yes. I'm sure she'd like to have a look down here." Eve led him back up the stairs as she spoke. Moments later the three of them stood outside the building on the narrow side-walk. She took his phone number. As she and Finch walked back along Claude Lane, she turned and waved a goodbye, then crossed onto Bush Street.

※

When Will and Eve returned to his condo in Mother Russia — the renovated Edwardian co-op house on the cusp of Nob Hill — Eve immediately unpacked her bag and set the contents on the living room coffee table.

"Two brandy snifters," she said as she lifted the ziploc bags which held the matching glasses. "A little love jism from the bedroom, and a pill which I'm certain will be identified as

Rohypnol."

"Maybe some of it will lead us to Fiona." Will shook his head and slumped into the sofa. He still felt partly responsible for Fiona's disappearance. After all, he'd implored her to stake out Justin Whitelaw in Café Claude and press him for an interview. Will even suggested she do it covertly. Without mentioning she was a journalist for the *SF eXpress,* lead Justin on with some flirtation, then grill him for whatever information he could provide about the murder of his sister Gianna Whitelaw. The fact that the cops hadn't questioned Finch about Fiona also troubled him. Almost a week had passed since she'd vanished. Why weren't they on the case?

"So, next steps." Eve carefully stored the stolen evidence in her shoulder bag. "Before I send this to Leanne in the forensics lab, you need to collect something to identify Fiona's DNA. And her fingerprints."

Will considered this. "You need both?"

"The DNA to match against the sample from the bed sheet and prints to compare to whoever held the snifter glasses. If either of them — or both — make a positive match, we'll have a lock on the case."

"All right. I'll go into the office this evening to see what I can find at her desk. Except for the nighthawks working the midnight shift, the building should be nearly deserted."

Finch felt a buzz in his pocket. His cell phone showed a text from Sochi: *We're in! Almost a new record for Rasputin: thirteen days, sixteen hours and twenty-two minutes to crack the password on the thumb drive. Well below the NASA job, but still a hard nut to crack. Details later.*

Finch smiled; finally some good news. One of his housemates, Sochi, specialized in quantum cryptography. He'd offered to use one of his software programs — Rasputin, as he called it — to crack open the password to the thumb drive which Eve had found in Gianna's condo the night of her murder. For almost two weeks, Rasputin had been stumped. The delay began to trouble Will and for a while he wondered if Sochi had broken the code and stolen the data on the drive. Simple paranoia, he told himself and read Sochi's message to Eve.

"That is good news." She smiled. "I didn't want to tell you this, but since I've never met Sochi, I was beginning to doubt him."

"Doubt him — or me?"

She reached across the sofa and set her hand on his thigh. "There's no doubt about you, darling. Not from me, anyway."

He knew she was referring to the night when Toby Squire bludgeoned her with a golf club and abandoned her to die in a locked cupboard swarming with rats. The thought made him shudder. After Finch rescued her, and when Eve realized that he'd saved her life, all the previous deceptions and uncertainties of their relationship dissolved.

Despite her infatuation, she pulled her hand from his leg and drew a long breath with a measure of self-control. "So what next? We wait for Sochi to reveal what's on the flash drive?"

He nodded. "It could change everything." But only if the thumb drive contained pertinent information, he thought. And what, exactly, could that amount to? He combed his fingers through his hair and tried to imagine the best-case scenarios. New information to explain Gianna's apparently senseless murder. Evidence proving fraud in the Whitelaw corporate empire. Documents. Photos. Transcripts.

Maybe.

CHAPTER FOUR

ALEXEI MALININ COMPLETED his degree in English Language and International Studies from Moscow State University in 1975. The following year he entered the 401st KGB training school in Okhta, Leningrad. There he met Vladimir Putin. After a few weeks they discovered that they shared the same birthday, October seventh, although Malinin was two years older than the future president of Russia. The coincidence provided reason enough to share a bottle of Stolichnaya and trade a few stories about their past and Putin's skill in Sambo, the Russian combat sport. Malinin was experimenting with Krav Maga, the Israeli martial art. Their promise to spar with one another never materialized and after Putin had been posted to East Germany, Malinin, who spoke excellent English, took a job in Ottawa. Following his assignment in Canada — where in 1981 he secretly filmed and discredited the Soviet cipher-turned-traitor, Igor Gouzenko — he was rewarded with a post in the Soviet embassy in Washington in 1982.

Over the next five years, Malinin developed a propaganda specialty filming ten-minute profiles of drug addicts, prostitutes, the unemployed, the homeless — and anyone else from the seemingly endless stream of individuals and families who had fallen through the American social safety net. His method was simple and effective. First, identify a trending theme, preferably something broad-based and intractable like racism, drug abuse, prostitution. Next, select a dozen victims willing to publicly indict their oppressors in his films. When he approached potential informants, most agreed to serve as sources. Especially if the offer included a free meal at the local bar and grill while they dished up the details of their destitution. Following these preliminary interviews, Malinin determined which candidates would provide the best testimonials. Then he sent in a film crew to record the allegations for syndicated broadcast.

Back in the embassy, Malinin edited the tapes to create a narrative spine, a storyline like those he'd seen on American TV. *60 Minutes* provided a good example, so he followed their formula. Why not, he thought; after all, they invented "gotcha journalism." The irony never ceased to amuse him. Finally, he translated all the dialogue into Russian and added his narrative perspective in a voice-over. After the master tapes were flown to Moscow, copies were translated into all the languages of the Soviet bloc in Europe and into Chinese, Korean, Vietnamese — and the languages of every nation the Soviets might be courting. From Berlin to Beijing, his films were broadcast to over five hundred million people. But in North America and Europe, except to the CIA and MI6, Alexei Malinin remained largely unknown.

In September 1987, Malinin met Stepan Krupin, the comrade assigned to support Malinin's expanding enterprise. Malinin had been ordered to train his new apprentice, the son of an apparatchik in the Kremlin recommended by the mayor of Moscow, Boris Yeltsin.

During their first month together Malinin realized that Krupin was the wrong man for the job. On three separate evenings, Malinin witnessed Krupin's alcoholic outbursts. A closet drunk whose initial geniality soon led to angry rants, Krupin often lost control of his temper in a single moment — as if someone flicked a switch and ignited a lunatic. But worst of all, Krupin was a sycophant: a yes-man who spat out the latest communist propaganda as if it provided a legitimate way to understand reality. As they said in America, "He drank the Kool-Aid." In Krupin's case, the preferred beverage was a double vodka martini. Stirred, not shaken.

Despite his concerns, Malinin followed his orders and attempted to shape Krupin into someone resembling a propaganda specialist. After two months, he realized the task was hopeless. Still, he decided to press ahead with a new challenge: Operation Black Night. It marked the beginning of the end of Malinin's career in the KGB and nearly cost him his life.

※

A little after six P.M. on November 26, as the afternoon faded into dusk, Krupin steered the embassy's Lincoln Continental onto Wisconsin Avenue and immediately turned left onto Massachusetts.

"Should we start looking in Baltimore?" His voice conveyed a note of vexed boredom.

"No." Alexei Malinin frowned in dismay. He'd already covered this with Krupin. Twice. "We have to make sure the

29

entire operation begins and ends in Washington D.C. Do you think anyone outside the Kremlin has heard of Baltimore? Russians only know of three American cities. New York, Los Angeles, Washington. Maybe four if you count Chicago. Everything else is a forgotten suburb. In other words, besides these cities, nothing else exists."

Krupin pressed his lips together as he drove on. "Got that wrong," he muttered under his breath. "Broadway, Hollywood, Las Vegas — nothing else matters."

Unable to make out these whispers, Malinin continued. "As I said before, we'll begin in Southeast Washington. Now turn around and head toward the Frederick Douglass Memorial Bridge."

"If you insist," Krupin muttered, the blade of anger barely sheathed in his voice.

"I do." Malinin decided he needed a distraction. He stared at two women crossing the street into the American University campus. Dressed in bright jackets and skirts designed to match the orange and red leaves dancing through the gusting autumn air, the women presented a subtle refinement, a careless comfort with wealth that Russian women could never imagine. Neither could their Russian husbands or boyfriends. After seventy years it was obvious that the revolution had failed to keep pace with the west. That's what General Secretary Mikhail Gorbachev, the coming man, maintained. All the leaders were desperate to find a new vocabulary to describe how the Soviet Union could still march forward. Expressions like "Perestroika" and "Glasnost." If all else failed, perhaps words alone might save them.

"But I know for a fact," Krupin insisted, "that Baltimore has more black citizens, more poverty, more homeless people than anywhere in Washington."

"Yes, your facts are correct," Malinin allowed, "but you refuse to think strategically." He rubbed a hand over his face and decided to try a new tack. "Listen, Stepan. Did you ever have a chess rating?"

"No, comrade." The angry tone had mutated to a kind of mockery. "Nothing like that."

Comrade. Malinin let out a gasp of exasperation. "Did you not play chess in school?"

"A little. Which way, then?"

"After you cross the bridge turn north onto the 295, then onto Good Hope Road. We'll start there." Malinin felt that Krupin was trying to ignore the point he was hoping to hammer into his skull. "When I was nineteen and I still had time for chess, my FIDE chess rating was twenty-two hundred and thirteen." He studied Krupin's face for a reaction. "Not that I'm fishing for compliments. Far from it. The issue is strategy. Strategy has to be our first consideration. It's the same thing in chess."

Krupin drove the Lincoln across the Anacostia River and made his way to Good Hope Road in silence. Suddenly they'd entered a forbidden zone. The street, the sidewalks, the shops — all of it gave the impression of disrepair and neglect. The pedestrians, all of them African-American, appeared to stroll along the sidewalk as if they were waiting for something, or someone, to provide a diversion from their despair.

Krupin pulled the car to the curb and pointed out a bar four doors along the sidewalk. Three men stood at alert next to the entrance, their eyes scanning the passersby. He cut the engine and said, "This place offers possibilities."

Malinin leaned forward and studied the broken awning over the front window. He studied the unlit "A" in the sign above the doorway: J-KE'S. "Maybe," he conceded and opened the door and stood on the sidewalk.

When a sheet of newspaper flew against his leg and he tried to shake it away, Krupin began to laugh. "Come on Alexei, I'll buy you a drink."

"Just remember: we speak English, only," Malinin said and followed his partner past the three men at the door and into the bar. His eyes took a moment to adjust to the darkness and the cigarette smoke that drifted through the room in a breathless fog. A crowd stood along the bar. A few men loitered next to a hallway that led to a back exit, another group stood beside the jukebox. George Michael's "I Want Your Sex" blasted from the dented chrome speakers. Krupin took a seat at a circular table next to a pool table where four negroes studied the disposition of a dozen pool balls at rest on the green felt. A moment later Malinin realized that he and Krupin were the only white people in the room.

"Yes. This will do," Krupin said. He flagged the bartender with his hand. When the barman shook his head, Krupin stood and glanced down at Malinin. "Vodka?"

"No." Better to drink something American, he thought. "Get me a Miller High Life."

As Krupin placed their orders at the bar, Malinin traded looks with the men surrounding the pool table.

"Looks like someone lost their way," one of them said. He wore a tight-knit, rainbow-striped cap.

Another took a shot with his pool cue and the heavy slap of balls clacked in the air. "Seems like," he said.

Malinin watched the seven ball drop into the corner pocket. He set a smile on his face. "Good shot," he offered.

Rainbow looked at his friends. "Good shot?"

Seven-ball laughed at this.

"You call that a good shot?" A third man grinned at Malinin. His nose slanted to the right below a bump of broken cartilage. "He just fuckin' sank Pinkie's ball."

"Ah. So that's *not* a good shot!" Malinin smiled again. "You want the truth?"

Nose looked at Rainbow with disbelief. "The truth?"

"Yes. I know absolutely nothing about this game!"

Pinkie stepped forward and studied Malinin a moment. "It's called eight-ball. Maybe you should play a round."

He shrugged. "If you teach me, yes?"

The men traded laughs and Rainbow stepped around the table. "Only if you got some wad. This table don't move without a little wad."

"Wad?"

"Yeah. Say what? A Jackson. Twenty bucks each. Winner takes all."

Krupin returned to the table and set four drinks down. Two shots of Smirnoff Vodka and two bottles of Miller High Life.

"Stepan, we're going to play eight-ball."

"To eight-ball!" Krupin raised a glass of Vodka to acknowledge their new friends and threw back the shot in one swallow.

Rainbow looked at him doubtfully, set a twenty dollar bill on the top rail and passed him his cue. "Where you from, friend?"

Krupin drew a breath of air to nip the heat in his throat. "Russia."

Rainbow seemed surprised.

"Born in Kaliningrad," Krupin added.

"Okay, Kalinstad." Rainbow traded smiles with the others. "Put your money on the table and we'll teach you a thing or two they probley don't show you back home."

Over the next hour Krupin lost a hundred and forty dollars and drank eight shots of vodka. Malinin enjoyed his two bottles of beer and bought a round for the boys. Because he saw it as a cost of doing business, Malinin didn't mind losing the money. Besides, his operating budget could cover this charge without questions being asked in the embassy. But when he saw Krupin teetering as he rounded the pool table to line up and sink the cue ball in the side pocket, Malinin knew he had to approach Rainbow and Pinkie about scheduling a taped interview before Krupin destroyed their credibility. Furthermore, Krupin had reverted to speaking exclusively in Russian, a procedural taboo. Time to act.

"Say boys, let's take a break. And I'm buying one more round," Malinin said and patted one of the chairs at his table.

Pinkie, Nose and Rainbow sat beside him.

Meanwhile Krupin made an elaborate gesture of bowing out and said in Russian, "Gotta piss." He stumbled down a hallway, then re-directed himself to the men's room. Seven Ball followed Krupin, one hand braced on the wall to steady

34

himself as he went.

By the time the bartender delivered a tray of drinks, Malinin had made his overture to the others. Had they ever considered telling their stories? Let the outside world know what the inside of their life really looked like? Explain what it meant to be penniless in a society run by money?

Rainbow leaned forward. "You mean being on some kind of TV show?"

"Exactly."

"Where on?" Pinkie asked as he leaned back in his chair and tried to fix Malinin in his narrow eyes. "What stations?"

"In Russia. Then Germany, Poland, Czechoslovakia, Korea, China." Malinin swept an open hand above the table. "Over twenty countries. I'll give you a complete list when we begin to record, yes?"

Rainbow let out a gasp of laughter. "You communist ain't you?"

Malinin sipped his beer and shrugged. He often had to make light of his political situation. He grinned. "Aren't we all at heart?"

"No, we fuckin' ain't." Pinkie's hand slammed the table with enough force to bounce Malinin's High Life onto the floor. Malinin looked at the broken bottle as a shallow pool of white foam bubbled around the shattered glass. The steady buzz and murmur in the bar paused a moment and then resumed.

"Pinkie's got that straight," Rainbow said. "You cain't turn none of us."

Seven Ball wobbled back to the table and sat in the fifth

chair. A fleck of blood sat on the edge of his lip. When he smiled at the Nose, Malinin could see red spittle smeared across his front teeth.

Malinin nodded, realized he and Krupin should leave as soon as possible. A clot of people stood idly at the front door, waiting for something. Waiting for a cue of some kind. Malinin looked past them, wondered if the back exit would be free.

Krupin re-appeared, his head tilted to one side. An angry twist contorted his mouth. He came up behind Seven Ball and snarled into the black man's ear: "Fuck your mother."

At least he's speaking English again, Malinin thought. He raised a hand and said, "Krupin, settle down."

"Say what?!" Seven Ball attempted to stand up but before he could rise, Krupin seized a pool cue from the table and lashed it against the side of Seven Ball's head. The sound of his cracking skull cut through the noise in the room and he crashed backwards from his chair onto the table. One by one the glasses and bottles teetered and smashed against the floor. The room exploded with cries of rage.

Malinin dodged a left hook from Rainbow, grabbed his sleeve and used the force of the round-house punch to pull the big man forward so that he landed on the floor. Next he seized Krupin by his collar and advanced five or six steps toward the rear exit. Pinkie charged after them and drove the butt of another pool cue into Krupin's lower back.

Krupin shuddered in pain, dropped away from Malinin's grasp and fell to the floor. A crowd of fifteen, twenty men surrounded them. Malinin placed well-aimed kicks into the knees of three attackers to create a small opening. He picked

Krupin off the floor, braced him under his arm and pressed ahead. Halfway to the door, Krupin recovered his strength, swung free and turned back to face the mob.

"Pozvol'te mne na nikh!" he screamed. He took a final step forward.

A blade swung from left to right and cut across Krupin's throat from his right ear down through his larynx. A jet of blood spurted from his head, subsided, and surged again. Complete silence filled the room. Everyone stood back as Krupin choked on his own blood.

Malinin took a step backwards, then another. He knew that Krupin would be dead within minutes. No way to staunch the bleeding, no tourniquet to apply, no means to plug the severed carotid artery. As he jogged toward the exit he could see the crash bar on the door ahead. Four, maybe five steps more and he'd be outside.

Then someone called to him, *"Hey, comrade!"*

Why he hesitated, he would never know. He turned and as he spun around the knife plunged through his jacket, through his shirt and into his belly. He felt the blade turn, cut across his stomach, and then slip out of his body.

Malinin slumped to the floor and the bartender ran towards him with a baseball bat clutched in his fist. Malinin was certain that he was about die. Then the bartender turned and swung the bat hard into Pinkie's hand. He cried in pain as the knife flew across the room and rattled against an overturned chair. The uproar of noise dropped to a collective gasp. As everyone raced for the exits, Malinin could hear the distant sound of sirens approaching.

Later the surgeon told him that his liver was nearly cut in two, scored from the top of the right lobe down to the gall bladder. The pain from the injury would last a very long time and require daily attention for years to come.

But compared to Krupin, Malinin knew he was lucky.

※

Alexei Malinin met Senator Franklin Whitelaw, then the rookie senator from California, in George Washington University Hospital on December third, 1987. The senator had suffered a ruptured appendix during a hunting trip in the Ozark mountains and been flown to the hospital in a military helicopter. Seated in hospital wheelchairs, the two men met in one of the day rooms where post-op patients could soak up some sunshine through the floor-to-ceiling windows overlooking Washington Circle.

When the senator learned that Malinin worked at the Soviet embassy he tried to cultivate a relationship. The following week Gorbachev would meet Reagan in Washington for an historic summit and the prospect of offering President Reagan some parallel support proved irresistible to Whitelaw. Besides, any media attention linking him to a victory in the cold war would be invaluable.

"You know, I've been warned not to talk to you," Senator Whitelaw said with a grin.

"No?" Malinin leaned forward in his chair to ease the strain of the sutures in his belly. "I can imagine."

"I've been told you're a spy." The senator's grin slowly enlarged into his trademark smile.

Malinin frowned. Despite his training it seemed ridiculous

to dispute the obvious, especially in his condition. Besides, while the embassy fixers had quietly shipped Krupin's corpse to Moscow without alerting the press, no one could ignore Malinin's race to the hospital in a screaming ambulance — nor the subsequent conjecture that he was a KBG operative. "And if I was a spy, it would make a difference?"

"Not if both our leaders sign the INF Treaty next week."

The Intermediate-Range Nuclear Forces Treaty. Malinin sneered at the mention of it. Everyone suspected that the cold war detente marked the beginning of the end for the Soviet Union. Ronald Reagan seduced Mikhail Gorbachev with money, power and a California surfer tan. His charms seemed irresistible, especially to the leaders of the Potemkin village that the Soviet Union had become.

Whitelaw and Malinin spoke quietly in front of the hospital windows, and then Malinin experienced something that could only happen in America. A squad of reporters burst into the day room and began an on-the-spot interview with the senator. Photographers took dozens of pictures, their flashbulbs popping like small-caliber handguns.

"Senator, how are they treating you?"

"Just fine. It was touch-and-go up in the Ozarks when my appendix burst, but once I arrived here I knew I was getting the best medical care in the world." His hundred-watt smile lit up the room. "And my friend here, Alexei Malinin from the Soviet Embassy, might say the same. Alexei?"

Caught off guard, Malinin turned away, then thought better of it. Whitelaw was playing a gambit of some sort. Just how good a chess player was he?

D. F. Bailey

"Yes, good. The staff has been helpful. Almost comparable to Soviet medicine." His face contracted as a new bolt of pain flew through his belly.

Still smiling, Senator Whitelaw turned to the photographers. "Want to see my scar?"

"Absolutely!" The media chorus was loud and enthusiastic. Some of them recalled President Lyndon Johnson displaying his scar following his gallbladder operation in 1965. It made for good politics and Whitelaw knew it.

The senator lifted the drape of his gown to display the row of tidy sutures below his ribs. More flashbulbs ignited.

"How about you, Alexei? Show 'em your scar." Despite the long reach across the two wheelchairs, the senator wrapped an arm around Malinin's shoulder to demonstrate their cama-raderie. "I'd say this gives east-west detente a whole new meaning. Don't you think?"

Malinin's face bore a worried look. "Did you arrange all this?" he whispered and waved a finger at the paparazzi who were still laughing at the senator's joke.

"An hour ago," the senator mumbled through his clenched smile.

Malinin knew that he could not back down. He lifted the edge of his shirt to reveal the crater of torn flesh above his liver. Again, a barrage of flashbulbs blazed through the room.

A reporter leaned toward Malinin and pressed a micro-phone to his mouth. "And what was the nature of your surgery, comrade?"

Comrade. He smiled. "To repair damages from a butcher knife thrust into my liver."

The reporter gasped. He seemed to have no idea how to continue.

"I was attacked by several homeless negroes. Blameless victims of hunger and want," he continued. "All of them citizens of your so-called *Great Society.*"

He notched a smile onto his lips and grinned at Senator Whitelaw. Malinin turned toward the senator's ear as the photographers took a final series of pictures of the two scarred bellies propped side-by-side in the wheelchairs.

"Checkmate," he chuckled, the smile still on his lips. "Let us keep in touch, senator. Yes?"

CHAPTER FIVE

AROUND EIGHT-THIRTY on Thursday evening Will Finch climbed the staircase to the *eXpress* office. He knew most of the staff would have shut down their computer terminals and shuffled off to their homes. Jeanine Fix the *eXpress* copy editor and web master would likely be putting the last edition to bed. And one or two of the unpaid interns might linger to impress the managing editor Wally Gimbel, but only if Wally himself remained at his desk.

As he turned the corner into the office, Finch made a cursory sweep of the reception area and the "wire room," where Jeanine and the tech staff designed and published the internet pages. He then turned toward the board room and Wally Gimbel's private office. Except for Jeanine, the premises appeared to be vacant.

More good luck, he whispered to himself when he saw Jeanine mesmerized by some task on her computer screen. He waved to her from a distance. When she failed to return his signal he walked into the bog, where the staff writers toiled in their cubicles during the day shift, and along the row of empty cubicles to Fiona Page's desk.

He settled in her chair and studied the surroundings. He'd sat here, beside her, dozens of times over the past year when Parson Media launched their internet news feed, the *San Francisco eXpress*, on the third floor of the building, just above the offices of their print edition, the *San Francisco Post.* But the transition from print to digital publishing required a corporate slight-of-hand. To staff the new internet news feed, Wally Gimbel poached six journalists from the *Post*. Fiona Page and Will Finch were his first recruits.

Whereas in the past Finch barely noticed the trinkets and do-dads that decorated Fiona's cubicle, he now studied them carefully. A dozen pencils and pens pointing tip-up in a ceramic coffee cup with a broken handle. A framed photograph of Fiona and her son Alexander in the bleachers at a San Francisco Giants baseball game. A clipping of her first front-page story from the *Post:* "Record-Breaking Drought Squeezes Bay Area Dry." A stained-glass mobile suspended from the retractable arm of her desk lamp. A coffee mug ("World's Best Mom") with a barely visible lipstick smudge. Bingo. Finch slipped a pencil through the handle, carefully tipped the mug into a baggie and eased it into his courier bag.

He opened the drawer under her telephone stand and scanned for more personal items. Thumbtacks, a stapler, paper-clips, erasers, highlighter pens. More pencils. Ah, a pair of tweezers. He held this to the light for a moment and wondered if it might provide an eyebrow hair or eyelash. Nothing. The second drawer held more promising prospects. A compact and mirror. An open tube of Lypsyl. He slipped the lip balm into another ziploc and leaned over the open drawer. Ah, here: a bamboo hair brush from the Body Shop. He lifted the brush in his hand and examined it carefully. Woven between the rows of teeth lay a knotted web of Fiona's hair. This would do it, he told himself and tugged the snarl of hair from the brush and dropped it into the ziploc baggie and placed it next to the first sample in his shoulder bag.

As he headed toward the exit he checked to see if Jeanine was at her desk. Her lamp was still on, but she'd disappeared. Had she seen him? Then again, it didn't matter, especially now as Wally Gimbel rolled into the office with a grim expression on his face.

"Will — surprised to see you here."

Finch shook his head with a disorientated frown. "Me too, I guess. Just trying to sort out some thoughts about Fiona. I figured if I sat at her desk, I might find something."

"And?"

He shrugged. "I don't know."

"Yeah, it's beyond horrible. Worse, I haven't heard any-thing from the police. How about you?"

"They haven't even contacted me."

"Maybe they got everything they need from the others." He swept his hand toward the empty room. "Look, you got another minute?"

Finch followed his boss into his private office and closed the door. They both sat. Wally looked at the ceiling as if he had to prepare what he was about to say.

"I just had a meeting with the Parson brothers. *The Brethren.*" He let out a long sigh. "Working with them is like trying to eat soup with a fork."

Will studied the editor's round, heavy face. Was he expected to interpret a special meaning from this?

"There's no easy way to say this, so I'll just say it. Effective tomorrow, they are shutting down the print edition."

"What?"

"The last edition of the *San Francisco Post* is being printed as we speak."

Finch glanced away. This was news he'd expected for almost three years. But hearing it now, he felt as if he'd been shoved over an invisible cliff. "Tonight?"

He nodded. "After a hundred and twenty-three years. One-two-three. Simple as that."

"What about us?" Will's gut tightened as if he were now about to smash onto the rocks below. "What about the *eXpress?*"

"Safe." He shrugged. "For now, anyway. Parson Media is giving the *eXpress* another six months to break even."

"And if we don't?"

"Try to sell us, I imagine. But they didn't commit to anything."

"They couldn't sell the *Post?*"

Wally gasped — a cynical laugh at his star reporter's naïveté. "That's like asking if Henry Ford sold his last horse. Or simply shot it."

Wally stood up and washed his hands over his face. He *looks ten years older,* Finch thought. *Completely exhausted.*

"Anyway, don't say anything until tomorrow. I'm calling a staff meeting first thing."

"It'll put the fear of God into everyone."

"I know." He looked away, studied a fleck of dirt on the wall. "It's like we're all one step away from the abyss."

※

Eve and Will sat together examining the articles he'd retrieved from Fiona's cubicle and the loot they'd stolen from Justin Whitelaw's apartment.

That should do it," Eve said. "I'll take everything to Leanne tomorrow. Depending on how busy she is in the forensics lab, it could take some time."

"Sure." Will knew that Eve couldn't hurry things along. Like a dozen other women who worked in the SFPD, Leanne Spratz maintained fierce loyalty to Eve and she provided discreet forensic services to her friend whenever Eve asked for a favor. A few years earlier, Eve had publicly exposed the "chilly climate" — a euphemism for pervasive sexual harassment — towards women in the force. Like most whistle-blowers, Eve had been demeaned and then terminated. More determined than ever to redeem her reputation, Eve won a wrongful dismissal case and the SFPD was forced to implement new gender policies and training for all staff. To everyone's surprise, a new era seemed to dawn in the SFPD. To the women who remained, Eve Noon became Saint Eve.

As he studied the objects in silence, a maze of dreams and fears crisscrossed through Will's mind. So strange to think that these few items were all that remained of Fiona. After a minute or two, a light tapping at the door interrupted his somber reverie.

Grateful for the relief it provided, Finch pulled himself from the sofa and opened the door. Before him stood Sochi.

Between his thumb and index finger, the redheaded cryptologist presented a memory stick as if it might be a magic crystal glowing in a beam of light.

"Ah, Moscow, you're home! I present to you a Russian doll, or the digital equivalent thereof," he said, his voice rising in poetic loftiness. Moscow, Finch's *nom de jeste,* had been embraced by all his house mates in Mother Russia.

"The flash drive contains one hundred and twenty-seven files, a website link and three executable programs," Sochi continued, "all of which are themselves locked and password-protected. In other words, the vault is open, but inside we find *more* locked repositories."

Finch stared at the flash drive, unsure how to respond. "Sochi. Come in," he said. "Let me introduce you to Eve Noon."

"Greetings." Sochi shook Eve's hand and as he sat in the wingback chair, Finch noticed that he'd woven six pea-sized wooden beads into strands of his beard that hung below his chin.

"So what does this mean?" Eve asked.

Sochi glanced at Finch, eyebrows raised with a look of doubt. "She knows what this is about?"

"Actually, the thumb drive belongs to me."

Finch nodded. "It's true. You can tell her everything."

Sochi leaned forward, his elbows perched on his knees. The data drive lay in his soft, pink palm. "Okay. First, whoever put this together is no amateur. As I said, access to the drive itself is protected by a thirty-two character password which I've printed for you."

He handed Finch a yellow sticky bearing a code printed in tiny but perfectly clear script: H4-nv34&9_Ee98<-Fi2trJA,<e/D76ME

"Hang onto it, but don't stick it on your computer monitor." He laughed as if this should be hilarious to anyone with a sense of humor bent in the just right direction. "But as I said, that password will only open the drive. All the files and programs inside are also locked."

"What kind of files are they?"

"All but four are data files. One of those is a password manager program." He tugged at the beaded strands of hair on his chin. "The second is a bitcoin wallet. The third looks like a software program, something called GIGcoin. The last one is a link to a site in the dark web. Which, by the way, is *not* encrypted."

A moment of silence enveloped them.

"All right … so where to begin?" Eve said. "First, what's a bitcoin wallet?"

"Think of it as a digital purse that can hold any number of bitcoins." Finch said.

"Very good," Sochi tipped his head to Finch. "That's a start. It's also a program which can send and receive bitcoins in encrypted transmissions to other bitcoin wallets anywhere in the world. At about thirty-two megabytes per second," he added with another burble of laughter that suggested the device contained magical powers. "But once the transmission is completed," he cautioned and held a finger aloft, "it cannot be recalled. Although the transactions are all confirmed and verified in a global block-chain ledger, the bitcoin wallet holders can remain anonymous. Finding an open bitcoin wallet today is the equivalent of stumbling over a pile of gold nuggets a hundred years ago. Who does the loot belong to? To whoever finds it. So if you lose the wallet, or forget the password.... Well, best not to dwell on such gloomy prospects."

"And you say the bitcoin wallet itself is locked. Can Rasputin unlock it?"

"Good lord, have you two joined a cult?" Eve shifted on the sofa. *"Who* is Rasputin?"

"Moscow, I wish you hadn't mentioned Rasputin to her." Sochi shook his head and his lips pursed together, almost invisible under his mustache.

"And why are you called Moscow?"

" … It's my code name." How to explain this kind of nonsense? Finch shrugged with a look of self-consciousness.

An embarrassed silence followed, then Sochi broke into laughter again. "All right. I can tell you about Rasputin, but not before you're initiated into Mother Russia," he said to Eve and waved a hand to suggest the entire building was an outpost of pre-soviet nostalgia. "Let's see. What's a suburb or a special part of Moscow?"

"Arbat," Eve offered. "Everyone knows it's *the* shopping district."

Sochi's eyes widened. "Perfect. And the most beautiful part of the city. Architectural gems throughout." He made the sign of the cross above her head in a summary christening. "Okay, Arbat, it is. *Now* I can tell you." His face appeared to soften as he glanced from Will to Eve.

"Rasputin is a quantum computer software tool I've created

to mount what are known as *brute force* attacks to crack pass-
words on locked files and devices like this." He handed the
thumb drive to her. "However, Rasputin is quite the sophisticated gentleman. He doesn't care for the term 'brute force.'
Thinks it's beneath him."

Eve examined the drive and then looked from Sochi to
Finch. "So. Can you — I mean, *Rasputin* — open the bitcoin
wallet?"

"Maybe. Maybe not. But it might be smarter to open the
password manager first." He leaned back in the chair, wove his
fingers into the mane of hair draped from the back of his head
and pondered the options. "Think a minute. If you were putting
all these files and a bitcoin wallet on the thumb drive, and you
had to lock them all, each with a unique password, then you'd
store them all in the password manager, right?"

"Right." Finch and Eve nodded in unison.

"So our first step should be to unlock the password manager," Eve continued. "And once we're in, we can unlock all the
other files.

"Now you're thinking like a Ruskie!" Sochi snapped his
fingers at Eve. *"And* we should explore the suspicious link."

"So can you do that? I mean, can you ask Rasputin to do
it?" Eve glanced at Finch with a shrug as if to ask, *Is this how
you play the game?*

Finch chuckled to himself and smiled.

"Maybe. It can take a long time. Weeks. And I can't promise anything. But for you, Arbat, I will try. I can begin explor-
ing the dark web link today."

"And the dark web is?..."

"The vast majority of internet sites that aren't indexed, or illuminated, by Google. Most of it is garbage. But some of it is truly dark. Full of drug trafficking, sex, child porn, murder for hire."

"So. You can handle this for me?"

"Good question. One which brings me to a business proposition. You are in possession of X, an unknown quantity." Sochi pointed to the thumb drive in Eve's hand. "I possess the means to quantify it and maybe — *just* maybe — I can access everything on it, too. If I can do that, then I'd like ten percent of the value of whatever is on the drive."

"That includes getting the key, or whatever it is, from the dark web?"

He smiled. "It includes everything needed to access all the contents of the thumb drive."

Eve glanced through the French doors leading onto the balcony. Then she looked at Finch before turning to Sochi. "We should put a time limit on this. How much do you need?"

Sochi shrugged. "Three weeks. If I can't break this open by then, nobody can."

"All right. Deal." She shook hands with Sochi. One pump: signed, sealed, delivered.

They all stood up and Eve passed the thumb drive back to Sochi and thanked him. A moment later he exited the apartment and they listened in silence to his heavy feet thunking along the hallway carpet to his condo.

A moment later Eve burst into laughter. "I can't believe you're living in the same building as this guy. It's like he's from the lost land of magic mushrooms. He's an elfin genie."

"Who looks like a Viking." Finch began laughing, too. "Or the Norse god, Odin, with hand-carved beads laced into his beard."

Eve wrapped her arms around Finch and kissed his cheek. For the first time in days they both felt an effervescent buoyancy; the gift of unrestrained laughter. Finch kissed her lips, pressed his body against her and slipped a hand under her blouse.

"Uh-uh. I've got to shower, first," she said. "I can still smell the mould from Justin Whitelaw's basement cavern all over my body."

Finch began to caress her tenderly.

"No, I mean it." She dragged his hand away. "Don't worry, it'll be worth the wait." She kissed him again.

"All right." He broke away. "Five minutes. Max."

"Ten. I promise," she said but before she could reach the bathroom, they heard another knock at the door.

Cursing under his breath Finch went to the heavy oak door and opened it. Before him stood Detective Damian Witowsky.

"Got a moment?" he asked.

※

Detective Witowsky settled into the wingback chair that Sochi had occupied less than five minutes earlier. Finch and Eve took up their previous stations at opposite ends of the sofa and glanced at one another with a sense of foreboding. The zest of their passionate energy dissipated as they studied Witowsky's etched face. How different their world had suddenly become. Instead of Sochi's sparkle and wit, they now confronted Witowsky's edgy grit.

"I wasn't expecting to see you here," Witowsky confessed to Eve. "It might be better if I talk to Mr. Finch on his own."

"If this is about Gianna, then Eve can stay," Finch said. Although Witowsky had been assigned to Gianna's murder, in the past three weeks he'd done nothing to uncover any new evidence — at least nothing that he'd revealed to Finch or the Bay Area media.

"And what about my phone?" Eve leaned in. "Did you get the guy in the red sports car? The one who shot Dean Whitelaw?"

"Last night. We just published a press release an hour ago. A college kid named Jack Querrey. When he saw the video from your phone he made a full confession. But his lawyer Chuck Zanes — remember him, Zany Zanes? — is claiming justification based on self defense. He cited Article 12 in the Universal Declaration of Human Rights." Witowsky shrugged as if that was inevitable. "No matter what, you know the forensics team will hang onto your phone until the sentencing wraps up and any appeals are exhausted. Could be months. Even then...." His voice trailed off without offering much hope.

"Some things never change." She slumped against the sofa and turned her head. "So what's this about?"

"Fiona Page."

"What?" Eve let out a skeptical laugh. "So you've been demoted from homicide to missing persons?"

"Just trying to rebalance the load, Eve. You know what it's like. Last week the guys in MP couldn't keep up. Captain asked me to step in for a while."

Witowsky set his eyes on Finch. "You work with Ms. Page

at the *eXpress,* right?"

"Yeah." Finch wove his fingers together. Finally Witowsky was getting to the point. "She works a few desks away from me. Maybe you heard." Will couldn't suppress the sarcasm in his voice.

The detective narrowed his eyes with a look of scorn. "Yeah, as I was just saying, things are busy. And just FYI, I've interviewed everyone else in your office." He briefly turned to Eve, then back to Will. "Now tell me, when did you last see her?"

"Last Monday. About a week and a half ago."

"What time?"

Finch raised a hand to the back of his neck as he pondered the question. "Three-thirty, maybe four."

"What story was she working on?"

"She wanted to interview Justin Whitelaw. Find out what he knew about Gianna's murder."

"Where were they going to meet?" Witowsky drew his chest up as if he might finally be closing in on some critical facts.

"Café Claude. Over in the French quarter."

"Were you helping with the story?"

"No more than normal. Just talking her through it. About how to approach Whitelaw."

"She'd met him before?"

"Once or twice, but he wouldn't talk to her."

"No? Did she have any concerns?"

"Of course. Every reporter has to figure out how to get a reluctant source to open up."

"So what was her plan?"

Will stalled a moment. "Just to talk him up."

"At the bar? Make like a hook-up?"

Finch tried to recall their last conversation. "We discussed that. My advice was never to trade sex, or even the hint of it, for an interview."

"Why was that?"

"What do you mean?"

Witowsky took a moment to ensure that he had Finch's attention and when he held his eyes, he asked, "Did you have a sexual relationship with Fiona Page?"

Will's head snapped back as if he'd taken a punch on the chin. *"What?"* He stood up and stepped to the side of the sofa.

"Damnit, Witowsky. You don't get to ask that." Eve spat out these words with contempt. "And *you* don't have to answer," she said to Will.

"No? I suggest you do. Mr. Finch where were you last Monday evening?"

Stunned, Finch tried to calculate his whereabouts. Then it came to him. "In the hospital." Another memory flashed through him. "Hell, *you* saw me there with Eve when you confiscated her cellphone!"

Witowsky smiled as he witnessed Finch scrambling to find an alibi that would eliminate him as a suspect.

"Witowsky, you're a complete embarrassment." Eve stood and crossed her arms. "Will had nothing to do with Fiona's disappearance and you know it."

"Yeah? Well, here's something I *do* know. I know that you two have been poking around this case down in the French quarter. Which two super heroes do you think you are? Cat Woman and Clark Kent? We do *not* need you to screw up another investigation like you did with Gianna Whitelaw. I'm telling you. *For the record,"* he said directly to Finch, "Back off."

"That's enough!" Eve pointed to the door and took a step toward Witowsky. Her voice lowered to a restrained growl. "Get the hell out of here, Witowsky."

The detective nodded and stood up. He stepped past Finch, who'd been standing next to the coffee table. Then Witowsky turned back to Eve and shook his head as if he still had lessons to teach her. Lessons about power. How to dominate anyone who crosses your path.

"Just routine, Eve. You know that." He walked towards the door, then paused and swiveled back to her. "Or maybe you forgot. I guess that can happen when you get out of practice."

Finch marched over to the door and waved Witowsky into the hallway. When he departed, Will slammed the door, strode across the room and punched a fist into the top of the wingback chair. An image of Witowsky's face rose in his mind. And Finch beating him to a pulp.

"You see what I had to put up with? Five years with ass-holes like that." Eve set her hand on his shoulder and sauntered toward the bathroom. "I'm going to take that shower. I've got to wash all this slime away. It's getting thicker by the minute." She looked back at him. "You all right?"

He waved a hand and sat down again. "I'm fine."

"Good. If anyone else knocks at the door, don't answer."

※

Once he had Rasputin up and running Sochi sat at his computer terminal and toyed with the search parameters which would unlock the password manager on Eve's data drive. First, he entered the password that unlocked the drive itself: H4-nv34&9_Ee98<-Fi2trJA,<e/D76ME. The drive returned a "wrong password" message. No surprise, Sochi murmured. Any cryptologist worth his salt would never employ the same password twice.

"But we are all creatures of habit," he whispered aloud. Since the correct password to the data drive was thirty-two characters, he reasoned there would be a better-than-even chance that the next password also contained thirty-two characters. He set Rasputin to search for a password of exactly that length. If Sochi's approach were correct, he could save Rasputin days, if not weeks. If incorrect, so be it. He'd simply eliminate all thirty-two character searches on the next pass.

"You see, my friend," he said to Rasputin once he'd initiated the search, "digital logic may be unassailable. But human habits? Not so much."

Satisfied that Rasputin's program was underway and functioning properly, Sochi turned his attention to the mysterious web link on the data drive. Did it provide the key to open the bitcoin wallet? Or was it a rabbit hole that would lead him, Moscow and Arbat into an abyss?

"Only one way to find out." He swiveled his chair to a second computer, this one wired to the internet, and launched his favorite IP address spoofer, a web browser that allowed him to surf the internet anonymously. No one could link back to him, identify him, his server, or even his location.

He clicked the link and a single text box appeared in the middle of a white screen. Below that a caption stated: *Enter your public encryption key. Assume that your adversary is capable of one trillion guesses per second.*

Sochi tipped his chair backward and wove his fingers through the mane of hair behind his head. He narrowed his eyes and stared at the screen. Whoever had patched this website together was no tin-hat trifler. Clearly, the programmer believed in three things: simplicity, security, and complete control.

Sochi stood up and walked into his kitchen. He boiled a kettle of water and set a bag of Earl Gray tea into his "thinking mug," a sixteen-ounce cup his brother had given him on his eighteenth birthday. As his tea steeped he sat on the sofa at the far end of the room and stared at his computer in the distance. You can do this now, he reasoned, or you can do it later. *Or you can walk away and never visit this site again.* Since there was no information he could gather that would aid his decision, the option to enter the web site now or later presented a false choice. Furthermore, Arbat had granted him three weeks to deliver his end of their bargain, therefore delay was impractical.

The only real choice you have available — to enter now or to walk away — ensures a missed opportunity if you walk away. He nodded his head in agreement. Once again, the logic was unassailable.

Sochi sipped his tea, walked back to his computer and settled in his chair. "And when, my friend," he asked himself, "have you ever tossed a new opportunity aside?

CHAPTER SIX

FIONA PAGE POUNDED the leg of the bed cot against the bed-spring coil. She'd been at it for twenty minutes, enough time to work up a light sweat, enough sweat for her to peel off her blouse so that she could continue hammering with renewed vigor. Today, she decided, she would break free.

In two days she'd made some progress in transforming the tip of the coil into a slotted screw driver that would fit the four screws that held the rack of bars to her cell window. After another five minutes battering the metal she wiped the perspiration from her eyebrows and held the flattened coil to the lower left screw. Almost, she murmured to herself and pressed the tip into the steel groove. To her surprise it fit.

"Gotcha!"

She leaned her weight into the coil and turned the screw ninety degrees to the right. As the screw eased out of the wood frame her heart began to race. Yes, you're going to make it!

She turned her attention to the lower right screw. A small burr in the slot seemed to block the fit. She scraped the loose material away with the coil and then pressed the tip into the slot. Yes! She turned it one full turn and then studied the top

59

two screws in the frame. Just out of reach. She stood on the edge of the cot and reached up to the top right screw and gave it a full turn.

Then she jumped off the cot and stood on the concrete floor to consider the last screw on the top left. She'd have to pull the cot from the wall, set it next to the sink and climb up from there. "Better to remove it first," she said aloud, "and then the others one at a time." Just in case the worm surprised her before she could complete the job.

He'd done that twice already, popped in during the middle of the day. The first time to bring her some disinfectant and a bandage for the cut he'd opened on her face. The second time to rape her.

She tried to think how many days she'd been held captive. Ten, maybe eleven. She wished she'd scratched the passing days on the wall under the cot. She that knew she'd been drugged and that he'd increased the dose as her perception of day and night merged into one long blur. But worst of all was his slow descent into naked brutality. What started with his insane courtship of her had regressed into mute violence as he defiled her day after day.

She pressed her teeth together and felt the pain coursing through her jaw. The pain was good; it enforced a discipline and resolve. She stood up and balanced on the end of the cot and fit the coil tip into the top right screw. "Today," she whispered, *"today* you are getting the hell out of here."

※

Fiona gasped and jumped from the cot to the floor. As the door swung open, she shoved her arms through the sleeves of her blouse and sat on the edge of the cot. No time to button up. In one hand she gathered the front flaps of the blouse together. With the other she tucked the screw driver under her right thigh.

Justin Whitelaw stood at the open door, waited for the spring mechanism to swing the barrier back into place. He listened to the bolt extension as it plunged into the strike box with its dull click. As he tested the deadbolt, he released the deadbolt key which recoiled on the steel cable into the fob on his belt. A look of satisfaction crossed his face and then turned his mouth in a cynical frown.

He wore a navy pinstripe suit. As usual, loose strands of his hair were combed over his bald patch. Premature male pattern baldness, she recalled. The technical terminology for early onset baldness. She'd written a health article about PMPB for the *eXpress* last month. But why — *why?* — was she thinking of that now? She tried to shake the thought from her head.

"What day is it?"

A dark look crossed his face.

"Look, I really need to know what day it is. Since I don't know where I am, you can at least tell me what day it is."

He sat on the far side of the cot. "Why is your blouse open?"

She couldn't think of an answer he'd accept and when she didn't reply, he leaned over and drew her hand away to examine her bra.

"What were you doing?"

She looked away.

"What?" his hand locked around her forearm.

"I was just going to wash up in the sink." She pulled free of his grasp and sneered.

He nodded. "Take your blouse off."

"Justin, please." She felt her eyes welling with tears. "Why don't we try to make this pleasant. For both of us."

"How would you do that, bitch?" He pressed his face next to her cheek.

She could smell cinnamon on his breath. As she tried to figure out why he smelled of cinnamon, the hopeless feeling swept through her again. There were no answers. No answers to anything. All she knew for certain was that she had to gather her strength for what was coming. But how?

"I said, tell me how you'd make it pleasant." His voice rose to a near scream as his hand grabbed her neck. "Tell me how you like it!"

"I don't know," she whimpered and slumped onto her side as his right hand pawed at her breasts.

His mouth began to root around the base of her neck and his cheek slipped back and forth against the side of her head. As she leaned back she felt the bedspring dig into her thigh. She pulled the coil free, held the spring in her clenched fist, the sharpened end pointing to the ceiling.

"You really think you can make it better?" he whispered into her ear.

She raised the coil behind his head.

"Make *this* better?" He thrust his hips toward her to let her know what would come next.

She rammed the sharp end of the coil into his neck, just below his left ear.

"What?" He let out a gasp, a wisp of surprise in his voice.

She pulled out the coil and thrust the tip into his flesh again.

"Shit!" He tried to wrench away, but this time she clasped her free arm around his shoulder and punched the coil into his neck once more. Then again. And again.

He dragged himself free and staggered to the sink with a hand clasped over the punctures in his neck. "Fuck," he whispered as he examined the blood in his palm. "What have you done?"

Fiona stood up, took a step toward him, the bedspring coil poised in her hand, a dagger eager for another try at him. "Give me the keys."

He wiped the palm of his hand over his neck, paused and then examined the blood seeping through his fingers.

"Give me the *God-damn keys!*" She thrust the coil under his throat and pressed the sharpened tip against the flesh above his larynx.

A look of terror swept through his eyes. He pulled the fob from his belt and passed it to her.

She grabbed it and turned to the door. Which one? A dozen silver and brass keys hung from the fob. She tried one. Another. Finally one fit. As she turned the key in the deadbolt, Justin tackled her, dragged her under his chest to the floor. She lashed away with the coil tip, striking for his eyes if she could find them. When she heard another wail she crawled from under him, pulled the door open and ran into the hall.

※

When Fiona reached the end of the unlit hallway she glanced

63

back at the basement cell. Behind her Justin Whitelaw hobbled through the door, took one halting step forward, then another. He lunged toward her, and stumbled along the corridor with a hand braced on the wall. She choked down a gulp of air, tried one door, tugged on another, swung it open and charged up a wooden staircase and onto the street.

"Help!" she screamed. "Please help me!" She swung about — no cars, no people — north, south? Where was she? The adrenalin pouring through her body propelled her down the street toward the sound of traffic. As her feet pounded against the sidewalk she felt alive. *Alive!* She would beat this. A fucking survivor!

Halfway down the block she felt the damp fog of the drugs sweep through her vision. She stumbled against a parked car and crashed onto the sidewalk. She glanced back only to see Whitelaw gaining on her. He looked drunk, disoriented. She grasped the open flaps of her blouse and tried to race forward. As she fumbled along the sidewalk, she remembered the sound of the wind whistling against her ears. The sound she recalled as a teenager running sprints around the track at Mountain View High School. Run — *run!*

She glanced at the street signs as she crossed an intersection. Grace and Mission Streets. Where? Her legs felt wobbly and she crashed against the hood of a parked pickup truck and fell to the sidewalk. Her ankle screamed with pain. Had she broken her foot in this mad panic? Once again she forced herself forward, limped through the traffic, her eyes alert for squad cars, fire trucks. Maybe someone would help her. Maybe someone would kill Justin Whitelaw. Nothing. No one to save her. She turned left on Mission and before she crossed 11th she stopped a moment, braced her hands on her knees and sucked in gulps of air while she scanned the street for Justin. *Christ, there he is!*

When she reached Market Street she realized where she was. She turned left and hobbled toward the Van Ness MUNI station and through the graffiti-lined cavern toward the subway entrance. As she hopped the gate control, the attendant let out a brief yelp but no alarm sounded, no alert to bring the cops chasing after her. What would it take? What did she have to do to get help?

Get on the subway, she screamed to herself as she clambered down the escalator, nudging people aside as she went, her hands clasped over her open blouse. "Excuse me, 'scuse me. Please help me!" Nothing. On the concourse, she looked around. There he was — at the top of the escalator — shoving his way into the bottleneck of passengers stepping onto the stairs. *No!*

Maybe a hundred, two hundred passengers loitered in front of the yellow stripe that separated them from the subway tracks. She pushed her way along the loading platform, weaving through the clot of commuters, transients, gangstas and their hooker girls, school kids, and tourists until she reached the end of the station. She hid behind a knot of tall, gangly skater boys dangling skateboards from their hands. Her ankle throbbed and she knew she couldn't run another step. She tried to button her blouse, but her fingers wouldn't cooperate. "Please," she moaned and clutched her open blouse with both hands. She felt her pulse drumming in her throat, sweat dripping from her face and chest. The cut on her face throbbed. All she could do now was wait.

Hearing the dull sound of a train chugging through the tunnel ahead, she peered along the length of the track. There he stood in the middle of the bay, twisting about, his head darting back and forth, a bloodhound trying to catch her scent. Now the light of the oncoming train illuminated the mouth of the subway tunnel. Justin turned to look at it, then back toward her. *He saw her* — his eyes bright with recognition. He took a step forward, then stalled as if something in him had failed. The blood loss? The will to pursue this madness?

"Help me!" she cried out.

Then, seemingly from nowhere, a security guard approached her. His head stood a foot above her and his eyes swept over her face. "Ma'am, can I help you?"

"Thank God," she whispered, unable to find her voice. She clutched his arm and turned back to look at Justin.

Now perhaps three hundred people edged toward the lip of the track. As the passengers prepared to mount the train she saw the look of utter despair on Justin Whitelaw's face. She saw his confusion, his lost hope, the collapse of his life. In the next instant he blinked, and without a backward glance he dove in front of the onrushing train, down onto the tracks where the front left wheel rolled over his body and severed his spine.

CHAPTER SEVEN

ALEXEI MALININ STOOD at the window in his Moskva-City office on the twenty-ninth floor of Tower 2000 and gazed at the rain pelting the black water of the Moscow River. He'd been an early investor in the urban development venture and lived to regret it. In the 1990s, Moskva-City promised to become the financial heart of the new Russia. Now the twelve-billion-dollar boondoggle suffered from a forty-five percent vacancy rate, just as eight *new* towers neared completion. The scale of incompetence reminded him of the late soviet era, except this time no one could honestly blame Yankee capitalism for their woes. The Russian oligarchs and technocrats were responsible for this mess — and the US dollars, Yen and Euros they borrowed to finance it could never be repaid in rubles.

Since the collapse of the price of oil, the economy had become an unmitigated disaster. With the financial system faltering, the currency in shreds, the media shackled and the political opposition in chains, the only solution was to rebuild the military and make a grab for old glory: Georgia, Crimea, the Ukraine. Next up, Syria and then the Baltic states. No wonder so many Russians had longed for the return of communism. Or at least for a strong man who could turn their heads away from the sight of their collective ruin.

Malinin expelled a long stream of air through his chapped lips and watched a cloud of condensation form on the window. Good, he thought, it blurs the premonition of catastrophe. He stepped over to the wall behind his desk, placed a hand over his head and stretched his back, part of a set of exercises he performed daily to release the tension from the stabbing and surgery he'd endured in 1987.

When Malinin completed the round of prescribed stretches, he returned to his desk and continued to work at his computer. The spreadsheets revealed catastrophe. No matter how he toyed with the set of financial inputs, he'd become insolvent within two months unless he found a new source of cash. But that likelihood diminished with each passing day since the murder of his American partner, Dean Whitelaw — Senator Franklin Whitelaw's step-brother.

He brushed a hand over his face. How had he allowed himself to bet everything on a single roll of the dice? Everything that he'd learned about diversification, about hedging risk, about the treachery of partnerships. He'd forgotten all of it when he first heard of a new enterprise that could change the world. The word itself seemed magical: GIGcoin.

The Whitelaw brothers had approached him about GIGcoin in 2010, two years after Wall Street's collapse, at a time when the American Federal Reserve printed trillions of dollars to halt the death spiral of the US economy. Their solution, quantitive easing, was little more than sorcery, a piece of legal legerdemain to keep the economy limping forward. The Fed's illusion could work for a few years, the Whitelaws maintained, but eventually a tinder box stuffed with so much printed paper would ignite an inflationary inferno that could never be contained.

Dean Whitelaw had explained the pending catastrophe as he envisioned it. "We've got four, maybe five years, before the whole mess blows. That's all the time we have to launch GIG-coin as an alternative currency. We're going to anchor it in the USA, the UK, Europe, Russia, China and Japan," he said as he lit another cigar. "With your background and your connections to Putin, we want you to take the lead in Moscow. Franklin will handle the politics in D.C. and we've got interested parties — well-connected parties — in the west. But we want you to bring in the key players from China and Japan."

Malinin had met with Dean and Franklin Whitelaw at the Royal Hawaiian Hotel in Honolulu. Hawaii provided Malinin with the easiest access to the USA and if he needed to, he could quickly submerge in the burgeoning community of Russian ex-pats who'd built a beach-head in Honolulu.

The three of them talked about strategy while they sipped Mai Tais and watched the surfers glide on the waves into Waikiki Beach. At the time they all felt like geniuses. A year earlier, in 2009, bitcoin had been launched to little fanfare. But as the world economy teetered, bitcoin gained notoriety. The digital currency couldn't be inflated. It didn't need banks, or bankers, for that matter. Nor countries, nor politicians to "fan the flames of inflation," as the senator said.

Then trouble came in spades: bitcoin was exploited for money laundering, drugs and weapon crimes. And in 2014 over four hundred and fifty million US dollars worth of bitcoin disappeared. Without a trace. Whoever lost it could never claim it. Whoever found it would never know to whom it once belonged. "Like finding gold coins buried under the roots of the Judas Tree," Dean Whitelaw claimed with a hint that he knew exactly where that tree stood and what kind of shovel he'd use to dig it up.

GIGcoin offered several important improvements on bitcoin. First, its mathematical algorithms could be modified annually. To ensure it provided enough currency to support an expanding global population, the accrued value of GIGcoin would be adjusted by the world GDP expressed in the value of Gold: GDP In Gold — or GIG. Furthermore, with the currency's governance managed by a sanctioned international group, the wild west scandals that plagued bitcoin could be eliminated. "Or reduced," the senator conceded.

The Whitelaws' finance mathematician, Raymond Toeplitz, had already constructed the framework and software to regulate GIGcoin. "He's a genius. Stanford PhD., post doc from Oxford. The works." Dean smiled at the Russian.

"So you hold the brains, the patents and the software for GIGcoin and I provide the Russian and Asian network," Malinin said after considering the offer of partnership. "But what are my guarantees?"

It took two more days to negotiate a solution. They agreed that in addition to his proportional shares in GIGcoin Corporation, Alexei Malinin would become Vice President of Operations and, most important, he'd be granted one of two digital keys that Toeplitz had invented. The keys were needed to launch the software program once all the partnerships were in place. That meant that GIGcoin required a two-step system to activate and modify the currency, much like two signatures required to validate a business check. And Malinin was assigned one of the signatures. He agreed to the offer and within three months he'd secured the alliances he needed in the Kremlin and the far east.

Finally everything was in place. The corporate headquarters of GIGcoin Bank and Exchange was registered in the Cayman Islands. The international cartel had signed off on the corporate structure and agreed to all operational terms and conditions. The nominal value was set at one billion dollars. The enterprise would ensure their personal wealth for generations. That was guaranteed.

Until Dean Whitelaw's murder. And the disappearance of the GIGcoin software. Now Malinin's only remaining business assets were a contract with a dead man and a digital key with no lock to open.

As he contemplated his situation, a window appeared on Malinin's computer screen. The header read: *Public Encryption Key Received.* His neck tilted backward as if someone had nudged him in the chest. He recovered his presence of mind, clicked on the message link and leaned toward the screen.

Six lines of code appeared, neatly stacked in vertical rows. No message, no hello. Most important, no suggestion of any error. He studied the code for a moment. Soon he understood that this string of letters and numbers could only originate from the link connected to the GIGcoin software.

Someone had discovered the link that Toeplitz had created

to initiate the GIGcoin launch sequence. Someone reaching out to him. Malinin did not yet know the visitor's name, where he lived, or how he'd discovered the GIGcoin files. Nonetheless, Malinin realized that he had lured a key player into his domain. The trap had sprung.

He would need to call in Marat to help with the computer coding and messaging. And Kirill to provide any muscle that might be required. They could be ready within twenty-four hours and meet with his associates in Honolulu. Then Malinin's final hunt could begin.

CHAPTER EIGHT

EVE NOON SAT next to Leanne Spratz in the booth at the far end of Lori's Diner on the corner of Powell and Sutter Streets. The fifties-style restaurant provided privacy in a very public place: ten or twelve separate booths in a busy restaurant open 24-7. The kitschy decor — black-and-white checkerboard linoleum flooring, red vinyl bar stools and booths, a mint green Ford Edsel parked next to the juke box, the gleam of polished chrome — all of it attracted a clientele of amused tourists looking for a nostalgic lark.

"Thanks, Leanne." Eve finished her coffee and set the cup aside. "You've been good to me over the past two years. I appreciate it."

"No worries." She waved a hand dismissively. "The last two years have been the best part of my career at the SFPD. Some of us still refer to you as Saint Eve."

Eve smiled and turned her head away. "It came at a hell of a price."

"I remember." Leanne studied her friend for a moment. "Okay. Change of topic: are you, or are you not, seeing someone?"

"What?"

"Someone who might cast that glow in your face. Maybe a new ... manly-man?"

Eve laughed and glanced at a family peering into the interior of the Ford Edsel.

"And if I am?"

Leanne shrugged. "Good for you. About time, if you ask me. Someone like you without a significant other in your life? Makes no sense. Either that or the universal mating system's completely broken."

"Well. Maybe it's not *completely* broken." Eve considered Leanne's twenty-one-year long marriage. According to what everyone said, she and her husband were still solid as a rock. Lucky girl.

"So." Eve raised her eyebrows; back to business. "You were able to run everything through your magic forensic lab?"

"It's not magic. Just science with a dash of intuition and fifteen years' experience." She drew a plastic shopping bag from under the table and passed it to Eve.

"What's the verdict?"

"I don't know what you were looking for, but I suspect this won't tell you much."

"No?" She opened the shopping bag and gazed at the contents: Separate vials containing the white cross-hatched pill and the sample of bodily fluids, a ziploc pouch with strands of Fiona Page's hair, two larger bags holding the twin brandy glasses, another containing a coffee mug that said "World's Best Mom," and a small ziploc bearing a tube of Lypsyl.

"So what's the run-down?" Eve set the shopping bag at her

feet and turned her attention to Leanne. As always, she expected an oral report. No written analysis, nothing to tie Leanne's forensics lab to Eve's freelance detective work.

"The pill is high-grade Rohypnol. The so-called date-rape drug."

"I suspected that."

"Yeah. The DNA signature on the Lypsyl stick matches the hair sample. But neither of them match anything in the national data base. So they're from the same person, but who knows who?"

"If you want to know — "

Leanne raised a hand. "Sorry. Game rules in play: the less I know the better."

Eve glanced away and nodded.

"The bodily fluid samples are typical bed sheet scat. One, sperm. The second, unidentifiable vaginal secretions. Again, nothing matches anyone in the data base."

"How old is the sample?"

"Hard to say. One week or two?"

"And none of it matches the DNA from hair or Lypsyl?"

"No. I made certain of that."

A look of disappointment crossed Eve's face.

"As to the two brandy glasses, there wasn't enough residual saliva to determine a DNA signature. But I did lift the fingerprints."

Eve tipped her head to one side. "And?"

"The prints are from two people. Neither match the prints on the coffee mug."

"Go on."

"The first set of prints didn't match anyone in the data base. But—"

"The other did?" She knew Leanne liked to play a game Eve called But-Now-What? — especially at the end of her reports. Perhaps all forensic techs enjoyed this moment, the denouement when they could divulge a clever surprise.

"Yeah. And guess who." Leanne inched forward. "It matches some prints in the excluded set."

Eve recalled how the system worked. Whenever a crime scene investigation called for a forensic sweep, all of the prints from the investigating officers would be excluded. The police fingerprints were stored on an internal data base that no one else could access.

"So who is it?"

Leanne paused and shook her head with a look of wariness. "Damian Witowsky," she whispered.

"Witowsky?"

"Yeah. It's a ten-point match. Statistically, a ninety-nine-point-nine precent probability."

She sat back to consider this. "So I've caught Witowsky sipping brandy. With someone you don't want to know about."

Leanne nodded. "Whatever he's done, you got him, girl. But be careful. Rumor is that IAD already has Witowsky in their sights."

"For an admin investigation — or criminal?"

Leanne closed her eyes and whispered, "Criminal. Supposedly."

Eve took a moment to mull over the implications. When Internal Affairs moves forward on a criminal investigation the result is almost always the same. A cop goes to jail. And there he will die.

"What did he do?"

She shrugged. "He crossed over."

Eve gazed at the front door as she considered the unwritten rules. Rule one: if you move to the dark side, no one else can know about it. Ever. Rule two: ensure you have enough money to last the rest of your life. Plus fifty percent. Rule three: if you need to, make sure you can cross back. Undetected.

"I wonder if he has enough money," Leanne said.

"He'd already be gone if he did." Eve checked her watch then gathered her purse and phone. She wanted to bring Will up to date as soon as possible.

"If not, then I'd consider him armed and dangerous. Especially if he thinks there's no way back into the box." Leanne rummaged through her purse for a credit card.

Back into the box. Meaning the SFPD coffin. Eve smiled at that. Once you were out who would ever want to climb back in?

※

As Will clicked off his phone, Eve walked through the door to his condo.

"That was Wally." Finch said. "They've found Fiona. Turns out she escaped."

"Escaped?"

"Yeah. She had this horrible chase into the Van Ness Metro. And get this" — he pulled both hands through his hair with a look of disbelief — *"Justin Whitelaw is dead."*

"Dead? What are you talking about?"

"It's unbelievable." He sat down and dropped his hands in his lap. "He was hit by a subway train rolling into the station. Fiona was *right there.*" He looked at Eve, his face a knot of confusion and relief.

"Is she all right?" She sat beside him, set a hand on his knee.

"I don't know. She's in the hospital. Wally wants me to see her." He pointed to his phone as if Wally might inhabit the inner wiring. "He wants me to get her story."

"Now?" Eve shook her head. "You guys are ruthless. Almost as bad as some cops I know. What's she in the hospital for?"

"Psychiatric assessment. Apparently she collapsed. A full-blown melt down." His shoulders sank as the weight of Fiona's catastrophe fell through him. "I can't believe it."

"I'm sorry, Will."

A weary exhalation slipped from his mouth. "At least she's alive."

A moment of silence drifted between them. Eve opened the shopping bag Leanne had returned to her. "So I've got some news," she said in a brighter voice.

"Uh-huh." Finch stared into his hands, gazed at the desolation slipping through his life. He could almost see it: the vague outline of emptiness.

"From Leanne." She waited for him to look at her. "She finished her analysis."

He raised his head, just now recalling that Eve had arranged an assessment of the materials they'd collected from Justin Whitelaw's hideaway and Fiona's cubicle at the *eXpress.*

"What did she tell you?"

"Not much." She shrugged. "Except for one thing."

Finch sat up now, his mood shifting to curiosity. "Okay. So tell all."

"First, as suspected, this is Rohypnol. And this is a mix of semen and vaginal fluid, unidentified." One by one, Eve lifted the items from the bag and set them on the teak table. "Leanne correctly matched the DNA from Fiona's hair to the Lypsyl. But the fingerprints on the mug don't match either of the prints on the brandy glasses."

Finch considered the implications. "So there's no evidence that Fiona was ever in Justin's apartment."

"Not based on what we have."

"No surprise, I guess. Turns out she was imprisoned miles away." He gazed at the ceiling, tried to fit the pieces together. "And none of the DNA or fingerprints identify anyone?"

"Well," she hesitated. "That's where the exception comes in."

"And?"

"The second glass. Guess whose prints are on the second glass."

"I give up."

When she didn't respond, he examined her face, sure that she was enjoying some pleasure in withholding a piece of evidence. "Okay. The flippin' Queen of Prussia?"

"Damian Witowsky."

"Witowsky?"

She nodded.

"Which means … what?"

"I was thinking about that on the way over here. Obviously, Justin Whitelaw knew Witowsky — well enough to invite him to his hideaway for a brandy. Naturally, Witowsky had to interview him about Fiona's disappearance. But why meet Witowsky there? Would Justin bring him into his secret world if Witowsky didn't know it already existed? In other words, they must have a previous relationship."

Finch gazed through the window and nodded.

"And think about how Witowsky delayed interviewing you after Fiona's abduction."

"Over a week later."

"But in that same time, he was socializing with her kidnapper."

Socializing? Not very likely. Finch struggled to make sense of it. "Maybe he was protecting Justin. Maybe even orchestrating some of this mess."

"It's possible. Leanne says there's a rumor that IAD is watching Witowsky."

"Internal Affairs? That's serious stuff."

She nodded.

"Combined with what we have, can't we report him?"

"It's a snake pit. Move too fast, and they'll bite your throat. Remember, Witowsky had legitimate cause. In fact, he was *required* to interview Justin Whitelaw."

"Interview, yes. But drink with him?"

She shrugged off the implication of a misdemeanor. "So yes, it's against protocol. But think a minute. That's all we could bust him for. No, we have to wait for another shoe to drop."

Finch felt another wave of inertia wash through him. "All right. In the meantime, I've got to see Fiona."

He stood up, slipped his phone into his pocket and hoisted his courier bag over his shoulder. He struggled to adjust the strap. Get on with it, he told himself. Go deal with the horror that has gripped Fiona's life. And take your share of responsibility for it.

"I could be several hours," he said. "If they let me see her. There's some Thai food in the fridge. Wait for me here?"

She stood beside him. "Of course."

They kissed.

"You're a hard one to part with, you know."

"Go." She pushed his arm toward the door. "I'm going to sleep for a day. And when I wake up, I'm going to take a nap."

※

When Finch arrived at the Trauma Center at the San Francisco General Hospital, the ward nurse told him that the medications that the psychiatrist had prescribed for Fiona were finally taking effect. Her blood pressure continued to drop and would soon approach the normal range. Most important, in the last six hours her emotional stability had leveled off and she could answer routine questions coherently.

"What's a routine question?" Finch asked.

"What would you like for lunch. Would you like to go for a walk."

Finch nodded, wondered if his sudden appearance could trigger an emotional outburst. "So it's okay if I see her."

"She's been asking for you. You can visit for ten minutes," Boveri told him. "Just let her know you care. That you're glad to see her and you'll be back soon. But *don't* ask her about the kidnapping. Understood?"

"Of course."

"She'll be in the acute psyche ward for at least a week while we assess her."

"What happens after that?"

"Depends on how far she comes along."

Finch considered the possibilities. "And what if she's not so far along?"

"Depends. Maybe extended care. If she can't recover, she may have to be committed." He shrugged. "We'll cross that bridge later, okay?" Boveri turned his attention back to the computer monitor on the nursing station desk.

As Finch followed Boveri's directions down the corridor he reminded himself that Toby Squire lay comatose in a secured room in the hospital brain injury ward. Wally had emailed him the news: two days earlier Squire had been transferred here from the Mount Zion Medical Center. A shiver ran though him as he recalled the brutal attack he'd inflicted on Eve — and chasing him in the dark across the lawn of Dean Whitelaw's Sausalito estate. Madness!

Eventually he found Fiona standing near a bench overlooking a courtyard garden. He imagined that the scene outside — serene, vacant, synthetically bucolic — provided an antidote to the horror that she'd endured. Hoping not to surprise her, he called from a short distance. "Fiona. Hi."

When she turned, he noticed the suture on her cheek. A tidy job, knitted softly in the center of a fading bruise.

"Glad I found you," he began.

The skin of her forehead furled. Her nose snuffled as if she was about to sneeze, and then she burst into tears and covered her face with her hands. Finch stood beside her and brought her into his arms. He felt the tears dampen his neck.

"I'm so sorry," he whispered. "I can't tell you how horrible I've felt."

"I promised myself I wouldn't cry," she said and broke into a new round of weeping. "Jeez, look at me. I'm a complete mess, Will."

"No, you're not. You're wonderful is what you are." He held her at arm's length and looked into her eyes. "More important, you're alive."

"Yeah." She nodded. "At least I made it."

"Thank God for that." He held her so that he could examine her. The whites of her eyes appeared to be wired with microscopic red filaments, her eyelashes clotted with tears ready to fall. Her lips, quivering, were chapped and split at the corners.

"I'll bring you a Lypsyl next time I come."

She managed a brief laugh. "Would you? I'm addicted to the stuff."

"Tomorrow. I promise."

Another tear jumped from her lashes directly to her chin. She looked into his eyes, held him there and then glanced away. "I can't talk about it, Will."

He nodded.

"I don't want to. I mean, I don't think I can."

"I know."

"Wally will want you to interview me."

Finch frowned and glanced away.

"Hell, he's already asked you, hasn't he?"

"Do you think he's that callous?"

She narrowed her eyes with a look of uncertainty. Her breathing steadied and she drew herself aside. "I don't know if I can go back."

"Back to what?"

"To work. To the *eXpress.*"

Finch took two steps and stood in front of the window. A child and his mother sauntered up the concrete stepping stones through the garden below. "Have you seen Alexander?"

"Once. My sister said she'll bring him around again this evening."

"Good." He turned around to face her. "Fiona, the head nurse told me not to ask you about what happened. And I'm not going to." He held up a hand, a crossing-guard stopping a line of traffic. "That's all in the past and if you never say a word to me about it, that's fine. In fact, don't ever talk to me about it, unless you really do want to confide in someone. And if you do, you'll have me — all my attention. And in complete confidence." He paused, thought a moment, and continued.

"But there's something more important than all that, Fiona. It's about tomorrow and the next few days. The nurse also told me they're going to assess you over the next week. It's like a test. One you really have to pass."

"What test?" Her eyes focused on him without blinking.

"They want to see if you can come back. Go back to Alexander. To be a mom, earn a living. *Provide.*"

Her chest deflated and she gazed at the floor tiles. Down the corridor the drone of a floor polisher hummed in the air as a maintenance worker swept the machine from side to side in long, heavy arcs.

"That means going back to work," he continued. "To the one thing you do so well."

She shook her head. "I don't know, Will."

"Well … that's the test. That's the one you have to pass."

She considered this a moment. "Okay."

"Good."

"And you'll visit again?"

"Absolutely. With a six-pack of Lypsyl."

"Okay." She smiled. "Can you bring me the Honeyberry flavor?"

He laughed, pleased that he could leave her enjoying a moment of reassurance. Somehow it relieved his feeling of guilt.

※

From the hospital, Finch drove downtown to the *eXpress* office. He settled into his cubicle and in twenty minutes wrote a brief summary of Fiona's abduction and escape. Next he pieced together an account of Justin Whitelaw's death in the Van Ness Metro Station. Since Fiona refused to discuss her experience, both stories contained nothing but the facts. The story was still fresh, and no one would expect much more at this point. Finch advised the *eXpress* webmaster to position the stories side-by-side and link them with a block headline above both articles: "Senator's Son, eXpress Reporter in Subway Tragedy." An intern would add photos of Fiona and Whitelaw to complete the page composition.

Ten minutes after he'd finished the reports, his desk phone

rang.

"I just read the stories." Wally's voice contained a breath of compassion. "Fiona wouldn't give you any more?"

"She's still struggling, Wally."

A pause. "That bad, huh?"

"Yes and no. She had the grit to stab Justin and break out of there. But they're doing a psyche assessment and if she doesn't get her life back on track she could be in trouble."

"What kind of trouble?"

"Nobody's saying. But she's not sure she can come back to work. So then it's like falling dominoes: no job, no money. No money, no rent. It could end up with her losing custody of her son Alexander to her OCD ex-husband. Crazy stuff like that."

"You can tell her for me there's no chance of her losing her job." Wally's voice rose with determined certainty. "I'll tell her myself in the next day or two."

"Maybe we should all visit her. Everyone in the office. One at a time."

Another pause. "Good idea. I'll ask Dixie to put together a staff roster of some kind. Get one or two people in there every day. Listen," his tone dropped a note, "what's the hard evidence linking Justin Whitelaw to Fiona's kidnapping at this point?"

"You mean apart from Fiona's sworn accusations?" He shook his head, still incredulous that her case had ground to a halt. "Okay, so I checked the SFPD half an hour ago and they aren't saying anything yet. Apparently they haven't been able to locate the cell where Justin held her. And Fiona was so dosed up on Rohypnol she can't point the way either. Therefore no physical evidence. Shirley Yates in SFPD media relations said they'll have a press conference tomorrow."

"You'll be there for that?"

"Yes." Finch nodded as he gazed at his computer screen. "You know there's something else about this story that's bothering me."

"What's that?"

"Damian Witowsky."

"The cop investigating the kidnapping?"

"Yeah. The same cop assigned to handle Dean Whitelaw's murder."

"A coincidence?"

"Maybe." Finch shifted the phone from his right ear to his left. "But when I was trying to track down Fiona, I came across some evidence that Witowsky and Justin Whitelaw were drinking together."

"What? Where?"

"Fingerprints on a brandy snifter with a ninety-nine percent match to Witowsky. In a shag-pad Whitelaw kept on Claude Lane in the French Quarter."

"And you know this, how?" Wally's voice contained a blend of doubt and admiration.

Finch shrugged. "The usual."

Wally let out a brief chortle and continued. "So ... Witowsky is friends with Fiona's kidnapper. The same jerk he was supposedly tracking for over a week."

"And get this. Seems he might be the subject of an IAD investigation."

"Really?"

Finch winced, hardly able to believe it himself.

"Okay. Keep him on your radar."

"All right."

"Is there anything you think I should take to Fiona?"

"There is." Finch smiled as he continued. "Take her a stick of Lypsyl. In fact, tell everyone in the office they *have* to give her a tube of Lypsyl. Everyone, no exceptions." He had a vision of boxes of Lypsyl lining her cubicle. "She fought like hell to get out of that freak-house. A lifetime supply of Lypsyl will give her a laugh."

※

Finch returned to his condo a little after eight that evening. When he opened the door he found Eve and Sochi engaged in a solemn discussion over the kitchen table.

"I don't know," Sochi said as he fingered the beads in his beard. The look on his face suggested that he was pondering a dilemma.

"It's time to move forward, Sochi," Eve said and waved Finch over to the table. "Not to hesitate. The three of us can handle this on our own."

"Who's *'us'?*" Finch asked. He leaned over and kissed Eve's forehead and sat beside her.

"You, me, and Sochi. He got a response from the mysterious link on the data drive. From the *dark web.*" She arched a brow in mock disdain.

"They're Russians. Likely mafia. And if they are, they don't play nice." Sochi tried to sip some tea from his mug, realized it was empty and poured a fresh cup from the teapot.

"Fill me in." Finch stretched his legs under the table and

attempted to make himself comfortable in the teak chair, a near impossibility. "And give me a shot of that brew, whatever it is you're drinking."

"It's called *Paris Afternoon,*" Sochi said. "My new favorite."

Eve took a mug from the cupboard and Sochi poured the tea.

"All right. So while Rasputin is busy cracking the code on the password manager on the data drive," Sochi continued, "I decided to find out what's on the other side of the link. It took me to a website asking for my public encryption key, which I sent."

"Your what?" Finch heeled off his shoes and pushed them under the table.

"Public encryption key." Eve pointed to a drawing on the table that Sochi had sketched out, a venn diagram illustrating the connections between private and public keys that enable secure communication over the internet. "Basically it allows Sochi to send and receive files in complete secrecy."

"Okay, enough you two. I've just had the longest day — in a very long week. Somebody just give me the Coles Notes version." Finch realized that he was beginning to sound like Wally; after all these years perhaps the old man's cocky superiority had become infectious.

Sochi offered a sympathetic nod and went on. "All right. Even though he tried to mask it, I discovered that the other guy is in Moscow. No idea who he is, so I named him Chekov."

"The short story writer." Finch sipped his tea.

"No, the navigator of Star Trek's USS Enterprise. So

Chekov plans to meet us next week in Honolulu. What he wants is the GIGcoin software. And the reason he wants it? He holds one of two keys required to launch the program."

"The program requires launch keys? Like missile launch codes?"

"There's two of them and Chekov holds one."

"And the second?"

"Who knows?" Sochi cast a glance at Eve while they considered the unknowns.

"And in exchange for the GIGcoin software, what do we get?"

He shrugged. "I guess that's still negotiable."

"Good." Finch glanced through the French doors that led to the balcony. In the dusk, he couldn't distinguish anything outside. Just like GIGcoin. It seemed impossible to determine what it really was, how many puzzle pieces it contained and who held them. "All right, I want you to get back to Chekov tonight. Tell him I want three items in return for the software. One, the name of the second key holder. Two, Chekov's real identity. Three, an on-the-record interview with both of them."

"That could tie it all together, couldn't it?" Eve said.

"Tie what together?" Sochi looked from Eve to Finch, a confused expression on his face.

"Motives for the murder of Raymond Toeplitz and the robbery of Gianna Whitelaw's condo." Finch leaned forward, arms propped on the table top. He knew he was closing in on the endgame: the answer to Wally's *what-the-fuck* question. "Toeplitz gave the thumb drive to Gianna. Then he drove up to Oregon for a final meeting with Senator Franklin Whitelaw, where he was shot by the local sheriff, Mark Gruman. The senator's brother then sent his driver, Toby Squire to retrieve the drive from Gianna's condo — but Eve beat him to it. And for reasons of demented insanity, which is no *reason* at all, Toby Squire drowned Gianna."

Sochi let out a gasp of despair. "Look, this is *way* over my head."

"But here's the crazy, improbable thing," Finch continued. "All of Toeplitz's estate went to Gianna. And when she died, Eve became her beneficiary and the inheritor of their combined assets. Hence, Eve is the legal owner of the flash drive and everything on it, including the GIGcoin software."

"Arbat, you're a pinball wizard." Sochi smiled at Eve and waited to see if anyone else found this amusing.

"Sochi, when I moved in here, you and everyone else in the building wanted someone *different.* Someone you thought *could make a difference in the real world.* That's what *you* said."

"Yeah." He shrugged. "Okay. I did."

"So that's why you have to come with us to Hawaii. We can't do this without you. We're going to break this ring of murder and conspiracy wide open and you've got to be part of it."

CHAPTER NINE

FINCH SETTLED INTO an aisle seat in the last row of metal folding chairs in the Media Relations room of the SFPD headquarters in the Hall of Justice. The exterior of the building, a seven-story concrete box with three elongated entry portals, resembled a Nazi-era monolith. The atmosphere in the press room felt even more oppressive. Dingy, windowless, badly lit and just plain media-phobic. Finch assumed the over-riding architectural intention was to flush the reporters out the doors ASAP.

Four cops entered the room and positioned themselves not far from the lectern, a security detail ready for action. Rarely did the police provide any extensive comments about suicides, but the fact that a prominent political family had lost three members in suspicious circumstances in less than a month required special attention.

As he waited for the press conference to begin Will pulled his phone from his pocket and sent a text to Dixie Lindstrom: *Ask an intern to compile a profile on GIGcoin. Patents, company registrations, legal titles, corporate officers. Plus all mentions in social media. By noon, if possible. Cheers, W.*

A moment later the SFPD media relations officer Shirley Yates marched into the hall with a small retinue of supporters. Beside her stood one of the junior medical examiners, Frank Larson, and Detective Damian Witowsky. Finch began to ponder the idea that Witowsky was being surveilled by IAD. Why would the captain allow one of his detectives under an internal investigation to make a public statement of any kind? Especially about one of the biggest stories in months. Unless they were trying to give Witowsky enough rope to lynch himself. Which meant IAD wasn't ready to tighten the noose. Not yet. Finch shook his head with a sense of exasperation. Who could fathom the depths of this sort of paranoia?

The middle of the room, occupied by roughly forty TV, radio, internet and press reporters, ignited with a volley of camera flashes as Yates stepped forward to address them. Finch used his phone to snap a few images. Even at a distance, the phone captured two decent pictures of Witowsky gazing mutely at Officer Yates with a look of gravitas.

Finch recalled that Eve Noon once had her job. Two or three times a month she'd brief the press standing in the exact spot where Shirley Yates now stood. Strange to think of Eve now sleeping in his bed.

"The report from the Chief Medical Examiner came to me less than a day ago," Yates began. "The conclusion is stated clearly and unequivocally." She turned to the report and read aloud into the microphone: "In the opinion of The Office of the Chief Medical Examiner of San Francisco, Mr. Justin Whitelaw died almost instantly from injuries sustained when he was struck by a train in the Van Ness station on Monday, June twenty-eight."

A murmur arose from the media brigade who stood in the aisles with their equipment silently recording Yates as she spoke. She shifted her weight from one foot to the next and her voice adopted a less formal tone. "At this point, however, we can't conclude that Mr. Whitelaw's death was a suicide. There are complicating factors. The forensic evidence suggests that just prior to his death he suffered multiple cuts to his neck. If these cuts had a mitigating influence on his judgment, on his ability to think clearly, then those factors have to be considered. As a result, the SFPD is investigating the events leading up to his death. Detective Damian Witowsky is here to speak to that side of this tragedy."

"So is it suicide, accident or homicide?" someone called from the front rows. "I have witnesses claiming he entered the Van Ness station covered in blood."

Yates ignored the question and stepped to the left of the lectern and made way for Witowsky to take her place.

"Thank you, Officer Yates. We'll take questions in a moment." Witowsky held a fist to his mouth and coughed into the microphone which responded with a searing burst of feedback. "I'm standing in for the captain who asked me to summarize our canvass of the witnesses to this shocking death. In short, our officers interviewed twenty-three bystanders so far. More are being interviewed as we speak. Most of them shared a similar view. Which is that Justin Whitelaw dove over the concourse edge onto the tracks in front of an on-coming train. Five of the statements came from witnesses who were within three feet of him when he fell. Three of them reported that they saw blood stains on his shirt before he fell. All of them said that he 'looked dazed' or 'appeared disoriented.' However, the ME report shows that his blood-alcohol level was zero-point-zero-two, which suggests he'd ingested some small amount of alcohol earlier in the day, or even late the previous evening. Dr. Carson" — he nodded to the ME officer who stood next to Shirley Yates — "do you want to add anything to that?" Witowsky's voice lifted hopefully, a tone that sounded like a plea to save him from having to continue on his own.

Dr. Carson moved to lectern. "As you are aware, I can't disclose the complete findings of the autopsy. However I can confirm everything you've heard so far. The cause of death was from the impact of the subway train. The autopsy revealed five shallow cuts to the region around his neck — "

"Cuts from a knife?" someone called out.

"Unknown." Carson hesitated. "But the cuts were neither deep, nor from a very sharp blade. Certainly they were not lethal. The instrument used to inflict the injuries is for the police to resolve. Beyond that I won't speculate." He stepped away from the lectern.

"Thanks, Dr. Carson." Witowsky frowned. "All right. The captain instructed me to remind you that the Whitelaw family has asked us to respect their privacy at this time. I'm sure all of us can appreciate their anguish after suffering three unexpected tragedies over such a brief period." He looked across the room. "So, there you have it. I'll take a few questions. Just two or three."

The room erupted in a cacophony of shouted questions. Arms flew into the air, hands waved with urgency. Witowsky shook his head in dismay, seemed to recognize a familiar face and pointed it out. "Frances, is it?"

"No, I'm Gerri Farmer from the *LA Times.*" Gerri stood, a notebook and pen in hand. Old school. "Detective, so far what have you done to determine if Mr. Whitelaw's death was an accident, homicide or suicide?"

Witowsky's expression seemed to wilt as he leaned away from the grill of the microphone. "We interviewed four family members and two of Justin's friends. None reported any signs of depression. Furthermore, he'd been to work that morning. None of his colleagues or staff reported anything to suggest a suicidal mood. However, as you've heard, eye witnesses agree that he jumped of his own volition onto the subway tracks. Which suggests suicide." He shrugged. "Next question. Second row, in the middle."

"I understand that the kidnapping victim, Fiona Page, was discovered in the same station waiting for the train that struck Justin Whitelaw. Is there anything that links these two cases?"

Witowsky glanced at Shirley Yates and Frank Larson. Both maintained their deadpan expressions. "I can't disclose that." He paused and a worried frown creased his face. "Ms. Page is currently undergoing medical assessment and until her doctors green-light us, we can't interview her. Rest assured, once she's recovered, we'll talk to her. Possibly as early as this afternoon."

A collective sigh deflated the room, a gasp of weariness and the recognition that once again the press corps were being fed a buffet of delay and deception. Finch seized the opportunity to stand. He braced a hand on the chair in front of him and called out. "Cut the crap, Witowsky! The first thing Fiona Page said to the attending medics was that Justin Whitelaw kidnapped and held her in captivity for over a week! Did you bother to interview *any of them?*"

A new round of outrage burst through the room as the reporters hurled their questions at the police. At the same time two cops with starched faces standing near the doorway shifted into gear. As they approached Finch, one assumed a look of malevolent pleasure. The other seemed to anticipate a fight he knew he would certainly win.

"Ladies, gentlemen ... I think that's it for today." Witowsky shrugged with relief. As he looked at the back of the room, his eyes lit on Finch. Witowsky smiled when he saw the cops' hands wrap around Finch's biceps as they frogged-marched him out the rear door.

"Hands off," Finch snarled and broke free of their clutches as the three of them strode down the hall toward the side exit. "I'm leaving under my own steam, okay? Let's try to keep this on a platonic level."

As they breezed down the corridor toward the steel doors, they took his arms into their hands again. His feet stumbled on the final rush through the door. Then the cops released him with a quick heave-ho and he tripped down the exterior steps and smacked onto the sidewalk with a sharp twist that tore open his pants at both knees.

He stood up and examined the twin wells of blood seeping through the tattered flaps on his khakis. "Bastards!" he yelled, but the heavy door slammed shut and Finch was left to wail his obscenities into the empty air. As he limped along the sidewalk to his car, Finch could almost hear Wally's voice echoing in his ears: *"We are going to take the bastards down!"*

During the drive back to the hospital he wondered just how much further down he'd have to go before he could stand upright again. But when he did, he'd chronicle this episode, blow for blow and get Lou Levine to sue the arse off everyone from the chief down to the two drones who'd tossed him onto the street.

※

Before he returned to the hospital, Finch stopped at his condo, washed the blood from his knees, applied a bandaid to each cut and changed his pants. By the time he entered Fiona's hospital room, his knees had swollen into two round lumps. He convinced himself that his stiff-legged limp would last no more than a day. He imagined soaking in a hot bath with Eve. No doubt that would cure him.

Fiona sat in a chair, a laptop computer perched on her thighs. She closed the lid and smiled. "Good to see you."

"You too. You look five hundred percent better." He studied her face. The bloodshot eyes were now clear, the tear-encrusted eyelashes bore a hint of mascara, and her cracked, blistered lips were almost smooth again.

"Getting there." She tipped her head to one side. "But I still have moments. A lot of them, to be honest."

"You working?" He sat on the edge of the bed and slipped his courier bag onto the floor.

"Wally came by. For almost an hour." She pointed to a vase of flowers. "He got me going again."

"Good. Looks like you've had a few other visitors too." He

pointed to seven or eight tubes of various brands of lip balm lying next to the vase.

"Yeah. Five so far. I can't quite believe it. Looks like you've successfully turned me into San Francisco's Lypsyl Queen." To prove the point, she drew a stick from her pocket and swept it over her lips in two strokes.

"And deservedly so." He tugged a box of twelve sticks from his courier bag and passed it to her. He'd tied an inch-wide ribbon around the package and knotted it with a clumsy bow.

She glanced at them and loosened the bow. "Honeyberry, too."

"Yeah. For the queen."

They shared a laugh as she set the package on a side table.

"So Wally got you back to work already."

She slipped her computer onto the side table. "Yes. And I thought a lot about what you said. About *the test.*"

"Mmm."

"I figured there's only one way forward. And that's straight through it." Her hand formed the shape of a blade and her arm pierced the air.

"Smart."

"Wally told me to write a feature. The complete story, five thousand words, guts, gore, and all. He said it would be a way to own what happened. And when you own it, you can destroy it."

Finch smiled. A typical Wally Gimbel quip. "He said something similar to me about the shooting up in Oregon." He brushed a finger over the missing tip to his earlobe. "In a way, it's true. You get to do a psychic purge."

"I know I need to. Besides," she hesitated as she drew another long breath, "the cops are going to interview me this afternoon. Writing about it might prepare me."

Finch looked away and then shifted to face her directly. He felt an obligation to tell her about the press conference. He described the SFPD's focus on Justin Whitelaw's dive onto the tracks, the evasive non-answers to direct questions from the press. The dispute about how to classify the case: homicide, suicide or accident. "Most important, they haven't formally linked Justin Whitelaw to you. I mean … to the fact that he kidnapped you."

"What?" A look of astonishment swept over her face.

"When I brought it up, they threw me out. Literally."

Her eyes wavered from side to side and she brushed a finger over her right eyelash. For a moment, Finch thought she might be having a relapse. Instead, she set her jaw and leaned forward.

"What else?"

"It's a dog's breakfast, Fiona. A mess. The ME report shows he'd ingested a trace amount of alcohol. Some witnesses saw bloodstains on his shirt. Others claim he was disoriented before he went over the edge. His family and work colleagues said he wasn't depressed, so he had no predisposition for suicide."

"No *predisposition?* " She glanced away as if the word was an impostor, a mask to cover the horror she'd experienced in the past week. "You're bloody right it's a mess."

Bloody right. She owned it. Completely.

"Will, there's something that happened on the subway platform, something I'm still not sure of." She shook her head. "I was at the far end of the station and he was in the middle. Maybe thirty feet away when he went over."

He waited for her to continue.

"But if nobody else saw this, I mean if none of the witnesses said anything, then I'm going to sound crazy if I tell it to the cops."

"What?"

"When he saw me. When he recognized me … he had this look of, I don't know, it sounds crazy. This look of epiphany."

"Epiphany?"

She blinked. "As if he realized what he'd done. He saw me standing next to the security guard and he realized it was over. His face lit up with this glow of recognition. Then he jumped."

Finch considered this, tried to imagine what someone might look like the moment before diving in front of a train. He shook his head with a sense of confusion. "There's also the question of the blood on Justin's shirt. Before he died."

"Yeah." She sank backwards into the chair. He sensed the ordeal had absorbed some vital part of her. "Okay, look…. There's one more thing."

Her head tipped up and down as if her body had to convince her soul to confess a hidden crime. "I stabbed him." She paused to study his face. She hesitated and then continued. "I stabbed Justin in his neck. Five or six times. With a bed spring that I'd sharpened into a point."

Two or three tears dotted each of her eyes and she wiped them away.

"Fiona … you had to."

"It was the only way I could escape." She sniffed and then set her teeth again.

"You had to do it. It was him or you and *you* were in the right." He reached over and took her hand. "Don't you see? It was the moral thing to do. And just like Wally said, you should write that, too. The guts and gore."

"That, too?"

"Exactly. And tell the same thing to the cops when they interview you. Tell them everything about Justin, okay? Consider it another part of the test."

※

As he walked through the *eXpress* doorway, Dixie Lindstrom waved Finch over to the reception desk.

"Gabe Finkleman gave it to me ten minutes ago." She handed him an inch-thick, sealed manilla envelope. A floral script that could have been hand-written by Martha Stewart herself was inscribed across the front cover: *Mr. Will Finch.*

"Who's Gabe Finkleman?"

"One of the Berkeley journalism interns."

"That would be me." A long-armed creature with a toothy smile grinned at Finch from his chair behind a computer monitor. He stood up and shook Finch's hand.

"That's everything I could find about GIGcoin. Ms. Lindstrom said you wanted it by noon today?" His voice rose and cracked on the word today. "Let me know if you need anything more." Finkleman flashed another eager smile and then slumped behind his monitor to continue his work on the endless stream of low-level demands that landed on his screen.

"Sure. Thanks." Finch turned back to Dixie. "Wally in?"

"At a meeting." She pointed downstairs, to the recently shuttered *San Francisco Post.* "Last rites, I think."

Finch frowned. "Right. Ask him to see me when he returns."

He continued down the aisle toward his cubicle in the bog. Three other writers were banging out copy on their terminals, their ears wrapped under noise-canceling headphones. Nothing had changed much. Even the dust balls under his desk remained in place. Some had apparently mated and borne offspring.

He turned on his computer and while the system sprung to life and loaded a fresh stream of email into his in-box, he opened the manila envelope and glanced at the contents. Finkleman had printed reams of material related to GIGcoin. A cover sheet provided his summary. An international corporation, GIGcoin Bank and Exchange, was registered in the Cayman Islands. So far the bank didn't have an internet presence, but all the requirements to launch a site were "in situ" (Finkleman's phrase). In other words, he said, the bank could be online and fully functional before the evening news. A "whois" search of the bank's internet identity was blocked, but somehow Finkleman had found the incorporating charter for the bank. The document, registered in George Town, one of the most secretive legal jurisdictions in the world, contained the few scant details required by Cayman law. Which included — and here lay the gold nuggets, Finch realized — the list of corporate directors and their national residences: Reginald Doncaster (England), Hans Hertel (Germany), Alexei Malinin

(Russia), Jerry Chi Chen (China), Hiroji Akihiro (Japan), and Dean Whitelaw (USA). And at the bottom of the list, signing on as a non-regional director: Senator Franklin Whitelaw.

In his mind he saw the pieces connecting Dean Whitelaw to the GIGcoin software lock into place. Furthermore, the Russian contact from Sochi's dark web link had to be Alexei Malinin: the answer to one of Finch's three questions.

Will looked over the cubicle barrier and scanned the office. The interns' desks tethered together behind Dixie's reception area stood empty. Damn.

"Finkleman!"

A moment later Finkleman's long right arm waved tentatively in the air as he emerged from the men's room. "Me?" he mouthed.

"Come here." Finch notched his voice a few decibels lower.

"Sorry," Finkleman said, "did I miss something? In that report?"

"No. But now I want you to produce a complete biography on these seven corporate directors. The first one on the Russian, Alexei Malinin. Can you get it to me by" — he checked the wall clock above Wally Gimbel's office — "say, four o'clock?"

He grimaced. "Maybe."

"Good. Three-thirty would be better."

The intern's eyes widened with doubt.

"Oh. One more thing, Finkleman. What's the best dining room in San Francisco? In your opinion."

He shrugged. "The Ritz-Carlton?"

"Good choice. Sometime, Finkleman — not today, but

soon, and definitely before you return to journalism classes in September — I'm going to buy you lunch at the Ritz-Carlton and you will tell me by what means of stealth and native cunning you acquired the incorporation documents for the GIG-coin Bank and Exchange in Grand Cayman."

※

Wally Gimbel staggered into his office, plunked himself down in his leather chair, tilted backwards as far as the counter-weight chair mechanisms would permit and then stared dizzy-eyed at the ceiling. Finch imagined this is how his boss might appear as he settled into a dentist's chair before a problematic root canal surgery.

"That bad?" Finch eased into one of the guest chairs opposite Wally's desk.

"Worse than I imagined." He pointed to the floor, a gesture everyone at the *eXpress* used to refer to the now-defunct daily newspaper one floor down. "Guys I've worked with for decades threatening lawsuits for their sudden dismissal. Hell, Parson Media is offering a week's pay per year of service. And their pensions remain fully vested."

"Sounds bleak." Finch calculated the benefits. In his case it would amount to a little over ten grand, less taxes, plus a pension he couldn't touch for another thirty years. With that kind of money he might survive for three months.

"The bleak part is seeing the anger the old boys have for me. It's not *my* fault that we've entered the twenty-first century." He tipped forward and set his hands on the desk. A look of surrender crossed his face. "At least we can help some of them."

"How?"

"We're bringing Stutz and Wengler on board the *eXpress.*"

Good. More writers. Once again the *eXpress* would scavenge the *Post* to staff the online editorial section. Stutz and Wengler were both competent. More than. Plus they'd fit into the digital ethos of the *eXpress*.

"Anyway, that's my day so far. How's your's shaping up?"

"Like always; ups and downs." Finch provided a summary of the SFPD press conference including his abrupt departure from the Hall of Justice, and the hour he spent with Fiona. "She's doing better. I think she's going to write the first-person piece on her abduction."

"And consequent serial rape." A look of horror crossed Wally's face.

Finch closed his eyes and turned his head away. "I feel so shitty about it. Wally ... I was the one who pushed her into it."

"No. I did." He shook his head. "And I just assigned her to chronicle the entire chain of events. To expose Justin Whitelaw's twisted mind. You know as well as I do, you track down the story wherever it leads and then you tell the world. That's what we do. *That's the job.* She knows it, too."

Of course. It takes someone half-insane to be so addicted to this kind of work, Finch thought. The adrenalin, the hunger for glory, the rat-like cunning, the relentless chase. Every reporter had to be part sociopath, part Hemingway, part MENSA master. And because it paid so badly, you had to disrespect the need for money. Or at least pretend to.

Wally drew a long breath as if he were preparing to run a second marathon in one day. "Okay, leave Fiona for me to handle." He paused. "Anything else for me?"

"As a matter of fact, there is."

"Lord help me."

"It's like a gourmet meal, Wally. And I've saved the best for last." Knowing he had to deflect Wally's exhaustion somehow, Finch smiled as he slid Finkleman's file across Wally's desk blotter. "Read the summary when you have two minutes. The new intern, Finkleman, did a decent job."

"Who?"

"The Berkeley intern Dixie brought in. Skinny kid."

Wally glared at it as if he couldn't bear the weight of any more trouble. "What's in it?"

"Okay, so this is a two-part story." Finch leaned closer, pointed to the file. "Part one is in there. Dean Whitelaw and five oligarchs from around the world have incorporated a private bank, GIGcoin Bank and Exchange, in the Cayman Islands. GIGcoin is a new digital currency set to launch any day."

"So why do we care? Dean Whitelaw's dead. This is nothing more than an obituary note. Forget it."

Finch held up a hand to stop any further objections. "Part two goes back to the flash drive that Toeplitz gave to Gianna. Which now legally belongs to Eve. We got one of your nephew's friends to crack it open."

"One of the kids from Mother Russia?" He barely stifled a laugh.

"Yeah." Finch smiled, conceding the joke. "Sochi. The flash drive also has a web link that led to one of the six partners, a Russian named Alexei Malinin, who holds one of two keys needed to unlock the GIGcoin software — and that software is also on Eve's flash drive."

This time Wally held up a hand. "Wait, wait, wait. So Eve has a software program, some kind of online money machine that Toeplitz developed. And the Russian has one of two keys needed to launch this thing. Sounds like nuclear weapons."

Finch let out an amused smile. That had been his first thought, too. "Close. More like nuclear money."

Wally looked away and studied the Diego Rivera painting on the far wall, The Flower Carrier, an image of a latino laborer dressed in white cotton and a yellow sombrero loaded with a massive basket of flowers as he crawls uphill on all fours. A modern Sisyphus.

After another moment Wally sat upright, startled by some inner revelation. "So this GIGcoin is — "

"That's right," Finch said. "GIGcoin is the answer to your what-the-fuck question."

Wally drew an hand over his mouth. "It's all about the software. Why Toeplitz was murdered. *Not* because he'd decided to testify for the DA in the case against Whitelaw, Whitelaw & Joss." He blinked as if more facts had just clicked into place. "And it's why Toby Squire broke into Gianna's condo. To steal the software."

"What threw me off," Finch admitted, "was Gianna's murder. But that wasn't really part of any scheme. Just part of Squire's madness." He sat back in the chair and wondered why he'd assumed her death was motivated by some criminal intention. There was no intention at all. Just random bad luck that morphed into insane depravity.

He considered this another moment and continued. "So I have an idea about how to find the second key."

"How's that?"

"Malinin wants to meet. He's sure to know who has the second key."

Wally's eyes cast a look of suspicion. "What's in it for him?"

"He wants the GIGcoin software."

"I bet he does." He glanced away and chuckled under his breath. "But I can't imagine that Eve will give it to him."

"Maybe not, but I want to interview him."

"All right. But Russian mafia? After what happened to Fiona, you have to take someone with you."

"Got it covered."

"Who are you thinking of?"

"Eve and Sochi."

"Where are you going to meet this Malinin?" He turned his wrist, adjusted his watchband.

"Honolulu."

Wally let out a snort of disbelief and then laughed as if he'd been ensnared in an elaborate practical joke.

"Give me a break, would you? A multi-million dollar newspaper collapses under my nose and the next day you expect me to finance an all-expenses-paid trip to Waikiki. Really?"

CHAPTER TEN

SOCHI CAME INTO Finch's condo with a look of triumph on his face. "Rasputin's done it again." He opened the palm of his right hand to reveal Eve's flash drive.

"Done what?" Eve struggled a moment with her suitcase clasp, then snapped it shut.

"Cracked the password to the password manager." He strolled into the living room, a duffle bag propped on his shoulder. "Just now," he added and pointed down the hall toward his condo.

Eve paused. "So. Does it open all the other files on the drive?"

"It does. I haven't examined the files, just ensured that they can launch. Exactly what we agreed to." He looked at her with a measure of pride. He'd accomplished his end of the bargain. It was up to Eve to determine the value of the files and then pay him his ten percent. "We could go through them now."

She heaved her suitcase from the sofa onto the floor. "How long will that take?"

He shrugged. "Couple of hours?"

"No time," Finch said. "Are you packed?"

"All set." He slapped the duffle bag with his free hand. "If you're not going to open it now, then you should take this." He passed her the thumb drive. "Store it someplace that's secure. And keep this password" — he gave her a yellow sticky note containing a long string of printed letters and numbers — "in a separate place. And don't tell anyone, including us, where the drive and password are. Either of them."

"All right." Eve thought a moment, took the drive and paper slip and walked into Finch's bedroom. Then she returned and tugged on her suitcase handle. "We'll meet you at the airport in an hour. Meantime, I've got to get something back at my condo. Will, can you drive me?"

※

Eve had booked three economy class seats from San Francisco International Airport to Honolulu. In the departure lounge, Finch received an email from Gabe Finkleman containing profiles of the six partners linked to GIGcoin Bank and Exchange. After the plane lifted into the air and looped over the bay, Alcatraz and the Golden Gate Bridge, he decided to get to work. He leaned under the seat and drew his laptop from his courier bag.

His challenge was to transform the conspiracy underlying an international business enterprise into a riveting story that the average reader could understand and want to read from beginning to end. Because he knew the plot would unravel in many layers and textures, Finch had to write an opening that grabbed readers by the throat and then screamed at them: *Read this. These bastards are screwing us all!* He closed his eyes and tuned his ears to the pitch of the jet engines as the plane climbed to thirty thousand feet.

"Aren't you glad I booked us in a day early?" Eve set her hand on his arm and smiled with a look of longing. "Imagine. A day on Waikiki Beach. When was the last time you sat on a beach, Will?"

"I dunno. Maybe somewhere in Iraq."

She frowned. "All right. So enough already! I've baked an actual vacation day into this trip and all you can do is joke about it."

"Okay, no jokes. I'm going to love a day at the beach with you. Really. But for now, I've got to write this story while it's percolating in my head."

"Percolating?"

"Just ignore me," he said. He drew the dinner tray out of the arm rest and set his computer in place. "I've got five hours to read Finkleman's research and crank out the beginning of the story for Wally."

"Okay, I won't let you touch me until we get to the hotel in Waikiki. But after that all bets are off. Besides, I've got my own reading to do." She pulled a book from her bag and flashed the cover at Finch. *Bitcoin for Dummies.* "Sochi's gift to me."

They glanced across the aisle at Sochi who occupied the far window seat. He sat hunched over his laptop, his long beard floating an inch or two above the keyboard. He plugged a flash drive into the USB slot on the laptop, typed in a series of keystrokes, unplugged the drive, inserted another and repeated the sequence.

"What's he doing?"

"No idea." Finch glanced up the aisle where the cabin crew prepared the coffee cart. He relished a fresh dose of caffeine and the fuel he needed to get to work.

He knew that readers needed a backgrounder to the GIG-coin story, so he began by drafting a side-bar: "Bitcoin Basics." He laid it out in five bullet-points:

• *Bitcoin is a digital currency that can be transferred globally from buyers to sellers without oversight by banks or governments. Consequently it is a currency of choice in the underground and criminal economy.*

• *Bitcoin can be exchanged via desktop computers or by smart phone apps called "bitcoin wallets." Millions of dollars can be transferred in bitcoin in under a minute. A "block-chain ledger" — bitcoin's most innovative contribution to financial technology — tracks each transaction using a distributed, de-centralized accounting system. However, it's impossible to identify all bitcoin buyers and sellers. Users can remain anonymous.*

• *Bitcoin can be exchanged for dollars, pounds, Euros and other fiat currencies at on-line bitcoin exchanges or corner store bitcoin ATMs. In April, 2014, one of the largest exchanges, Mt. Gox, headquartered in Japan, lost 850,000 bitcoins from their client accounts. Valued at over $450 million at the time, the loss has never been recovered.*

• *Bitcoin was launched on the internet on January 9, 2009 by Satoshi Nakamoto to little fanfare. On 17 November 2013 its value peaked at US$1,216.73 per bitcoin. It now trades for just under $400 per unit.*

• *Satoshi Nakamoto's identity is a mystery. Newsweek Magazine's March 6, 2014 cover story purportedly unmasked the bitcoin creator, but the article was immediately dismissed by industry insiders. Other outings have proven equally fruitless. From 2009 until 2011, Nakamoto communicated only by email. As the currency caught fire, all contact with him stopped and he vanished from the public eye. Experts speculate that "Satoshi Nakamoto" is a pseudonym for a group of elite cryptocurrency experts who remain unknown.*

After scanning the sidebar, Will turned his attention to Finkleman's file. Except for a ten-minute break to eat something that almost resembled camembert cheese and some broken European crackers, he worked without a break until the plane descended over the north shore of Oahu and landed in Honolulu. As they touched down he ran a word count on the two articles he'd drafted. Twenty-five hundred, sixty-three words. Not bad for first drafts. From these two stories he could build the series that he knew would smash down the front gates to the GIGcoin palace. And once inside, who knew what he'd discover?

※

Finch lifted his head from the blanket and looked past the potato-white flesh of his toes to the surf as it crashed onto the hot sand of Waikiki Beach. Eve was right, their one-day vacation was a triumph of self-indulgence. He couldn't believe his luck.

"Come on in, Will!" Eve hitched the straps on her bathing suit over her shoulders and waved a hand. A new swell rose behind her and hoisted her up and down. A roller-coaster ride.

He jumped up, dashed forward, jumped over a falling breaker and dove head first into the trough of water beside a gang of six teenage boys and girls holding hands in a circle. He paddled hard and fast, propelling himself underwater until he could see Eve's green one-piece a few feet ahead. He could hear her scream with delight as he wound his arm around her and pulled her under.

As they broke the surface he spat out a long jet of water and splashed his hand in a slant that sprayed the water past her face.

"You will pay for this!"

"Promise?"

"I was trying to keep my hair dry!" She paddled beside him and kissed his cheek, then wrapped her legs around his waist and braced herself so that she could sweep her hair over her shoulders with both hands.

He locked his arms around her back and held her there. "This is like our first time."

She laughed. "You're so sentimental. I feel like I'm in a Deborah Kerr movie."

"Careful. I don't think that flick ended so well for her."

"Maybe if we make love right away, then everything will turn out perfect."

"Right away? Like, right here?"

She glanced toward the Moana Surfrider Hotel, a 1930s architectural gem that sat above the long flank of sand just above the tide line. She pointed to their corner room on the top floor, the open window she'd pulled ajar to admit the sea air just after they'd checked into the hotel. "No. I'm not some crazy exhibitionist. I mean up there."

He turned his head.

"In our bedroom."

He saw the curtain flap rustle. Could a breeze be tugging at the dark fabric? In this still air?

"All right. But only if we order room service tonight."

"Sure." She smiled and kissed him again. "If you think you'll still be in a mood for eating."

He laughed at that, at the gift Eve had for spinning almost any topic into sexual innuendo. He knew she was falling in love and he realized he was getting there, too. It was all so different than his marriage to Cecily with its weight of domesticity. A child to mind, the worries about tomorrow, the weary routines. No, there was none of that now. Eve had a talent for living in the moment and she invited him to share every minute with her.

He took her hand and they stumbled out of the ocean, picked up their towels and made their way to the patio at the back of the hotel, through the lobby and into an empty elevator car.

Eve leaned against his chest and whispered into his ear. "I've got a special surprise for you."

"A surprise? I love surprises."

"I know you do."

"Mmm. So what is it?"

"Not telling." The tip of her tongue traced the lobe of his ear.

By the time he opened the door to their room, he couldn't

contain his passion for her. Maybe she was right after all; maybe they wouldn't have time for dinner tonight. Or anything else.

※

The next morning Finch and Eve met Sochi for breakfast in the Surfrider Cafe. Finch watched in amusement as Sochi unfurled the top of a flexible bag and pulled out a flash drive.

"You're always bringing a new device into the game, Sochi. What've you got this time?"

"It's called a Faraday bag." He opened the top to reveal the mesh interior. "Looks like a shaving kit, but it provides electro-magnetic shielding for electronic devices. Phones, computers, laptops. And thumb drives." He smiled as if the bag possessed innate intelligence. He set the flash drive on the table.

"Good." Finch sipped his coffee. "But we won't need the drive this morning."

"Right." Sochi nodded and slipped the device back into the bag. He glanced over a shoulder. "Unless the plan changes."

"Nothing's changed." Will wondered how Sochi would react to a last-minute shift to their schedule. He had a touch of obsessive-compulsiveness, a need to ensure life maintained a predictable order and sequence. From what he'd observed, it was a common neurosis amongst the technorati — the minions who engineered the world's digital cogs and gears.

"So how did you sleep last night, Sochi?"

"Perfect." He pointed through the open-air cafe to the beach. "It's the surf. I think it might be harmonic with my REM-wave patterns."

Eve smiled and checked her watch. "So. It's almost eleven

o'clock. Time to go." She glanced at Finch and turned back to reassure Sochi. "I'll text you when the meeting's over and then we'll see you in your room, okay?"

He shrugged and toyed with the beads knotted in his beard. His expression suggested that her comment was unnecessary. Almost coddling.

As they left the restaurant, Eve leaned next to Finch and whispered, "He's nervous."

"Yeah." He didn't tell her that despite their night together, a night that should have dispelled all cares, he felt some anxiety, too.

※

Finch walked past the giant Banyan tree along Kalakaua Avenue, the air clean in his lungs and the sun warm on his skin. The tide was up and he could hear the rollers breaking on the beach where he and Eve had lingered yesterday. Between the ocean and the sidewalk, the beachfront shops were preparing for business. A crowd of tourists with hotel towels draped over their shoulders waited at the open-air counters. The men wore thigh-length swim trunks. The younger women wore thong bikinis. Tattoos wound around thighs, up arms, over bellies. Inside the stalls long-haired boys in surfer shorts rented surf boards, umbrellas and collapsable loungers for a few dollars an hour. A breeze lightly scented with coconut oil wafted past him. He felt as if he'd stumbled into an endless summer.

As he approached the covered pavilion opposite the Aston Waikiki Circle Hotel he paused and studied the passing crowds. No one bore a hint of agitation or concern. The perfect place to meet. At the far end of the pavilion he saw the line of picnic tables. Every other bench was occupied by tourists and topped with clothing, portable ice boxes, towels, newspapers — all you'd need for a day in paradise. Next to the chess board sat a heavy-set man in his mid-thirties. He wore a linen jacket and a monochrome green tie, sunglasses, no hat. Nothing ostentatious. Only the scar along the length of his jaw betrayed him.

Finch approached the bench and studied the board. All the pieces in place, ready to begin. "Do you play the Sicilian Defense?"

The stranger lifted his head and studied Finch. "Never on Monday." A Russian accent, Chekov from Star Trek.

Finch nodded. The greeting matched the prepared script word-for-word.

"Do you have software?"

"Maybe. And you have the key?"

"Maybe. Maybe not." Chekov narrowed his eyes. As he leaned backward his neck thickened above his collar. Finch guessed that he'd trained with weights when he was younger, likely won a tournament or two.

"So. It's all guesswork then." In the near distance, next to the banyan tree, he could see Eve watching them. He frowned and leaned forward to speak under his breath. "I want to meet Alexei Malinin."

Chekhov smirked at this. "He talks through me. Me only."

Finch studied the men on the board. The black pieces were on his side suggesting he play defense. Each stood perfectly aligned, the four knights nosed straight forward, the notches parallel in each bishop's miter, the kings' crosses squared. He wondered how a bull like Chekhov could possess such a tidy sense of order. Had he set up the board, or had someone else?

He said, "Are you wearing a wire?"

"A what?"

"A microphone." He fluttered his fingers and thumb together, a pantomime of lips flapping in the breeze.

When Chekhov didn't seem to comprehend, Finch leaned forward, his head a foot away from the big man's jacket lapel. "Alexei Malinin. If you want the GIGcoin software, then you have to meet me. In person. In the flesh. No later than six o'clock tonight. This is a one-time offer. Take it — or I leave this evening and you never see me again."

Chekhov nodded with a look of contempt. "You want meeting? Okay. Three o'clock outside the Princess Iolani Palace. In the gazebo." His accent sank on the *zee*. "Bring software. And no trouble."

"All right." Finally some progress. "In the meantime, what do you say we have a friendly game." He tipped his chin to the chess board.

Chekhov shrugged as if he had no idea how to begin.

Finch advanced the black king's pawn two squares.

The big man smiled, almost let out a laugh. "White goes first, always."

"Not today, my friend. Starting today, we play by new rules."

※

On the eighth floor balcony of the Aston Waikiki Circle Hotel Alexei Malinin pulled the headset from his ears. He'd heard enough. The reporter knew his name already. No surprise.

Their next meeting was set and Kirill had done his job well. To look strong, impenetrable, controlled — that was enough for now. Later, if the need arose, he could unleash the big man against his adversaries.

Malinin closed the file folder containing the confidential documents on Finch and Eve Noon. Back in Moscow his old colleagues in the FSB had provided everything he needed to know about the reporter. Since his discharge from the US Army, Finch had maintained the charade that he'd served in Public Affairs, a cover for his assignment in Military Intelligence. At least the man could keep a secret, a rare quality in anyone these days.

Malinin walked to the open window and pressed the Zeiss binoculars to his eyes to study Finch. He clearly resembled the photograph in the file. He was taller than Malinin imagined, and heavier in his arms and legs. Perhaps the reporter had lost some of the physical agility he possessed during his tour in Iraq. Ten years later, that would be natural. But his instincts might be sharper, his senses more tuned, his stamina deeper. Malinin watched him jump a black pawn forward two squares on the chess board. Absurd. Who ever starts a fight with a left hook?

He shifted the binoculars a few degrees to the east until he spied Eve Noon pacing under the Banyan tree. Despite the concern drawn in her face, she was a beautiful specimen. Tall, robust — yet elegant. She possessed the self-assured reserve of a runway model. Perhaps because she was once a cop. How strange when beauty and iron discipline are wed in one woman. What man would not want to savor this fantasy for a night or two?

He turned back to examine Finch as he walked away from the table under the pavilion and ambled down to the beach. Why did Finch want to stand against him now? Except for the few who endured through sheer spite, all the reporters in Russia had been imprisoned, intimidated, or simply liquidated. But despite their assurances to him, the Whitelaw brothers had failed to eliminate Finch.

Perhaps one had to take great precaution with such a man, an extra measure of care.

※

The gazebo provided a whimsical air to the clipped-and-pruned Victorian landscape surrounding the Princess Iolani Palace. As he led Eve and Sochi up the steps to the covered platform Finch wondered if they'd stumbled into the gardens of Alice in Wonderland.

But when he saw Alexei Malinin and his team ahead, his wonder turned to more pragmatic considerations. He found himself assigning pros and cons to the venue. Pros: One, a public space distant from any eavesdroppers. Two, a location miles from Waikiki neighborhood snoops who might recall Finch's previous meeting. Three, a decent vantage-point to detect approaching intruders. Cons: One, only a single access point in and out. Two, Chekov guarding that access point. Three, the contented look of anticipation on Alexei Malinin's face.

"Ah, Mr. Finch. We meet at last." Malinin crossed from the far side of the gazebo, his hand extended in greeting. He shook hands and turned to Eve. "And you must be Eve Noon."

"Indeed." She shook his hand.

"Well, I'm always pleased to meet new business partners." He swung around to introduce his team. "This is Kirill, who you met this afternoon" — he waved a hand toward the unsmiling bull Finch had dubbed Chekov — "and Marat, my tech specialist."

"Hallo," Marat mumbled and glanced away.

Malinin paused to smile and after a brief hesitation ticked his hand toward Sochi. "And this is?"

"Our tech specialist. Sochi."

"Sochi?" Malinin's face brightened with an air of surprise. He stepped forward and shook Sochi's hand with brisk formality. "Do you speak Russian?"

"No, not a word." Sochi looked away.

"Ah. Well. Sochi is one of our most beautiful cities. In the Crimea."

Except for a few mispronunciations, the Russian's English was near-flawless, his accent flat, mid-western. Finch was impressed. So far Malinin behaved as if he'd convened a Christmas meeting of the board of directors to announce a special gift for a children's charity.

"Please. Come, over here." Malinin waved a hand and led them to a cluster of chairs in the shade of the gazebo roof. "Kirill will ensure we have privacy."

They sat, three facing two: Finch, Eve, Sochi versus Malinin and Marat. Despite their shared expertise, Marat could not look less like Sochi. His face appeared sallow, almost unnourished. His fingers were stained with nicotine, his jaundiced eyes sunk deep in his face. With a nervous tic he raked thin strands of his hair to one side. Finch wondered if he had cirrhosis of the liver, or if some form of hepatitis had sipped the lifeblood from his being.

"I hope you don't find me too expedient, but I suggest we get straight to business."

"Of course." Finch adjusted his chair so that he could keep Kirill in sight. The man rolled back and forth on the balls of his heels at the top of the stairs. His arms crossed over his belly, probably to screen a pistol tucked under his linen jacket.

"Good. To begin, let me say that I believe you are in possession of software that belongs to our company."

"You mean GIGcoin Bank and Exchange?"

Malinin's bonhomie vanished in an instant. He looked away and then turned back to Finch with a serious turn in his jaw. "Yes. GIGcoin."

Finch leaned back in his chair and glanced at Eve. "Gee, I wasn't aware of a change in ownership. My understanding is that the software belongs to Eve Noon."

"Yes." Eve uncrossed her legs and leaned in. "It was given to me by Gianna Whitelaw. I'm also the beneficiary of her estate and that of Raymond Toeplitz. The lawyers are probating the estates as we speak."

"Any way you look at it, Alexei, Eve has the law on her side here." Finch lifted a hand, a gesture that called for capitulation.

"Not if the property was stolen."

"Stolen?" Eve feigned surprise.

"And you have some alternate proof of ownership?" Finch said.

"Of course." Malinin lifted a briefcase onto his lap and carefully rotated the spindles on a four-cylinder lock located under the leather handle. The latch snapped open with authority. He withdrew a three-page legal document with an embossed seal imprinted on the bottom of each page next to a series of signatures. He passed the papers to Eve. "As a former police officer, I'm sure you can testify to its validity."

Finch watched as she studied the signatures and read the summary paragraphs at the beginning and end of the document. The fact that Malinin knew her background showed that he'd done his research, too. No surprise.

"As you can see," Malinin continued, "Raymond Toeplitz entered into a contract with GIGcoin Bank and Exchange to develop the GIGcoin software for the exclusive use of our company. For this he was paid handsomely. If you are the beneficiary of his estate, Ms. Noon, then congratulations. You will live comfortably for the rest of your life. As to the legal rights to the property, there is not a court in the USA, or Russia for that matter" — he laughed and looked away — "that would dismiss this contact and assign the software to you."

"Maybe." Eve handed the contract back to Malinin. "But as a cop I can assure you that once the lawyers stir the pot, anything can happen. Especially when it comes to assigning the property of a US citizen to a foreigner." She glanced at Finch and continued, "So. Let's talk about the software key. Two of them are required to initialize the program. You hold one. I assume the other belongs to the Whitelaws."

He stared at her without answering. By now his amiable look had shifted to something more sinister.

"I'd like to propose another option that might satisfy both of us. A compromise."

Malinin scowled. "There is no compromise to outright ownership."

Finch watched as Kirill adjusted his weight and took a step toward the staircase. He felt the urge to change the mood. "Why not hear what she's proposing?"

Malinin nodded and waved a hand as if he were shooing a dog across the street. "Go on."

Eve leaned in again. "I will give you a copy of my software and you will give me a copy of your key."

"What?"

"That way we each get what we want and keep what we already have. And neither of us can move forward without the second key."

Malinin's eyes narrowed and he settled the palms of his hands on his thighs. As he moved, the stick man, Marat, touched his shoulder and whispered into his ear.

Malinin held a hand aloft. "A moment." They spoke in whispered phrases, in Russian.

Meanwhile Sochi drew Eve and Finch into a huddle. "He's going for it," he murmured and drew a hand through the mane of hair on his shoulders.

A minute passed as Malinin continued his conference. "All right," he said at last. "Marat can arrange for the exchange tomorrow morning."

"Sochi," Eve asked, "can you prepare for the transfer by ten A.M?"

Sochi shifted his shoulders from side to side, weighing the

possibilities. "Yes. But I'll want to verify that the Russian key is valid before I transfer the software."

Malinin looked at Marat. He nodded.

"Then we are agreed?"

"Not yet." Finch set a smile on his lips. "I have two other conditions."

"What conditions?"

"You and me. We talk for an hour." His hand waved back and forth between them. "An interview. On the record. Before we exchange the key and the software."

"And the other?"

"You confirm who holds the second key."

Malinin wiped a hand over his face to cover his look of amazement. He shook his head, unsure how to reply. "Okay. You want to talk, we'll talk. I'll tell you anything you want to know. I used to do the same thing when I worked at the Soviet embassy in Washington." He grinned, his mood had shifted again, back to the social niceties appropriate to the chairman of the board. "I always did my interviews over a meal. We'll meet at six for dinner at the Shorebird. Then at ten tomorrow morning Sochi and Marat do the exchange in Maunakea Marketplace in Chinatown. In the courtyard where everything is in the open. After that, we are done. As to who has the second key, I will tell you this evening."

CHAPTER ELEVEN

MALININ SAT AT a window seat overlooking Waikiki Beach. When he saw Finch approach, he set aside the newspaper he was reading and waved a hand at the empty chair. "Mr. Finch. Please. Join me."

Finch studied him a moment then sat in the slatted deck chair and gazed at the ocean views. In the distance Diamond Head towered over the grassy slopes and palm trees. Past the open window the breeze tugged at the line of beach umbrellas next to the tide line. A tropical paradise. No wonder Eve wanted to live here.

"I hope you don't mind buffet dining, yes?" Malinin said. "I thought it best; no interruptions from nosy waiters."

"Good idea." He took his phone from his pocket and set it on the table. "You mind if I record this?"

"For your paper?"

He nodded. "Except we don't use actual paper anymore."

"Fine." Malinin shrugged. "First, let's get some food, shall we? I'm very hungry."

Finch decided to eat light so that he could focus on the interview. He took a chicken kabob and some Caesar salad.

The Russian settled in for a full meal: mahimahi, baked potato, mushrooms and onions, garlic bread, a glass of chablis.

"You seem to know your way around here," Finch began.

"My favorite American city." Malinin slipped some fish into his mouth and contemplated the flavor for a moment. "There's no place this warm anywhere in Russia. And Hawaii has fewer Americans than Florida or California."

"That's a positive?"

He ignored the question. "It may surprise you to know there's a real Russian community here. Over two thousand ex-pats."

"And Russian mafia, too."

"Mafia." He scoffed and tested the baked potato with a fork. "You Americans like to use words like mafia, gang, and syndicate whenever someone tries to pull himself out of the ditch. When was the last time you had to kill an animal to feed your family?"

Finch shook his head.

"I, myself have done this." He ate some potato and washed it down with the chablis. "When your national economy dis-solves, your expression 'dog eat dog' gains literal meaning, yes?" He pointed his fork at Finch and continued. "The moral man does his best to live in harmony with others, but there are times...." He let the thought hang and turned his attention to his meal.

"Where were you when the Soviet Union collapsed?"

"Where? In Moscow. And when times required it, I moved to my family dacha four hours' drive from the city. When I needed to, I could hunt. I'm good at it. My grandfather called me Lone Hunter. When you know how to live on the land, there's always something out there to keep you alive."

"Lone Hunter." Finch jotted the words into his spiral notepad. "How did you make the jump to international banking?"

Malinin let out a short laugh and set his knife and fork on the table. "I had friends. Connections who needed someone to create good publicity."

"Former KGB friends? Or have they all moved over to the FSB now that Russia is a democracy?"

Malinin studied the distant clouds over the ocean. The sun had slipped behind a rising storm and the effect sent a cool breeze along the beachfront. "I could either lie to you, Mr. Finch, or say nothing. Since I don't want to lie to you, let's leave it at that."

"One of them was Senator Franklin Whitelaw."

"I see you've researched this. Good. I met the senator in a Washington hospital in 1987. We became friends. After the Soviet collapse, he called me. I became his liaison for corporations looking for a way to expand into Russia and Asia generally."

"And that led to GIGcoin?"

"Indirectly." He finished the last piece of mahimahi. "Before that I had to do a lot of what you call bootstrapping."

"So you consider yourself a self-made man."

"Don't you?" He tore a piece of bread and dragged it across his plate to swab up the sauce from his dinner. "You were once part of military intelligence, discharged from the army, studied journalism at Berkeley, had a wife, Cecily, and a son. Buddy, yes? Both of them only to die, I'm sorry to say. Yet here you are now. You've re-made yourself, have you not?"

Finch blinked and looked away. Occasionally people tried to turn an interview inside-out. Make him the subject of probing questions. But no one had ever dug this deep, never probed his pain so skillfully.

"I'm sorry." He popped the sopping bread into his mouth. "Are you all right?"

"What do you want, Malinin?"

He shrugged again, a habit that Finch recognized for a cultivated indifference. The gesture struck him as more Gallic than Russian, but Finch now realized he wasn't dealing in stereotypes. Malinin possessed a carefully disguised, but pinprick sharp, masochistic streak.

"I suppose I want the same thing as you Americans. Life. Liberty. Pursuit of happiness." A glib smile fixed on his lips and he pushed his plate away. "You haven't touched your food. Is everything okay?"

"I mean from GIGcoin. What do you want from GIGcoin?"

"Ah, finally a real question." He leaned closer and pointed to the cell phone. "If you want an answer, turn off the recorder. The interview part of the evening is over. Let's get down to business."

Finch paused the recording app and turned his phone face down on the table.

"You know, when you make a deal with the devil," Malinin said, "always be sure to check the fine print."

"And what does the fine print say?"

Malinin brushed a finger under his nose and began to speak

in a low voice. "That our contract, *this* contract" — he pointed to the table with his index finger — "is guaranteed by MAD."

Finch's head ticked to one side. "MAD?"

"Mutual Assured Destruction." He inched closer still. "At the height of the cold war, what kept everyone completely sober about the threat of nuclear war was the certainty that if the Americans launched a missile, the Soviets would retaliate with annihilating force. And vice-versa."

Finch searched Malinin's face for an explanation. "And this applies to us?"

He lifted a hand, palm up, as if it contained a precious coin. "Everyone on the GIGcoin board understands that if one partner is betrayed, the remaining players will extract immediate … compensation."

"Why the drama, Alexei? What's the deal about GIGcoin that drives everyone to extremes?"

"Have you not been paying attention? Do you have any idea what it will mean when the USA defaults on the seventeen trillion dollars of monopoly money it printed to create this illusion of prosperity?" His hand swept across the room pointing to the linen table cloths, the crystal glassware, the inlaid floors. "And the Europeans, the British, the Japanese — and now the Chinese of all people — have all done the same thing. None of you — *none* — has experienced the hunger that forces you to comb through your neighbor's garbage for a scrap of bread! GIGcoin, Mr. Finch, *GIGcoin* provides an alternative to all this. The algorithms are incorruptible."

Finch shook his head. Malinin's vision revealed a paranoid megalomania. Despite his doubts about the Russian's sanity, he knew he had to press on. "Maybe the algorithms are incorruptible," he conceded, "but not the men who run it."

Malinin turned his head to one side and narrowed his eyes with a grimace of contempt.

Finch moved on. "And all this applies to Senator Whitelaw?"

"You're trying to be too clever." Now a refreshing smile returned to his face. The man was a psychological chameleon, able to shift his mood and demeanor from moment to moment. As a result, everything about him was forged, distorted, a lie. "You want to ensnare the senator to boost the circulation in your paper. But all his assets are in a blind trust. He has very little to do with all this."

"No? You're telling me that as Chairman of the United States Committee on Banking, Housing, and Urban Affairs he won't play his assigned role to assure GIGcoin is accepted as a viable currency to backstop the world economy?"

Malinin scoffed at this and for a moment the two men sat in silence. When Finch realized that Malinin refused to implicate the senator in any way, he decided to press for more information about his step-brother.

"And what did the board decide when Dean Whitelaw was murdered?"

Malinin shrugged yet again. "That was unfortunate. No one anticipated his death."

"Or the disappearance of the GIGcoin software?"

"No. But thanks to you, we're about to recover it tomorrow morning." He smiled with a false look of compassion. Despite his deception, the grin provided a modicum of comfort.

"And what's become of the second key? Does the senator have it?"

A pause. A nod of the head. "Yes. I understand it came into his possession following his brother's death."

Finch felt his pulse quicken. He was closing in on all three goals he'd set out. Identify the owner of the first key: Malinin. Interview him: job done. Identify the owner of the second key: Franklin Whitelaw. But now a new challenge arose: how to arrange a final interview with the Senator?

"Let's return to fundamentals, Mr. Finch. When we make our exchange you and Eve and Sochi enter the same covenant that binds us all. Any betrayal will be dealt with immediately. Possibly within minutes. Do you understand?"

Finch tried to weigh the risks. "There will be no betrayals."

"Good." He glanced around the room. The restaurant was full and a line of ten or twelve customers waited at the entrance. It was almost eight o'clock. In a little over fourteen hours the deal would be completed. "As long as we all understand one another, yes?"

Finch tucked his phone and notepad into his courier bag, slipped the strap over his shoulder and stood. Despite his hunger, he hadn't touched his food. A matter of taste, he decided. There was something so repulsive about Malinin that he'd turned everything near him to shit. Including the food.

※

After Eve finished her half-hour run along the waterfront and around the perimeter of Kapiolani Park she returned to her room in the Moana Surfrider Hotel, showered, dried her hair and prepared to polish her nails. Just as she set out the polish,

Sochi knocked at her door. She tied her bathrobe across her waist and let him in.

"What's wrong?"

"Nothing." He pressed a finger to his lips and whispered, "Ssshh. Can you step outside?"

She blinked. Had he missed the obvious? "I just had a shower."

"Grab your keycard."

"What?"

He took her room pass from the dresser and drew her into the hallway by her elbow. "Listen. We've got problems."

"What problems?" She gathered the collar of her bathrobe together at her throat and glanced along the hall.

He opened his fist. In his hand sat a black micro video recorder. "A surveillance bug. And it's no toy." His voice dropped a tone. "God-damned Russians."

The look of anger in his face caught her by surprise. She felt a creeping sense of distrust. "Where did you find it?"

"In the smoke detector. I swept my whole room. This is the only one I could find."

"Do you think there's one in our room, too?"

"I can check."

She paused to think a moment. "All right. Let me get dressed and grab a few things. Then sweep the room. I'll meet you downstairs."

After she dressed, she made her way down to the lobby and sat on the sofa opposite the piano. While she waited she tried to recall all that she'd said to Finch in the room since they'd checked into the hotel. If their suite was bugged, someone would get an earful. Ten minutes later Sochi entered the lounge. She could read the news on his face as he approached.

"Us, too?"

He nodded. "I think we should discuss this outside."

Crowds of tourists swept along the sidewalks beside Kalakaua Avenue but eventually they found a vacant park bench facing the surf. Across the lawn a trio played traditional hula songs on ukuleles. The evening air felt warm and humid. In the distance she could see heavy cumulonimbus clouds rising above the ocean.

Sochi showed her the device he'd extracted from her room. "It's the same bug. Also in the smoke detector."

"You think the Russians did this?"

"Who else could it be?"

As Eve examined it, a new thought struck her. "Is this audio only, or does it have a camera, too?"

"Both."

"Unbelievable." She let out a false laugh. "Will's going to be pleased."

"Yeah?" Sochi seemed unable to decode her meaning.

"Never mind. Look, I'm going to text him. When he's finished his interview with Malinin, let's meet in the beach bar of the hotel. In the meantime, try to identify this thing. We need to know who makes it, what it can do, and most important — who planted it."

※

Eve arrived at the Beach Cafe twenty minutes before Sochi. When he appeared at the top of the staircase leading down to the patio he looked jet-lagged, as if he hadn't adapted to the time-zone shift. He wore a pair of surfer shorts, a long-sleeve tie-dyed hippie shirt and a hand-stitched leather vest. Everything about him looked mismatched: his clothes, his hair and beard, the look of ambivalence on his face. All of it suggested confusion. The man is a study in contrasts, Eve told herself as she waved him over to her table.

"What did you find out?"

"Everything." Sochi ducked under the patio umbrella, sat beside Eve and set his laptop on the table. They faced the stage where two musicians had just finished a set and were preparing to take a break. "Before I get into that, I want to establish the protocols for transferring the GIGcoin software key once I get it from the Russian."

"I thought we already discussed all that."

Sochi frowned. "We did. But given what we know now, I want a faster hand-off."

"All right. So what does that mean?"

"I need a dormant email address." He tugged at the tip of his beard and when Eve didn't respond, he added, "One you never use and that no one associates with you."

Eve raised her hands and glanced around the cafe with a look of despondency. So much of Sochi's world involved game-play. Was this more of the same? "Why do you need this now?"

"As soon as I validate the software key tomorrow I want to email it to an address that no one else can access."

"Well … I can't think of one right now." She saw Finch approaching from the hotel lobby and signaled him as he reached the staircase. Despite the bad news she had to reveal about the surveillance bug, she felt relieved to see him. Maybe he could figure out how to deal with this mess.

"How're we doing?" He made an effort to smile and sat beside Eve.

"Not good. You want the bad news first — or the pressing news?"

"Roll the dice." He shrugged. "Guess I'll take the pressing news first."

Eve pointed to Sochi. "Over to you, comrade."

"We need an email address that neither of you has ever used and that no one else can access."

Finch cast his eyes to the underside of the umbrella. A light rain began to pit against the nylon shell. "How about Gianna?" He looked at Eve. "Is her email still working?"

Eve's face lit up. "Yeah. I think it is."

"Type it in here." Sochi passed his computer to her. "I'll set up an automated routine for the hand-off later tonight."

"Why?" Finch looked from Eve to Sochi and back.

"I'll tell you later." She typed Gianna's email address into Sochi's computer and passed it back to him. "Now for the bad news. Sochi, show him the bug."

Sochi closed the cover of his computer and set it aside. Then he dug two identical spy cameras from his vest pockets. With a measure of discretion he opened his palms to reveal them, one in each hand. "These are covert DVR video cameras that I extracted from the smoke detectors in our rooms."

"What?" Finch felt his stomach sink as he considered the implications. "Okay. So give me the details."

"The Russians installed one in each of our rooms. Simply

put, they can record seventy-two hours of hi-def, full-audio movies of everything we've said and done since we checked in." Sochi tucked them back into his pockets. "Up until an hour ago Malinin and company have seen and heard everything we've done since we checked into our rooms."

"How do you know Malinin is involved?"

A look of astonishment crossed Sochi's face. "Who else could it be?"

Finch glanced at Eve. She shook her head with a bewildered look. What had Malinin said about betrayal? That it would be dealt with immediately. Within minutes. He took a moment to absorb the implications. "I guess this means we're … completely screwed."

"Will, please." Eve closed her eyes in an effort to banish the image. "Those are the exact two words I am trying not to visualize."

※

Five minutes later Eve made her way to the bathroom to find some relief from the implications of Sochi's discovery. She sat on the toilet and dropped her face in her hands. She tried to imagine the images of her and Will making love through the night. Had she switched off the lights? No, of course not. After a few moments of self-loathing, she flushed the toilet and opened the stall door. She stood at the sink and stared at her weary eyes in the mirror. Convinced that she could do nothing to retrieve the video, she carefully dampened her cheeks with a moist paper towel and then applied a clear gloss to her lips.

Another woman slipped into the bathroom and before the door closed behind her, Eve caught a glimpse of a familiar face as a man turned along the exterior corridor. But who? She often had trouble identifying people when she saw someone out of context. Normally she'd simply release the feeling of ambivalence and walk on. But *this face* troubled her. She decided to follow him. Ahead she saw the slouching shoulders, the salt-and-pepper hair — and when he turned into the hotel lobby — the toothbrush mustache. Damian Witowsky.

She stopped, felt her heart thrum, then jogged after him. When she caught his elbow, he swung around with a look of surprise, a look that immediately shifted to suspicion.

"Knew I'd see you here," he said.

"You did?" Her eyes narrowed. "So what? Now you're tailing me?"

Witowsky scanned the room, wary of being watched. "Look, not here in the lobby. Let's take this outside."

As she followed him onto the sidewalk and along Kalakaua Avenue she wondered how he'd found her, but immediately let the question go. As an SFPD cop he could track her down using any of a dozen tools: monitoring the GPS on her cell phone or the trail of her credit card purchases. What troubled her more were her paranoid suspicions about his motivation. Witowsky had followed her to do what exactly? Arrest her for leaving the scene of Dean Whitelaw's murder? To question her about Gianna's estate? Or to seize the GIGcoin flash drive?

He turned a corner onto Lewers Street, glanced over both shoulders and, satisfied that no one had followed them, he settled on an empty bench under an awning. A light rain drizzled from the canopy onto the sidewalk just past their feet.

"So. What's this about, Witowsky?" She sat beside him and

looked into his eyes. He glanced away. "All right. Now I know I'm about to get a load of BS topped with a fresh layer of horse shit. Can't you be straight for once?"

"I'm here for the same reason you are, Eve." He glanced past her shoulder to the end of the street. "Alexei Malinin."

The answer surprised her.

"How did you know he was here?"

"Flight manifest flagged him."

"And why are you interested in him? He hasn't committed any crimes in San Francisco."

"Hasn't he?" He smiled. "You know I don't have to tell you anything."

"No? What if I gave IAD a call and let them know where you are?"

"IAD? What do they care?" He sniffed and tipped his head to one side.

"I heard they're nosing through your case files. A few people say you crossed over."

"Bullshit." He scuffed his heel against the pavement. "You think I'd have access to the Surveillance and Monitoring network if IAD were on me?"

S-and-M as the old boys called it. She coughed up a bleak laugh as she considered this. True enough. Maybe Leanne's rumor was just another paranoid lie that slithered through the SFPD every other month. Suddenly the rainstorm broke open with a blaze of lightning and a baritone thunder clap. She turned her attention back to Witowsky.

"It's because you need me, don't you? That's why you're here. You need me to get to Malinin." She leaned forward, pressed him to look squarely at her, but his eyes snaked away again. "What do you know about Malinin?"

"A hell of a lot more than you, apparently. Otherwise you wouldn't be here with no one else besides Clark Kent and Captain Gizmo." He crooked his thumb in the direction of her hotel.

Eve looked away and studied the rain as it slashed down on the street. For the first time in years she felt out of her depth. The Russians filming her making love with Will was bad enough, but now Witowsky seemed to know everything about her, Will, and Sochi. And their rendezvous with Malinin.

"Okay. Pants down. You caught me." She laughed a genuine, almost inviting laugh to suggest that Witowsky held some pretty good cards.

"You're in way over your head, Eve. Way over."

"Maybe."

"No, not maybe." He lit a cigarette and blew the smoke away from her. "For real. Why do you think Malinin wants to meet here? And it ain't for the golden sunshine." He drew on his cigarette and continued. "Because Honolulu is a center of Russian mafia. He does his deal and snap" — his fingers clicked in the air — "his fixers come by to clean up the chills and spills while he disappears."

"So what do you want from me?"

"I want you to work with me. On Malinin." A cloud of smoke drifted from his mouth. "In exchange, I'll provide some backup when you need it."

"First tell me why you want him."

Ever alert for some unknown danger, Witowsky peered up

the road and then turned back to Eve. "Sorry, I can't tell you that."

"Then fuck you, Witowsky."

She stood up. He gripped her elbow and pulled her back beside him.

"All right." He squeezed the half-finished cigarette under his heel. "It goes back to the Toeplitz and Whitelaw murders. Last week our tech team scanned all their computers. Then we discovered something called GIGcoin." He paused to gauge her reaction.

"Go on."

"It's digital currency like bitcoin. Something that Toeplitz engineered for Whitelaw and an international syndicate. And my Assistant Captain thinks all of it's tied to Malinin."

"And?"

"We know in order for Malinin to go forward with GIGcoin without Whitelaw and Toeplitz, he needs something." Finally able to hold her gaze, he stared into her face. "Something that I know you've got, Eve."

"You think so?"

"Yeah. And I think that's why you're here. But make no mistake, he'll kill you for it. Whether you give it to him or he has to take it from you. Once he has it he'll take you out. You and your two friends."

Eve looked along the length of the street. It was lined with high-end shops and hotels. A few tourists willing to brave the steady shower ducked from the protection of one awning to another. If Witowsky could provide backup, what would it cost her? In the past she'd never agree to work with him. But now, with the risks mounting, he could prove useful.

"All right, Witowsky. Whatever it is you think I might possess is irrelevant for now. But if you want Malinin, then show up at the Maunakea Market in Chinatown tomorrow morning. Ten A.M. sharp."

※

While Sochi and Finch waited for Eve to return to their table, Finch brooded over the events of the past day. First the news from Eve and Sochi that they'd been surveilled by the Russians. Well, maybe. After his dinner at the Shorebird Finch knew that Malinin possessed the local resources to manage any kind of spy craft. He could pay for intelligence, hire some muscle from the local Russian mafia, bribe the desk staff to reveal Finch's room number, monitor his movements in and out of the hotel, and install the bug without leaving a trace. Standard FSB operations. But what of his talk about betrayal? Of mutual assured destruction. Surely he knew that if Finch discovered the spy cams, Malinin could lose his only chance to retrieve the GIGcoin software.

Furthermore, Sochi made a convincing argument that any high school senior with a modicum of tech smarts could mail-order the electronic components and install two spy cams in under five minutes.

After considering the possibilities, Finch tried to clarify their situation. "So in fact, the Russians *might not* be the bad guys."

"I wouldn't say that. I'm saying setting up the web cams is dead-beat easy." His head turned from left to right, scanning the cocktail lounge for Malinin, Kirill or Marat. "And if they toy with us again," he said, "I will completely screw them."

"Careful." Finch's tone was apprehensive. "Malinin doesn't tolerate any betrayal. He laid out a clear warning to me tonight."

Sochi sneered at that, a look of anger Finch hadn't seen from him before. "Don't worry. I can fix it so they won't even know what's happened. They'll be rubbing the round part of their asses wondering who poked them. Meanwhile we'll be back in San Fran."

Minutes later Eve returned to the lounge with her news about bumping into Witowsky and that the grizzled old cop had tracked her down in Waikiki. As she spoke, Finch studied her with a look of disbelief.

After she explained the little she knew about Witowsky's interest in Malinin, Sochi pushed off for an early night. "Besides," he said, "I need to make some final tweaks to the software. Before I meet the Ruskies tomorrow, I want to have plans A, B, and C lined up to deal with any contingencies."

"Don't make this unnecessarily complex," Finch warned him. "Remember, all you have to do is exchange flash drives and check to ensure Marat is giving you a valid key. It's really that simple."

"Is it?" Sochi drew the two web cams from his pocket and held them aloft as if he were displaying evidence to a jury. "I rest my case." He turned and walked across the outdoor patio, trying to dodge the rain that poured between the umbrellas.

"What's he really up to?" Finch asked when they'd returned to their hotel room.

"Sochi?"

"Him, too. But more important, Witowsky." Finch locked the door and dropped his courier bag to the floor.

"He says it's all about Malinin. But I don't trust him."

"Me neither." Finch recalled Witowsky grilling him after Dean Whitelaw's murder. And again, in the hospital when he produced a warrant and confiscated Eve's phone. Then came the interrogation — a week too late — about Fiona's kidnapping. And now he appears at the Moana Surfrider in Honolulu. A string of unlucky coincidences? Impossible.

He went into the bathroom and brushed his teeth.

Eve leaned on the door, hesitated, and then said, "Trust him or not, I asked him to cover us tomorrow in Chinatown."

"You what?" He rinsed out his mouth and turned to her.

"We need him, Will. Don't you see it? We're completely outgunned. If Malinin put together this surveillance operation" — she pointed to the ceiling smoke detector — "it means he's playing in a bigger league than us. And probably with twice as many players."

He sauntered over to the bed, a heavy weariness dragging through his feet. "You brought your .38?"

"It's in the case." She tipped her chin towards the locked, hardshell box in the closet. As a registered PI she'd simply followed standard protocols and checked it in with her luggage during the preflight clearance. "But if Witowsky's right about Malinin, a .38 is more a liability than a threat."

No doubt about it, he thought. Once someone draws a pistol, all the halfway options vanish. The middle ground disappears and whatever talk remains runs to extremes. The only important question then is, who has the bigger gun?

"You think he can bring in the Honolulu police if we need them?"

"If it were me, I'd have a SWAT team in place. Ready, set, locked and loaded."

"Right." Finch tugged off his shirt and pants, flopped onto the bed, stretched out his legs and turned his head toward her. His eyelids felt heavy, trance-like. "Except he's not like you. He's Witowsky."

"Sadly." She shrugged and began to unbutton her blouse.

He listened to the rain beating against the windows, the wind slapping the palm tree limbs together. Despite the violent weather, he sensed a peace of mind approaching, the void that follows complete exhaustion. He pulled the sheet over his chest and watched Eve undress through his half-closed eyes. He liked to see the clothes slip away from her body, gaze at her breasts as she strolled naked through the room, watch her apply various creams to her hands and face, brush out her hair. It provided a marvelous distraction, a glimpse into a private world that she seemed more than happy to reveal.

But soon the abyss called to him and dragged him under. Before she'd removed her bra — before she'd even unhitched the clasp — he fell into the vast emptiness and didn't budge for another seven hours.

※

The morning heat in Chinatown began to cook the air. A stew of fragrances from the vegetable, meat and seafood stalls drifted through the streets leading to Maunakea Marketplace. Rows of bananas, papaya, pineapple, mangos, kiwis and dozens of foreign, exotic fruits and vegetables lined the exterior walls of shops along the crowded streets. As the fast food chefs prepared for the noon-hour rush, the burst of flavors from stir-fried meats and fish sent an intoxicating plume through Finch's nostrils.

He walked along the open plaza in the heart of the market, past the statue of a standing buddha and settled into a chair in the shade of the east wall. He found a local newspaper that had been abandoned on a nearby table and began to leaf through its pages. On the second floor promenade above the market court-yard, Eve leaned against the railing. Below her, opposite Finch's position, Sochi sat on a clay stool next to a table covered by a green sun umbrella. Finch studied Sochi's face as he gazed across the patio. Even in his surfer shorts, t-shirt and leather vest he still resembled a cross between a Viking and a Canadian logger. Finch had to agree with Eve; Sochi was a quirk wandering in an anomaly lost in an aberration. And yet so brilliant.

He glanced at Eve again as she walked the length of the upper promenade, her hand trailing along the balustrade. No trace of the .38 under her vest. They nodded to one another. Steady, ready.

Finch continued to scan the crowds. Witowsky, if he was present, had made himself invisible. Same with Malinin, Marat and Kirill. The mid-morning shoppers were already swarming around the vendors hawking hand-made jewelry, knock-off jade carvings, burnished ukuleles, wood flutes and whistles, and a sea of plastic knick-knacks imported from China. What had become of the world, Finch wondered. Everyone up to the their chins in debt — just so they could purchase the endless stream of junk needed to keep the economy afloat. What if everyone simply agreed to stop the nonsense and —

Marat.

Finch snapped out of his reverie when he glimpsed the young Russian approaching the market courtyard through the south concourse. Impossible as it seemed, Marat looked more jaundiced than yesterday. His skin had the color of cold urine and the flesh on his face hung from his cheekbones and jaw. As he walked across the red brick courtyard toward the Buddha statue his eyes seemed to peer at the world from a distant place, as if he might be witnessing this life from a bottomless hole.

Despite his illness, Marat had no trouble finding the standing buddha. Sochi nodded to him. Marat said nothing and sat beside him. He drew a laptop from his shoulder bag, lifted the cover and turned it on.

He drew heavily on a cigarette and flicked the butt to one side. After a moment he turned his eyes to Sochi and began the final negotiations.

※

"You have flash drive?"

"Yes." Sochi took a moment to study the Russian, to assess the extent of his broken health. Something about Marat bothered Sochi — something out of place, even alien. Why had Malinin assigned this half-living soul to test the validity of the software?

The Russian wagged a finger. "Then give."

Sochi pretended to fumble for the flash drive in his vest pocket, and as he fussed, he caught sight of Finch walking beside a fruit stall on the far side of the plaza. Eve leaned on

149

the rail on the second floor concourse above him. So far no sign of the monster, Kirill, or Malinin himself. As for Witowsky, who knew?

He held the GIGcoin drive in his fingers as if he were tempting a child. "And yours?"

"Is here." Marat drew a metal stick from his shirt pocket.

For a moment they held the two drives a few inches apart. Sochi felt as if he were preparing for a hockey face-off. He nodded. The two men traded the drives and Marat immediately plugged the GIGcoin drive into his computer and began to type a series of keystrokes. Sochi could tell at a glance that the Russian had prepared a set of validity tests to determine if the GIGcoin software was authentic. As he completed each one he nodded as if he were assessing the sequence of moves in a chess game. With each nod he mumbled, "Mmm. Mmm."

Because Sochi only had to evaluate the viability of the key his assessment consisted of answering two questions. One, did the key fit one of the two locks? Yes, it did. Two, could the key engage, or "turn," the start-up protocols in the software. Yes, it did that too. He could see at once that only a second key would be needed to launch the entire program. With the Russian's key now verified, he attached the file to the prepared email and sent it to Gianna's address. As the message window spiraled forward, he glanced at Finch and nodded his head. Finch returned the signal and nodded to Eve at her station next to the railing. Sochi turned back to his laptop screen to see the critical email notification: "Message sent."

He pulled the stick drive from his computer and shut the lid. "Well, that's me," he said under his breath and tried to stand.

Marat's hand reached across the table and pinned Sochi's forearm to the table. The sudden display of strength and agility caught him by surprise.

"Wait. Test not complete."

Sochi tried to free his arm but Marat held fast.

"All right. No rush, my friend." When he relaxed his arm, the Russian released him and returned to tapping his computer and uttering low grunts of approval. But after a few moments his breathing turned to elongated sighs, deeper tones that suggested some discontent.

Sochi glanced up at Finch with a look of confusion. The longer Marat took — two minutes, then five — Sochi's mood turned to concern and then a gnawing anxiety set in.

After another growl, Marat closed his laptop and stared at Sochi, the whites of his eyes now the color of cold butter. "Smart," he whispered, "or maybe not." Then he turned the collar of his shirt up to his lips and whispered a few words in Russian, concluding with the only word that Sochi understood: "Nyet."

"Are you wired?"

When Marat failed to respond, Sochi stood up, tipping his chair backward as he rose. The hollow frame crashed onto the patio with a metallic clatter.

"You're fucking wired, aren't you?"

Marat stood and stepped away from the table. This time Sochi grabbed the Russian's arm. In an instant, Marat swung his free hand behind Sochi's wrist in a swift judo countermove that released Marat's arm. He then snapped his fist forward with a brisk chop to the center of Sochi's throat. Sochi dropped his laptop and doubled over clasping at his neck, gasping for air.

"What the fuck?" Sochi wheezed as he tried to breathe.

Eve saw the altercation and ran along the upper promenade, down the staircase and across the patio. When she reached Sochi, she eased him into a chair and began to massage his neck and throat.

From where he stood next to the fruit stalls, Finch tracked Marat's movements as he scuttled back through the south gate of the Marketplace. When he saw the Russian plunge through the crowd Finch ran through the gate after him.

※

The open market flowed into the bottle neck of the south gate, an enclosed space lined by dozens of trinket stalls and food kiosks. The crowds immediately swallowed Finch, forcing him to slow his jog to a brisk walk. Twenty feet ahead he could see Marat slipping through the crush of pedestrians, each of them pausing to consider earrings or necklaces, stir-fried rice or sushi. The Russian disappeared, bobbed up and down, an abandoned buoy bouncing among the waves of shoppers, tourists and merchants.

Then a shock of recognition brought Finch to a halt. Thirty feet ahead Damian Witowsky was approaching. Finch shuddered when he saw the determined look on the cop's face. He realized that Witowsky had corralled Marat between himself and Finch, and that the Russian would have to decide to squeeze past Witowsky or turn and face Will. Marat's head briefly rose a few inches above the crowd and then submerged again. Then Finch heard three muffled pops — *pup, pup, pup* — a deep howl of pain and the cries of several women.

A moment later Witowsky pressed through the crowd towards the open plaza where Sochi and the Russian had exchanged flash drives moments earlier. Witowsky's mouth knotted into a dark snarl when he saw Finch. At first Witowsky glanced away, but as the crowd stumbled backward from Marat's corpse, the cop crashed against Finch's chest.

"Get the fuck outta here," he barked into Finch's ear. His voice carried a hard, uneven edge. When he stepped back, Finch saw the veins in Witowsky's neck tighten into long cords. Everything about him seethed with adrenalin. "Grab Eve and the tech geek and get the fuck back to Frisco."

"What?"

Witowsky swept past him without another word. Finch turned and saw a dash of blood sprayed along Witowsky's shirt sleeve and shoulder bag. He called after him, but the cop disappeared in the chaos.

At first a ring of bystanders edged forward to stare at Marat sprawled on the ground. But as the gravity of the crime weighed on everyone, they tore themselves away, many of them running with a hand across their mouths to stifle their screams.

After a few moments the crowd had almost dispersed through the south gate corridor. Ten feet ahead Finch could see Marat stretched out on the concrete floor. Finch limped forward as if he'd been struck in the knees. As he approached the Russian, he saw Marat's shirt ripped open above his chest. Marat held a flap of the shirt in his left hand; he must have torn the shirt away thinking he could staunch the bleeding with his hand. Through three separate holes next to his heart a gush of blood pulsed onto the ground in an ever-widening pool. Beside his right foot lay a small-caliber revolver with a torn gray rag bound around the pistol grip. A paper carton of fried noodles lay beside his head. His jaundiced eyes were frozen in a look of surprise, his head turned at an awkward angle toward the floor boards of the merchants' ramshackle stalls.

Finch knelt beside him and pressed two fingers to Marat's carotid artery. Nothing. If Marat wasn't dead already, he soon would be. "Christ," he whispered. He drew his cell phone from his pocket and dialed 9-1-1.

Ten minutes later an ambulance arrived followed by two HPD squad cars. One cop busied himself surrounding the zone with crime-scene tape. Once the CSI team completed their assessments, the ambulance attendants bundled Marat's corpse onto a gurney and into the rear of their van. A second cop, heavy-set, balding — an old hand, obviously weary of it all — approached Finch and led him to a take-out booth where they found two chairs and sat.

"You call this in?" He opened a note pad and with a glance, tried to take stock of Finch.

He nodded.

"Your name."

"Finch. Will Finch."

"Did you see what happened?"

"No. Not until everyone cleared away. I just tried to help."

"You live around here?"

"No. San Francisco. I've been here three days."

The cop made a series of notes as he spoke. "But did you see the shooting?"

"No."

"You know him?" He tipped his chin toward the pool of blood on the floor.

Finch shook his head, paused to study the cop's shield: Officer White. A black cop named White. He could imagine the taunts.

"Is that a no?"

"Sorry. Guess I'm a little shaken." He tried to think his way through the coming questions, the traps to avoid. "I saw him before, but no, I don't know him."

White cocked his head. "You've seen him, but you don't know him. How's that?"

"Back in the market." Finch pointed over his shoulder. "I was standing on the plaza near the fruit stands. I saw him sitting at one of the tables. Next to the buddha statue."

A skeptical look passed over White's face. "And you remember him?"

"Yeah. I'm a journalist. *San Francisco eXpress.*" He shrugged. "I remember things."

White made another note on his pad. "What exactly was he doing that made him so memorable?"

This is where the clever traps lay. Finch raised his eyebrows and glanced about. The vendors and tourists had all disappeared. A faulty overhead lamp buzzed sporadically.

"He was sitting at a table, working on his laptop. It seemed odd. Everyone else here is a tourist. This guy's working on a spreadsheet or something."

"You saw what he was working on?"

"No. Just a guess."

Another look of doubt. "All right. This will all go on the file. We might have to talk to you later. Depending on how things shake out, you may have to file a sworn affidavit. Depending on the DA, likely you could do it from Frisco. You got a card?"

Finch dug a business card out of his courier bag and handed it to the cop.

White was about to turn away when a thought struck him. "Mr. Finch, you said he had a computer. But I don't see a laptop around here. And none of the chasers or the CSI guys took one in the ambulance. You sure about that? Sure he had a laptop?"

"Yeah. I'm sure." Finch pulled a hand over the top of his head as he scanned the length of the empty mall corridor. The crowded market had become a deserted mausoleum. Despite the shock of seeing the Russian's corpse so raw and graceless, Finch now realized that Marat had been robbed before Finch arrived at his side.

The GIGcoin software and one launch key. Both gone.

※

Sochi felt rattled. The news from Finch — that Marat had been shot three times in the heart and left for dead — didn't buoy his mood. He felt as if something unimaginable had happened to him personally. He was the last person Marat had spoken to, the last person he'd touched, the last person who'd looked into his godforsaken eyes. Sochi had become a last outpost, a final call on another human being's journey into ... what?

He had no vision of what might lie beyond his own life, except for emptiness. If the question is, is there a life after death? Sochi's answer remained agnostic: None that I can see.

And that conclusion troubled him. Troubled him in his guts, in his heart, in the complex circuitry of his thoughts where he'd managed to answer almost every other question he'd ever encountered.

"You all right, Sochi?"

Eve studied Sochi's pale face as he pulled the strands of his beard under his chin and massaged the bruised flesh where Marat had driven his fist into Sochi's throat.

"Yeah," he coughed. He turned his head to one side and saw a wave of tourists flood through the airport entrance and stream toward the departures concourse. He tried again: "I'll be okay in a day or two."

"I saw it happen. All of it," Finch said and gathered his boarding pass and bag in his hand and guided everyone toward Gate 11. "For a guy who looked so wasted, Marat hit you pretty hard. Make no mistake, he knew what he was doing. At some point Marat did some serious fight training."

Sochi nodded with a feeble grimace, unable to engage in further conversation. He grappled with his duffle bag as they strolled toward the gate. Then he paused and crooked a thumb toward the entrance to the men's room. "Later," he mumbled.

"Sure." Eve smiled sympathetically and took Finch's free hand as they continued along the airport corridor.

Sochi made his way to the end of the row of closed stalls and pushed on the last door. It swung open. The toilet looked clean, the seat unstained. A ten-inch length of tissues dangled from the toilet paper dispenser. He closed and locked the door, pushed his duffle bag to the side and took the toilet tissue in his hand. He wiped his brow. Surprised by the dampness, he took another band of paper, wrapped it around his fingers and patted his face dry. Then he squatted on the toilet seat and gazed at the facing door. No graffiti. He wondered what he would write if he had a sharpie with him. He dismissed the first impulses: *fuck, shit.* Then something slightly more imaginative came to mind: *What am I doing here?* Another question he could not answer.

He sat gazing at the emptiness for another four or five minutes until he heard a flight announcement: "Qantas Airlines flight 121 to Fiji, now commencing boarding from gate 5."

Fiji. *Fucking Fiji.* As a child growing up in Arizona, he'd often fantasized about Fiji. The beaches, the tropical breeze, the native women, their innocent nakedness, the complete idleness of life lived through the flesh from day to day to day…. In an instant, he realized that Fiji provided an answer to the unknowns in his life.

Q: What are you doing here?

A: I'm on the way to Fiji.

Q: What follows life in this world?

A: A good death in Fiji.

"Go tell Moscow and Arbat," he whispered aloud. He stood up and unlocked the stall door, tugged the duffle bag over to the row of steel sinks arrayed beneath the washroom mirrors. He could probably exchange his ticket to San Francisco for one to Fiji. Today. *Right now.* Why not? As he washed his hands, he studied his face. He decided he would cut his hair, shave his beard. Throw away his cell phone. Stop working with computers. "And start living again!" he shouted through the sharp rasp in his throat.

As he dried his hands under the blower, four men entered the washroom, each going their separate ways to the urinals and stalls. One — burly, thick set, dark hair cut tight, tattooed arms — bumped into Sochi as he backed away from the hand drier.

When he felt a deep pinch on the cheek of his ass he turned to confront the bastard. But too late. The bull had come and gone in an instant. Disappeared. He heard a light clatter on the floor tiles leading out to the main concourse. When he looked around the corner he saw another man lean over and pick up a discarded umbrella lying next to the wall.

"This yours?" he asked.

Sochi's right buttock stung and he grasped it in the palm of his hand and tried to massage the glute muscle. "No," he gasped and limped out to the concourse in search of Gate 11.

By the time he joined Eve and Will he felt disoriented. "Someone pinched me," he complained to Will privately. "In the ass."

"What?"

"I don't know." He waved a hand and hoped that by ignoring the pain it would dissipate.

"Look, I've got to tell you both something." He pulled Eve by the elbow and led Will to the far wall.

"What is it?" A look of concern crossed Eve's face.

"I think I might have done ... something crazy," he confessed with an anxious laugh. A brief shudder coursed through his body.

"Hey." Eve took his hand. "Don't worry about it."

"No. Listen." He squeezed her fingers and released them. "The software. I spiked the software. The copy I gave to Marat. To the Russians. It won't work. *I spiked it.*"

"Spiked it. What does that mean?"

"You mean like a cannon?" Finch felt a ripple of fear sink through his stomach. This could only lead to something very unpleasant.

"Yes." He wiped a smudge of perspiration from his forehead. "I spiked both locks on their copy of GIGcoin. Neither of the keys can launch the software I gave to Marat."

"Sochi … why did you do that?" Eve's voice faltered and she glanced away.

A wave of confusion swept his face, as if he couldn't possibly explain the rationale for his actions. "Because of what they did to us. Because of the spy cams."

The overhead speakers announced their final boarding call and Sochi adjusted his shoulder bag strap and nodded toward the gate. "Let's go," he muttered. "I have to sit down."

After he boarded the plane and found his seat, Sochi suspected that the stranger had injected him with something. When the 737 to San Francisco reached thirty thousand feet he limped over to the washroom, pulled down his pants and swung around until he could glimpse a bright red pimple the size of a pea on his gluteus maximus. It looked like an insect bite. A sting of some kind.

CHAPTER TWELVE

ON THE FLIGHT back to San Francisco, Finch and Eve found themselves sitting ten rows ahead of Sochi. Although Sochi didn't object to his seat assignment, whenever Will turned around he noticed the worried expression on Sochi's face. His rising anxiety suggested he regretted everything to do with Finch, Eve and GIGcoin. Maybe it's even worse than that, Finch concluded. Much worse.

"I can't believe what he did," he said to Eve as they unbuckled their seat belts following the crew's all-clear announcements. "Something's wrong with him."

"No, *everything's* wrong." She fixed him with an angry look. "Marat's dead, Sochi betrayed Malinin, and you and I were filmed screwing our heads off. Tell me, Will, which part of all that went *right?"*

The shrillness in her voice turned him away and he gazed through the cabin window onto the Pacific. The ocean was heavy with rolling waves and white caps that dotted the dark surface.

After a moment he said, "Look. We got the three things we set out for. You got the first key that unlocks the GIGcoin software. I got an interview with Malinin. And now we know who holds the second key. The other stuff, that's the price that had to be paid."

"*The other stuff?* You mean shooting Marat?"

He studied the frown on her face. Was it remorse — or fear? "Eve, you're going soft."

"Soft?" She narrowed her lips as if she might be assessing the aftertaste of cheap white wine. "No one's ever said that to me before."

"No. I can't imagine anyone has." He shrugged and set his laptop on the fold-down dinner tray.

"You know what the worst part is?" She crossed her arms and clenched her fists.

He shook his head.

"I can't stand that Witowsky stole from us."

"You mean Marat's laptop?" He tapped the keys and opened a new text file.

"That and everything else. Don't you see it? That string of coincidences was an elaborate ruse. He played on my fears to reveal where we were meeting with Malinin. Then he shot Marat to steal his computer after Sochi gave him the GIGcoin software. Jeezus, he's been playing us since he came to interview you about Fiona."

"Yeah, but I didn't actually see Witowsky shoot Marat. I didn't see who threw the pistol to the ground. And I didn't see what happened to Marat's laptop."

"All right." She took a moment to weigh the options. "So anyone could have it. Malinin, Witowsky. Some kid who snatched it off the ground."

Finch was pleased to hear her talking like a cop again. "Right. And there was nothing I could do to save Marat. Nothing I could tell the Honolulu police that would help him. Or them." He felt as if he had to justify his actions. Not that Eve or Sochi had accused him of abandoning the Russian. Nonetheless he felt a kind of guilt by association.

She sighed and nuzzled her chin onto his shoulder. "I know. I know how these things are." She took his hand into her own.

As the plane banked to the left they were offered a view of the Pacific below. They peered through the window, absorbing the magic of this life: the vast expanse of the ocean, the modern marvel of a 737 lifting them above the world from one destination to the next. Somehow it all seemed impossible, yet absolutely necessary. A perfect moment.

The plane leveled again and Finch pulled away from Eve. "I need to get to work."

"I guess you do." She glanced down the aisle. Sochi sat in the chair in front of the emergency exit. "You know, he doesn't look that well."

"Maybe you should walk over and see how he's doing." His voice grew distant as he began to type a line of words.

"Okay." She pulled herself from the seat. A few moments later she returned.

"He's got a fever," she said.

"A fever?"

"I asked an attendant to bring him some cold compresses. Maybe he'll feel better by the time we land."

Finch peered over the seat back. He watched the attendant pass two damp face clothes to Sochi. "I think he'll be okay. I'll check on him in an hour or so."

"Good." She pulled a blanket over her torso. "I'm going to nap."

"Excellent idea." He turned on the overhead spot light and adjusted the computer screen.

"Wake me when the coffee cart comes around."

He felt like posting a *Do Not Disturb* sign on the back of the neighboring head rest. Instead, he opened the cellophane packet containing a pair of orange foam earplugs that the steward had given him and inserted them into his ears. He considered the writers back in the bog and their noise-canceling headphones. Finally, he was one with them.

He spent the next two hours writing the profile of Malinin and the corporate connections linking him to GIGcoin and Senator Franklin Whitelaw. Despite Malinin's instincts to protect Whitelaw, Finch had gathered enough information to make the allegations against Whitelaw indictable offenses. But the complete Malinin story, while critical to the overall picture, wasn't required right away. What Finch needed first was an opening lead, two paragraphs that he could email to the senator. They would be a battering ram to smash the barricade to the senator's world and let Finch into the center of the story he'd worked on for months. With the first draft completed, he returned to the opening lines to tweak the sequence of words that he hoped would shatter Whitelaw's empire of corruption.

A Russian oligarch has identified Senator Franklin Whitelaw as a key partner in an international banking scheme headquartered in the Grand Cayman Islands. In an exclusive

interview with the eXpress, Alexei Malinin, an ex-KGB opera-
tive once assigned to the Soviet Embassy in Washington, con-
firmed that Whitelaw, the senior US Senator from California, is
one of seven principals who signed the incorporation papers of
GIGcoin Bank and Exchange.

GIGcoin is a cryptocurrency set to launch this year and
compete for supremacy with bitcoin, the digital currency asso-
ciated with the disappearance of over $450,000,000 in March
2014. The eXpress has acquired copies of the GIGcoin incor-
poration papers which confirm Malinin's statement. Whitelaw
first met Malinin in 1987 at the height of the Cold War. Follow-
ing the collapse of the Soviet Union in 1991, the two men have
maintained a business and personal relationship.

※

By the time the 737 touched down at SFO, Sochi's fever had
spiked above one hundred and three degrees. His face bore a
gray pallor that sunk beneath his red hair and beard. His eyes
couldn't focus on any objects more that a few feet away. When
he lurched into a trash can outside the departure gate Finch had
to grasp him around his shoulders and pull him away from the
luggage claim ramp.

"Sochi, you're soaking wet!" Finch rubbed his damp hands
against the legs of his pants.

"I know. Something's wrong."

They could barely hear him. Eve held a hand to his forehead and pulled it away in shock. "Let's get him to a hospital."

He raised an arm to object, then relented. "Okay," he
wheezed and then tried to tug his duffle bag behind him.

"Let me get this," Finch said and heaved the bag onto a cart and set Eve's luggage and his own onto the rack and wheeled the carrier toward the airport exit.

As Sochi stumbled forward, Eve wrapped her arm around his waist and steered him along the sidewalk to a taxi. Before he could climb into the back seat he leaned over the curb and vomited into the gutter.

Fortunately the emergency ward at the San Francisco General Hospital was experiencing a brief lull. Within ten minutes Sochi was guided through the admission process, whisked behind the reception desk and led toward a bed with a pull-around privacy curtain. Finch helped him strip and then dressed him in a vented hospital gown. An orderly settled him onto a gurney. Soon an array of wires connected him to a monitor that clicked and beeped above his bed. Eve and Finch were told to wait in the reception area.

But before he could sit down, Will's phone pinged with an in-coming text message.

"Wally. Somehow I imagined I'd get an hour to myself." He read the text and glanced at Eve with a look of resignation. "I've got to go to the office."

"Go." She slumped into the chair next to the water cooler and set her bag at her feet. "I knew you'd have to. But someone should stay with Sochi. Me, obviously. At least until we know what's happened to him." She dug through her purse and pulled out her tablet and tapped the cover with a fingernail. "Besides, I've got to sort out a ton of email with Gianna's estate lawyer."

He leaned over and kissed her.

She wrapped a hand around his neck and pulled him in close.

"I love you, you know."

He wasn't expecting to hear this. Not now.

"So don't fuck this up. Okay?"

"Okay. I won't." He laughed with a genuine brightness and kissed her again. "I promise."

※

Finch loaded the three bags into a taxi, drove them back to Mother Russia, carried the luggage up to his condo, had a quick shower, shaved, and took the Powell-Mason cable car down to Geary Street. As he marched the three blocks over to the *eXpress* office he considered his next moves and tried to imagine a sequence that would lock all the puzzle pieces into place.

As he walked toward his desk in the bog he passed Fiona's pod. Her computer was on, the cursor blinked mutely. Her collection of Lypsyl sticks stood in a row behind her telephone. A cotton sweater lay draped over the back of her chair. He dashed off a note to her and stuck it onto her monitor: *Welcome home. Come and find me. W.*

Back at his station, he tugged his laptop from his bag and plugged it into the server lines. Minutes later he was up and running. He pulled up the Malinin file that he'd written on the flight back to SFO and emailed it to Wally with a brief query: *I'll send the first two 'graphs to Whitelaw to pry a response out of him. What do you think?*

Less than a minute later his desk phone buzzed. He checked the caller ID: W. Gimbel. "Finch, my office. Now," Wally growled.

"Nice to hear from you," he replied with a false decorum.

A pause. "Right. Welcome back. Now get over here pronto, amigo."

When Finch swung open the door to his boss's office he saw Wally Gimbel standing next to a new wall-mounted TV monitor. Fiona sat in one of the three chairs facing Wally's desk. As Finch passed behind her he squeezed her shoulder.

"Good to see you," he said under his breath.

She set her hand on his, then let it slip away. "You too."

"Wally, you got a new video monitor?"

"Scavenged it from the editor's office in the *Post.*" He frowned and pointed to the floors below the *eXpress*. "The day after they closed down. Okay, let me replay this," he continued without missing a beat. He pressed the rewind button on his remote clicker. As the gray-scale images whizzed past, Finch thought they could be watching reruns of a grainy 1950s TV show.

"All right. This is security footage of the Van Ness subway station captured during the two-hour slot when Fiona managed to escape from Justin Whitelaw."

"Impressive. How did you get this?"

"Can't reveal my sources." Wally turned and fixed them with his cheshire grin. "If I did, my ex's ex would feel a certain level of betrayal."

"Your ex's *ex?*" Fiona' asked.

"My first wife is a serial monogamist. Five times down the aisle," he said without a hint of irony. "Her third husband, who works for MUNI, still bears a grudge. Okay Will, this is our second go-round with this. Fiona says she saw Justin at the edge of the platform right here." He advanced the video and stopped it at the time marked 11.36.42.

"Could be him," Finch said. "Looking a little rough, I'd say."

Fiona said, "No, that's definitely him. You can't see his face very well, especially in the crowd, but that's his shirt. And see" — she pointed with her hand — "the blood on his shirt. That's from...."

She looked away, unable to complete her thought. Given what she'd been through, Finch was impressed by her composure. She'd dug down deep to be able to come back to work and watch this video so soon after her imprisonment and escape.

"Now watch this." Wally advanced the video in slow-motion, describing the images as they progressed. "The subway car enters the station. Then Justin seems frozen in place. Then *here* — look carefully — he simply turns and dives onto the tracks."

He let the video run as the three of them watched the disaster unfold. Justin's arms slumped forward as if he were about to dive into a pool. He fell across the track, face-down, his belly atop the left rail. A second later the train rushed over him and Justin disappeared.

"Unbelievable," Finch whispered.

"While you were gone," Wally continued, "everyone agreed it was suicide. When you see this, there's no doubt. The official rationale runs like this: the deaths of his sister and uncle led Justin into an acute depression. Then his desperate act. When Fiona escaped he knew it was the end."

Finch nodded. There was Cecily's death and then Buddy.

He knew more than a little about acute depression. "So the cops finally confirmed his link to Fiona?"

"Yeah. Right after they interviewed me. I guess they wanted to get it out before I did."

"They scooped us?" Finch let out a mock laugh.

"I guess they did." She shrugged. "I just wasn't ready, Will."

"Of course. Sorry, Fiona ... I didn't mean...." Finch tried to backpedal, realized it was impossible and decided to switch the discussion back to the suicide.

"So now it's all about Justin's depression. The SFPD claimed the exact opposite at the media session just last week. That he wasn't depressed, I mean."

"You know how it works. Second opinion."

"And the forensic psychologist confirmed the diagnosis this morning," Fiona added.

"That's what the family said about Gianna. Depression, then suicide." Finch turned away in disgust. Their collective delusion sickened him with its perverse self-pity. "What is it about the Whitelaws?"

"Hard to say." Wally turned off the monitor and settled into his chair. "The senator has gone to ground. Hiding in his condo in D.C., apparently. It wouldn't surprise me if he's had a complete breakdown. Losing two children separately within two months? And his step-brother. Most parents would completely collapse. I know I would."

Finch took a moment to assess the implications. "Okay, I've got a lot to fill you in about Hawaii. Fiona, you want to stick around for this?"

"I would, but I'm finishing my feature story." She stood. "I want it ready before I go to the police press conference at the Palace of Justice." She checked her watch. "In two hours. I think they're trying to wrap it up. Stamp 'case cleared' on Justin's file and bury it in the archives."

"Your first-person account?" Finch asked.

She nodded.

"Go." Wally tipped his head toward the door. "If there's anything you need to know, I'll fill you in. And Fiona." He paused. "Everyone knows you've done a helluva job with this."

Her face churned with a twist of pain and pride and she slipped out of the room.

※

Finch spent the next hour with Wally. Given Malinin's history, the murder of Marat following the exchange of flash drives, the illicit web cams, Witowsky's involvement with it all, and Sochi's sudden illness — Wally sat riveted by Finch's story. The only episode he omitted was about Sochi spiking the software. Since Will didn't know the implications, he decided to ignore it for now.

When he concluded, Wally believed they were poised to smash open an international financial conspiracy. Only one question remained: how to reveal the scheme in the right se-quence to ensure that one source didn't jeopardize another and immediately kill the entire operation.

"We have to publish this all at once." he announced. "A complete A-to-Z box-set exposé. No drip feed with this thing."

"To do that, I have to talk to Senator Whitelaw."

Wally looked away with a frown.

"Did you read my last email?" Will pointed to his boss's computer. "I sent you the story on Malinin. But I want to send the first two paragraphs to Whitelaw. If he doesn't consent to an interview with me, the implications of his silence will be brutal. It'll mean the end of his career. Most likely he'll be imprisoned. His only hope is to go on record and clear his name of any involvement with GIGcoin. The question is, how do I get him to read it?"

Wally peered into this monitor and read the opening paragraphs. Then he set his elbows on the desk, tented his fingers over his mouth and thought a moment more. "Leave that to me," he sighed. "I should have an answer for you in a day or two. Meanwhile write all the backgrounders to the story so we can publish everything after you talk to Whitelaw."

"And if he refuses an interview?"

"Then we publish without him. But he'll talk. He's smart enough to know he has to get in front of this story. Like you say, it's his only way to survive."

"Okay." Finch stood up.

"By the way, you said that friend of my nephew got sick in Hawaii?"

"Yeah, Sochi. On the flight back from Honolulu. Instant flu syndrome, I guess. Fever and some vomiting. But the guy's built like a Viking. I'm sure he'll be fine in a few days." He swung open the door but before he could leave, Wally called him back.

"One more thing." Wally held a finger in the air. "New orders from Lou Levine in Legal. Every *eXpress* reporter is now required to install a security app on their phones before they conduct another in-person interview. It's called *Stand Up 4 Justice.*"

"What?"

"Since Fiona was abducted. You'll find instructions in an email from me with a link to the app. In an emergency it automatically captures a video on your phone, sends the recording to Dropbox and a text to me. If you're in trouble, I'll know it and we'll have documented video proof of whatever went down."

※

When Finch scrolled through the screens of email back at his desk, he was pleasantly surprised to find no emergencies waiting to snap at him. He sorted the new messages by the sender's name to identify anything important: one each from Wally and Fiona, another from the new intern, Gabe Finkleman.

As promised, the note from Wally contained the "legal requirement" to install *Stand Up 4 Justice* on his phone. Despite his doubts, he installed the app as requested, taking a moment to scan the user tips as the program loaded on his Samsung. The app had been inspired by the murders of US citizens by cops. 2015 would mark a record year if the trend continued: one thousand people shot dead during arrest procedures. Everywhere you looked it seemed like the police were out of control. Did the intake process not include some kind of psychopath screening? Or maybe psychopathology was now a requirement for new recruits.

He opened the email from the ever-eager-to-please Finkleman: "Just checking to see if I can help."

Finch replied: "Yes, you can. Dig up any and all info on

GIGcoin patents, copyrights and trademarks. Email results directly to me. Thanks, W."

From Fiona he found something much more personal, written several days earlier when she was still in the hospital.

Will, thanks for the pep talk last night. After crying myself to sleep I woke up realizing that you're right. I can eat the rapes and beatings I took or let them eat me. (Good old Niet- zsche, right?) So I started writing the first-person feature story that Wally assigned to me. Began with me breaking out of Justin's make-shift prison and running for my life to the Van Ness station. Then I looped the story-line back to the night when I met him for a drink at Café Claude, thinking I could interview him to get the inside scoop on Gianna and Dean Whitelaw and his crazy driver, Toby Squire. (Who lies in a coma, in a locked room three floors above me....) I haven't finished writing yet, but the story will end with Justin's death in the subway. Kind of a full-circle thing.

Anyway this isn't supposed to be about my story. It's more about how you helped guide me out of the maze I was in. I know in some way you blame yourself for what happened. But that's not accurate. I went to meet Justin knowing there was a risk. Both you and Wally warned me, but it was my call. What I couldn't do on my own — and where I needed help — was to find my way back to something resembling 'normal.' But you did. You came to me and you got me out. Thank-you. Fiona. PS — I owe you one. Lunch some day? On me.

Finch read the note a second time and was about to reply

with a snappy come-back, something to diminish the weight of emotion — so that they could, as she said, put the "normal" back in their working relationship — when his phone buzzed with a text message from Eve: *Sochi's taken a bad turn. Can you swing by?*

Finch wavered between the two messages, both demanding something from him. There'd been a time in his life, in his early twenties, when he would have ignored both women and simply moved on. But that was when he needed to deny their power. It also meant that he had to deny what he needed — and what they offered and possessed. He now believed that denial was somehow tied to personal destruction. To say "no" to someone in need is like summoning death in a whisper. And there was plenty of that going around these days.

First he responded to Fiona, one sentence that he hoped would keep their bond alive: *Fiona, you are the most normal person I know and if you think that feeding me lunch can prove it, then simply name the time and place.*

Then he took his phone and replied to Eve's text: *I'll be there in an hour.*

CHAPTER THIRTEEN

W<small>HEN</small> F<small>INCH</small> <small>MET</small> Eve in the hospital lobby, he felt concerned the moment he saw her face.

"Sochi's been moved to ICU." She bore a worried look, as if some threads of her life had slipped beyond her reach and she didn't know how to pull them back under control.

"Intensive Care? I thought he had a bad flu." Finch scanned the hallways, seeking out a sign pointing the way to ICU. "Where is he?"

Eve led the way along the hall and up an elevator to the third floor. As they marched along the antiseptic-smelling corridor she explained the little she knew about Sochi's condition. "Apparently his fever has spiked and there's been more vomiting and diarrhea. The orderlies let me walk along the gurney beside him as they moved him up here. All he could say was that he's been poisoned."

"Poisoned?" They stood at the counter in front of a nursing station that also served as a barrier to the doors marked Trauma Center.

"He said he was injected with something in the washroom before we took off from Honolulu."

Finch's mind drifted back to the moments he and Eve waited for him in the departure lounge at Gate 11. "Right. I remember that seemed to take a while. Then he told me something about being pinched. But not injected with poison."

A nurse slid open a glass security pane and observed Eve with a serious expression. "Dr. Henney finished a minor surgical procedure half an hour ago. Once they complete the specimen analysis he'll want to talk to you."

Eve nodded. "Is he all right?"

"Mr. Pocklington is resting comfortably. You can wait in the lounge." She pointed her pen to an open room opposite the doors to the Trauma Center.

They sat in matching chrome chairs next to the windows overlooking Potrero Avenue. Artificial plants stood in dusty pots beside a water cooler.

"All right. So, who's Pocklington?" Finch asked.

"You don't know his real name, do you?" Eve shook her head.

He nodded and turned his head away with a sheepish air. True enough. After all this time, how could he not know Sochi's name?

"It's Pocklington. Oscar Pocklington."

"Oscar Pocklington?" Finch studied her face a moment, seeking a trace of humor, a flinch that would betray her solemnity. After a moment he let out a laugh. "You're serious?"

She nodded, allowed a smile. "I saw it on the patient chart. I guess they pulled it from his heath insurance card."

"Oscar *Fucking* Pocklington. No wonder he changed his name!"

"Stop it!" She tried to muffle her laughter. "You're terrible. And he's seriously ill."

"Yeah ... well." Finch's mood shifted to something more reflective and for a moment he tried to imagine Sochi's inner world. For years he'd inhabited an elaborately constructed mirage. Even his adopted name suggested that he lived in a fantasy land so vast and sprawling that reality itself remained a distant illusion. But the encounter with the Russians had cracked the veneer of his mask and now Finch could recognize the mix of emotions that had washed through Sochi when they were preparing for their final meeting in Chinatown: shame at being duped by the surveillance camera, anger at the Russians, boyish bravado as he contemplated his revenge. Beneath the flux, Finch detected a base of fear. Like most of us, Sochi tried to bury the creeping fear that preys on all doubt and insecurity.

From across the hallway, they heard the click and bang of the trauma unit doors as they opened and then slammed shut. A moment later Dr. Henney appeared in a white coat, a stethoscope draped around his neck. Classic, Finch thought as he stood to shake the doctor's hand.

"Let me be frank," he said and pulled a chair beside Eve. Everyone sat. "I understand there is no next of kin?"

Finch shook his head. "We're close friends," he said and looked at Eve.

"Well, Mr. Pocklington is in serious condition. In addition to the vomiting, diarrhea and fever, he complained of a sharp pain in his buttocks. When we scanned it with ultrasound, we could see what appeared to be a metallic sliver under his gluteus maximus. About the size of a grain of rice." The doctor held up his thumb and index finger. A quarter inch separated them. "I made a small incision, extracted the particle and sent it down to the pathology lab for analysis." He paused and held them with a steady gaze.

"And?"

"It was a perforated pellet containing ricin."

"Ricin." Finch leaned forward. "That's toxic, isn't it?"

"Very." Henney nodded with a bleak look. "It appears that the pellet itself is composed of platinum and iridium. By the time I removed it, the complete dose of ricin had been released."

Eve held a hand to her mouth. "What can you do now?"

"Watch. Wait." He shrugged. "Things might be different if he'd inhaled it. But there's no antidote for injected ricin."

"No antidote." Finch repeated in a whisper and looked at Eve. He couldn't think of anything more to say. He stood, shoved his hands into his pockets and walked to the window.

"There is something else," Henney continued.

Finch turned to face the doctor.

"Obviously this was an attempted murder. So far. But barring a miracle, within a few days it will be murder pure and simple. One that employed a weaponized poison. I'm required to inform the authorities — in fact, I already have. The FBI has asked me to advise you to make yourselves available to them and not to leave here until an officer speaks to you."

Eve nodded as if all this had now become inevitable. "Can we see him?"

"Yes. He isn't infectious." Henney sighed. "But bear in mind that he's starting to experience seizures. They'll only get worse, I'm afraid."

Finch shook his head and walked back to Eve and the doctor. Once more the burden of guilt weighed on his shoulders. He felt it pressing him, shoving him back into the chair. He dropped forward at a sharp angle, his elbow cracking onto the chrome arm rest. He let out a yelp.

"You all right?" Henney set a hand on Finch's arm and helped settle him.

"I'm fine." He nodded. "Funny bone."

"Right." Dr. Henney let out a laugh. "Okay, I'll get the nurse to tell you when you can visit your friend."

※

"The FBI." Finch washed his hands over his face. If he could, he'd wash away the remorse he felt about Fiona and Sochi. "I never thought it would get to this. Honestly, Eve, which corner did we turn that led to this bloody place?" He swept a hand around the hospital lounge and stood up again. He walked over to the window and stared at the traffic sweeping along Potrero Avenue. In the falling dusk a few drivers began to click on their headlights.

She joined him at the window and looped her hand around his elbow and pulled his arm against her. "Just about every corner we took, I guess."

"And next up, the FBI. Hell, if they think we're involved with a ricin poisoning, they'll put us in jail." He tried to steel himself. "What do we tell them?"

"The truth. They'll get it out of us no matter what we say. Besides, we have nothing to hide. I imagine they'll interview Sochi while he's still able to talk. Then each of us separately.

First time out they'll serve coffee and donuts and assure us we're all on the same side. Then they'll compare notes, find the discrepancies and start to press us wherever they find deviations. Expect them to play hardball. Weaponized ricin is no joke. So the only thing we can do to live another day is to be dead honest."

"What about Witowsky? You going to tell the FBI about him?"

She turned to face him, leaned against the wall. "It may be the only way to keep Witowsky at bay."

"What do you mean?"

"I mean that Witowsky may be a bigger threat than Malinin. If I can get the FBI to run interference against both of them while we try to cinch the knot around Senator Whitelaw, maybe — if we don't run out of time first — we can finally bring this all to an end."

Finch tried to conceive of an end game that would save them from Malinin and Witowsky — and keep them out of prison.

"Come here." She led him back to the chairs and they sat down. "So. I've had all day to work this through. Every turn we make, who's there? Witowsky. Think a minute: he was the cop assigned to churn through Raymond Toeplitz's estate, his house, his car. And his computer. He told me that's how he stumbled on the GIGcoin software. Even a boob like Witowsky could see that it's worth billions."

Finch listened in silence as she continued.

"Remember my friend in the forensics unit told me he's being watched by IAD. Why? My guess is because they think

181

he's making a grab for GIGcoin. Let's assume he is. Knowing we're a step ahead of him, he starts tracking us. The SFPD has all the digital spyware they need to follow our every move. A single cop with a few in-house friends can track anyone wherever he wants. So he caught wind of our meeting in Honolulu and arrived there before us, set up the surveillance cameras and heard every word of our preparations."

"So Witowsky, not Malinin, tapped into our room at the Moana Surfrider. He learned that Sochi would get the key and Malinin would get the software."

"Exactly. Then he duped me into revealing when and where the exchange would happen." Eve shook her head with remorse, still astounded by her own gullibility. "By now he's probably determined that Sochi spiked the software on Marat's laptop."

She narrowed her eyes as if she were preparing for an impending battle. "Now he knows we have the software and one key. That means he'll come after us next."

"Or maybe the senator, who has the second key." Finch's voice carried a note of false hope. "Except that we're the softer target."

"By far."

"Do you think Witowsky injected the ricin pellet into Sochi?"

She shook her head. "Too sophisticated. Could he shoot Marat three times in the chest at close range? Absolutely. Cops train for it routinely. But this other thing? No way. You know, I remember a ricin poisoning in England decades ago. Some iron-curtain, Soviet espionage."

She drew her phone from her purse and began to key-in a search. After a moment she turned back to Finch. "Here it is. Bulgarian stuff back in 1978. The Brits claimed the ricin pellet was prepared by the KGB. And exactly how Dr. Henney described it, too. A platinum and iridium shell holding the ricin until it's released in the body."

Finch read over the article. "Unbelievable. The ricin pellet was injected into the victim using the tip of an umbrella."

"Did Sochi mention anything about an umbrella to you?"

"I don't think so." Finch shrugged. "But this definitely has the stench of the old KGB. And 1978 was back in Malinin's heyday. He could have worked on the ricin pellet himself. So Malinin took out Sochi because he spiked the GIGcoin software —"

"For revenge. Because Marat was killed by someone directly linked to us. Or to me, at least." Eve gazed into the distance.

"Let it go, Eve. Witowsky started this, not you."

"I know."

Finch turned his attention back to the problem at hand. Slowly he could see the pieces link together. "It's just as Malinin promised: *Any betrayal will be dealt with immediately.*"

"You know something else?" Eve had a hopeful look in her eyes. "It could be that Malinin doesn't know who Witowsky is. His name, the fact that he's a cop. None of it."

"And maybe Witowsky doesn't know what happened to Sochi." Finch doubted that either of these two possibilities could help them very much. But at least he and Eve could see all the cards the other players held. An advantage that no one else possessed.

※

"The Russians...." Sochi whispered through the mesh of his beard and mustache, his voice barely audible under the steady buzz of medical machinery humming on the walls of the room.

Finch drew closer to the hospital bed and leaned on a side rail that had been raised and locked into place to prevent Sochi from tumbling onto the floor during a seizure. "What about the Russians?"

He churned his head on the pillow and gasped. "Shit." His eyes filled with a look of exasperation.

Eve touched Finch's arm and pulled him back a step. "Sochi," she said. "You've been poisoned."

"I know. With ricin." He found his voice now and seemed to realize that Eve and Finch were there to help him.

"Someone from the FBI is going to interview you."

He nodded. "They already have," he whispered. He paused to catch his breath. "But you" — he leaned toward Eve — "you have the original GIGcoin software at home?"

"Yes. I hid it where no one can find it."

"Good." He nodded. "And the key I got from Marat works. You only need the second key now."

"I know. We're close." Finch released Sochi's hand and brushed aside a strand of red hair that had fallen across his face.

"There's one more thing." Another spasm tore through him. Sochi blinked and had to work to focus his eyes. "The software on the flash drive is like a gate. The complete system software is installed on a server somewhere."

Finch felt a sense of impending collapse. Another disastrous turn ahead? "On a server? Where's the server, Sochi?"

"I don't know." His head turned on the pillow. "It doesn't matter. But when you find the second key to unlock the software, make sure the flash drive is connected to the internet. It's a gate," he repeated. "Plug the drive into the internet and engage both keys. Then the gate opens."

Finch turned to Eve and gave her a distant look. Despite his coherency, Sochi seemed to have entered a delirium, another realm of the make-believe that governed so much of his world.

"Time to rest," she said and ran her hand along his wrist. The stroking seemed to calm him and he closed his eyes.

A moment later the door swung open. Dr. Henney crossed the room. Two others followed him, a man and woman dressed in suits, their hair slicked back, their faces resolute.

"Eve Noon, Will Finch," he said and swung an arm to the FBI operatives in tow, "let me introduce Agents Lavigne and Sterne."

Sterne stepped forward and shook Eve's hand, glanced at Finch and nodded. "I've heard of you. Ex-SFPD, right?"

She glanced away. "Once upon a time."

He turned to Finch. "And you're the reporter, right? I've seen you on CNN. That bear story. Quite something." His lips curled together in a sneer as if he'd accidentally bitten into a lemon seed. As if crime reporters were the lowest form of human waste imaginable.

※

Some people referred to the San Francisco FBI field office as an eminent example of urban modernist architecture. But to Finch, the Phil Burton Building was simply another late-50s box, a steel-and-glass government hive on the edge of the Tenderloin District. He imagined that a directive from President Eisenhower had deliberately located the building on Golden Gate Avenue next to the most impoverished neighborhood on the west coast. Occasionally federal employees might search their pockets for spare change to toss into the outstretched hands of the destitute souls squatting on the sidewalks. An example of trickle-down economics in action.

As they entered the building Agent Lavigne tried to bring Finch and Eve onside. "Since we're all working on this together," she said, "I think we should just help one another." Her voice almost conveyed a hint of sincerity.

"Of course," Eve said as she smiled at Finch. "We can use all the help we can get."

They took an elevator car up to the thirteenth floor and as Eve had predicted, they were provided with hot coffee and fresh donuts. Moments later they were introduced to the FBI field office chief, Bert Clemens. He shook their hands and turned to four men who'd followed him into the staff lounge.

"This is Jerzy Linka and Bill Mason, forensic specialists from Homeland Security, and two men you may know from the SFPD," he said looking at Eve, "Walt Mobley and Juan Morales."

"From IAD, right?"

Morales nodded. "Good to see you again, Eve."

"I'm not required to tell you this," Clemens said, "but as a courtesy, I'm advising you that we'll be listening to your interviews through the one-way glass. Rest easy, this is just about information gathering. We're all on the same team and no one suspects you of any criminal activity."

With that, Finch and Eve were separated and escorted into adjacent interview rooms. The game was on.

※

"I know you want to find out how this happened to Mr. Pocklington as much as we do." Lavigne waved to a chair and sat opposite Finch.

The straight-back chairs and table were made of steel, the one-way mirrors framed in steel, and the door reinforced with a veneer of steel scratched and scarred from decades of abuse. Finding any comfort here would be a challenge, he realized.

"So," she continued as she set up the interview recording system, "what can you tell me about Oscar Pocklington?"

Try as he might, Finch couldn't get used to calling Sochi, Oscar Pocklington. It was a fraud. A ruse. Which was why, perhaps, that Sochi had discarded his given name years ago.

"Where do you want me to start?"

"Let's start in Honolulu." Her face took on an open expression. He noticed that her eyebrows were brown, her hair-job a dusty blond with dark roots. "I've read the report from the HPD. Apparently you were cooperative with them. You called in the murder of this man, Marat?"

"I was there, but I didn't see the shooting."

"I get that," she said and leaned forward, relaxed her arms on the steel table between them. "What I need to know was how this happened. Why were you, Eve and Oscar in Honolulu? And what did it have to do with Marat?"

"You want the full picture?"

"All of it." She looked in his eyes. "From the beginning."

187

Finch took a sip of his coffee and tried to relax his back. Okay, here we go, he told himself.

"There's a digital currency called bitcoin. And another dozen contenders trying to steal bitcoin's market share. One of the contenders is called GIGcoin. It's a scheme run out of the Cayman Islands controlled by Alexei Malinin, an ex-KGB Russian oligarch, the recently murdered Dean Whitelaw and his brother, Senator Franklin Whitelaw."

Agent Lavigne sat back, brushed a strand of dyed hair from her eyes and whispered, "All right, you've got my attention. Go on."

※

Two hours later Finch was escorted to the men's washroom and offered a fresh cup of coffee and more donuts. He was then directed back to his interview room and joined by Agent Sterne.

Finch smiled to provide a sense of camaraderie. "So now we get the good-cop, bad-cop switch?" A joke. Hopefully Sterne would laugh.

"Maybe. But which is which? Did Agent Lavigne treat you well?"

"No complaints." He adjusted his weight in the chair.

"Then I guess it won't take long to figure my approach." With a superior-looking frown on his lips, Sterne slapped a thick file folder on the table. "Maybe you don't know as much about investigative journalism as you think."

Finch took a thin sip of coffee and set the mug aside. "No?"

"This is the file on Oscar Pocklington. Read it and you might find out why he called himself Sochi No-name."

Finch opened the cover and glanced at the first page. The top of the sheet read "CRIMINAL SUMMARY." He closed it. "Okay. So give me the Twitter version."

Sterne tugged the folder across the table, flipped it around to face him and scanned a briefing sheet. "Five years ago it seems that he devised a sports scam involving on-line bets in Curacao. He'd place a dozen bets a day, all under pseudonyms, then hack into their computer system, cancel his losing bets after eight P.M. when the bank wire-service closed — but before the wagers were settled. The winning bets he'd collect on, the losers would be cancelled. Turns out he had a hundred percent winning streak."

A new ghost from Sochi's secret past. Finch tried to mask his surprise.

"Tell me you knew about this."

Finch tried a deflection. "Does your file also reveal that he worked for NASA?"

Sterne nodded. "Yeah. That's in here."

"Good ole Sochi." Finch decided to take Sterne on a horse-and-buggy ride. Make him taste the horse shit. He clicked his lips, cowboy-style. Giddy-up. "That Sochi is one smart cookie."

"Damn you, Finch!" He slammed the palm of his hand on the table.

"What?"

"I need to know everything you know about Oscar Pocklington!" Sterne's face turned a shade darker. A vein in his neck throbbed.

Finch waited a moment, let a beat pass, then another. "All

right," he said in a near whisper. "I met him when I took a sublet in his building." From there Finch continued to fill in the gaps and revealed what he knew about a man he knew very little about. When he reached their point of departure from Honolulu, he held his arms up and shrugged. "That's it, I'm afraid."

"You didn't see him injected with ricin?"

"No. I thought he had a bad flu until Dr. Henney told us he'd been poisoned."

Sterne pushed the file folder aside. "All right, let's move on. What about Malinin? I understand you had dinner with him. Tell me what he said."

Finch brushed a hand over his mouth. He'd been down this road before: a challenge to his first amendment rights. Now would be a good time to probe his limits with Sterne. "You can read about it in the *eXpress. Malinin's a protected source for my story."

"A protected source?" Sterne eased back in his chair. "Let me advise you not to test me on this. Your friend" — he pointed to Sochi's file — "is going to die from weaponized ricin. That's one hundred percent guaranteed. Do you think for a moment that Homeland Security will tolerate two seconds of bullshit about protected sources if they think you know where Malinin scored this ricin?"

Finch considered the threat for a moment. The situation reminded him of Iraq. People he knew disappeared. Friends' records were simply expunged. He recalled Eve's guiding strategy: use the FBI to run interference against Malinin and Witowsky. And live to fight another day.

"Okay, I'll tell you everything you want to know." He began the narrative about his meeting with Malinin in the gazebo outside the Iolani Palace, then his private dinner at the Shorebird. He laid on as much detail as he could. It was like writing a first-person story for his college newspaper. The more color the better.

"What about the ricin?" Sterne asked when Finch finished his tale.

"The ricin pellet has old-school KGB written all over it. Malinin's alma mater. You know that. There's nothing I can add."

"Did Malinin mention ricin to you?"

"No. But he made it clear that any betrayal would result in instant retribution."

"And did you betray him?"

"Not until now. It was a formal news interview, pure and simple."

"Did Oscar?"

"I don't know." As much as the steel-framed chair permitted, Will set his shoulders back and tried to relax.

"No?"

Finch shrugged, struck by an intuition that any condemnation of Sochi could hurt them all.

Sterne let out a long sigh. "Okay. Let's talk about Witowsky."

"I'd rather not. The guy's a sociopathic criminal posing as a distinguished cop."

"Maybe, maybe not. Eve Noon knows him from her days with the SFPD. She also said he probably killed Malinin's geek, Marat."

"Be nice to prove that, but I didn't see it happen."

"But you told Agent Sterne that you saw Witowsky flee the market seconds after Marat was shot."

"I did. And I heard three shots fired and counted three holes in Marat's chest."

"What else did you see, Finch?"

He closed his eyes, shook his head in exasperation.

"Come on, Finch!" Sterne slammed Sochi's file folder on the table. As it skidded past him papers flew into the air and scattered onto the floor. "Fuckin' help me here! *What did you see?*"

To Finch's surprise the tantrum had some effect. He remembered Witowsky brushing past him, advising him to flee with Eve and Sochi. Then Finch turned to see Witowsky whisk through the crowd, a dash of blood on his sleeve and a bag slung over his shoulder.

"He stole Marat's shoulder bag. And Marat's computer. It's the one thing the HPD couldn't figure out. What happened to Marat's laptop."

"All right. What else, Finch? I need to know everything you've got."

Finch shrugged and shook his head with weariness. He took another thirty minutes to elaborate each encounter he'd suffered through with Witowsky. The night he'd first met the grizzled old cop following Dean Whitelaw's murder. In the hospital as Eve recovered from her coma. Again at his apartment following Fiona's kidnapping. Then at the SFPD media briefing. Finally, in the market after Marat's murder. Each lap backward in time required him to provide context: people, places, dates, motives. And on each occasion he supplied layer after layer of detail pointing to Witowsky's criminal intentions.

But never did he reveal that Sochi had spiked the software. Better not to let the FBI think Witowsky possessed a broken package, he decided. Let them think that once Witowsky acquires the second key, he'll win the game. Make them want to reel him in first.

※

An hour later Finch and Eve were escorted down the elevator, through the front doors and into a taxi. As Lavigne held the door open to the cab, she said, "Thanks for your cooperation, Ms. Noon. Fare's on us."

"Right," Eve said with a wave of her hand. "Keep us posted on Witowsky and Malinin."

"You'll be the first to know," Sterne said with a brisk nod of his head. "But it works both ways. Here, give me your phone."

Eve passed her phone to Sterne with a wary look. The cop punched a series of numbers into the contact file.

"There. That's my number. You call me," he said. "You may need me sooner than you think."

As the car pulled away from the curb Finch rolled his eyes dismissively. "Sure thing. First to know." He glanced around to find his bearings. Once they turned onto Turk Street, he leaned over the seat back. "Take us up to Nob Hill," he told the cabbie.

"Make that Union Square," Eve drew Finch away by his elbow and held a finger to her lips: *Hush.* "I'm famished," she continued. "Let's grab some take-out and sit in the square."

"Good call." Finch studied the serious expression on her face. "Great night for it."

"Wherever you want," the driver said in a dull, heavy voice. "It's the same twenty bucks to me no matter where you get to."

When they climbed out of the taxi at the corner of Stockton and Geary, Finch drew her aside. "What's up?"

"In a minute," she said in the same conspiratorial tone and led him across the street up the concrete stairs and into the square. Every day of the year the park throbbed with tourists, but Finch and Eve managed to find an empty space on a long low wall under a few palm trees. A team of elaborately costumed Korean dancers were busy preparing the nearby stage with props. A crowd of sightseers with matching outfits began to gather and settle into place.

"Sorry for the spy-craft," she said. She glanced over her shoulders to ensure they had a measure of privacy. "The cab driver's probably an agent. If not, then he'll be on the FBI payroll. And you can bet your condo is wired, too. And my place. Our phones, everything." She waved a hand in the air with a look of defeat. "So. Going forward we have to expect to be monitored and likely tailed."

Finch blinked. Of course. He watched an overloaded cable car climb up the Powell Street hill. A dozen people snapped selfies as they hung from the exterior grab-bars. Ambling along beside the cable car, a gang of Brit drunkards sang soccer chants as if they'd just won the World Cup.

"Were you able to feed Lavigne and Sterne any bait?"

"A couple of times. Especially after Sterne threw Sochi's file across the room. I had to get him mad before he thought he could trust me."

"Cops." She laughed with some apprehension. "A lot of them won't believe what they hear unless it's preceded by pain. Or humiliation."

"AGS."

"What's that?"

"Abu Graib Syndrome. Back in Iraq. The brass refused to believe any intel unless somebody cracked open a skull first."

"Okay. AGS it is." She glanced away for a moment. "Look, there's something else I found out from Lavigne."

"Yeah?"

"She let slip that Damian Witowsky's gone AWOL. He hasn't checked in with his unit since Hawaii and nobody can track him down."

"That would explain why IAD monitored our interviews through the one-way glass. So, he's gone rogue?"

"It means he's after one thing only. GIGcoin."

As Finch considered this he felt they'd entered a passage without side streets or alleyways — and definitely no way to double back. The only escape lay straight ahead along a dim road with no discernible end. "Are you still all right with this?"

"What are our choices? Once Witowsky discovers his copy of GIGcoin is spiked, he'll come for us." She stared at Will and then blinked. "You know, I think I agree with them."

"With who? About what?"

"Sterne and Lavigne. They see us as hapless fools, over our heads in a scheme beyond our control."

195

"Maybe we are." He lifted her hand and caressed her wrist with his thumb. "Need some sleep?"

"Not as much as I need to get back to Sochi."

"Let's get that meal first. Then, Sochi. Then sleep."

※

Finch and Eve returned to the San Francisco General Hospital a little after eleven o'clock that evening. Finch hoped that Sochi might have slipped off to sleep and he imagined that for an hour at least, Sochi could enjoy a reprieve from the poison, a chance to renew his energy in order to prepare for the struggle ahead.

But when Finch entered his room he was shocked to see a skull-like grimace stretched over Sochi's face. His skin had become a bleached parchment pulled tight from ear to ear and from his forehead down to his lips. The tautness in his flesh suggested an inner ghost waiting to tear through the thin filament of his flesh and then float away. Even his long, red beard looked thinner. A few strands, long curling strings of rusty hair, lay on the bedsheets.

"Sochi," Finch said as he lifted Sochi's right hand into his fingers.

"Can you talk, Sochi?" Eve ran her fingers over the sheet covering his chest.

His head swiveled heavily on the pillow. A look of recognition brightened his face. "Dunno," he whispered.

"Did you get some sleep?" Eve stroked the back of her hand across his forehead.

"Maybe." A heavy shudder rolled through him. "It's crazy."

"What's crazy?" Finch smiled and squeezed his hand.

"When I close my eyes … I can see my brain."

Finch glanced at Eve, then turned back to Sochi as another convulsion struck his belly and legs, and then released him.

"Jesus. I'm so scared."

Finch felt the fear course through Sochi's hand into his own. The jolt was electric, visceral. He looked into Sochi's eyes. "At least you can see it. That's the first step in beating back the fear. Seeing it right in front of you."

"No," he gasped. "I'm really scared, Will."

Finally. The first time Sochi had referred to Finch by his given name.

Dr. Henney pushed open the door and approached the foot of the bed. He studied the readouts on the monitors and nodded, not with a look of hope, but with a sense that Sochi's condition was following a predictable course.

He said, "We're keeping him hydrated with the IV drip. I've also got him on some medication to elevate his blood pressure. And we're monitoring the convulsions — they seem to come in cycles — and modifying the anti-seizure meds to keep him as comfortable as possible. Unfortunately, that can increase the delusional episodes."

Finch gazed at the overhead monitors. He could make out a few readings: blood pressure, heart rate, temperature.

"Any change in prognosis?" Eve asked.

The doctor shook his head and glanced at the clock. "Let's step into the hall while we talk and give Oscar some rest."

He led the way into the corridor and continued. "It's been what? Thirty hours since the attack? He's entering the normal range of terminal expectancy."

The normal range of terminal expectancy. Finch grimaced at the psychobabble. But who could blame them? Like everyone else, physicians took shelter behind a wall of jargon.

"Seventy-two hours would be remarkable," Henney continued. "Anything less will be a blessing."

"A blessing?" Eve took a step toward the doctor. "Look, I don't want to sound intrusive, but I checked this out on the internet. Isn't the CDC working on a ricin antidote?"

Henney seemed glad to hear the question, a distraction from the intractable problem facing Sochi. "Yes and no. I was on the phone with the CDC this morning. Yes, the military is experimenting with something. But no, they're not even close to sorting out human trials."

"Couldn't they try whatever they've got on Sochi right now?" Even as he asked this Finch expected a rebuttal. "Good Christ, the way it stands he either dies from the ricin, or the antidote that could save him."

Henney shrugged as if he heard this sort of logic every day. "You'd think so, but it doesn't work that way."

Finch felt a rush of anger bolt through his blood. *"Well how the hell does it work?!"* He clenched both hands in the air as if he might erase every word he'd just said. He swung around in a full circle and shook his head to clear his despair. "Sorry. Look … I know you're trying."

Henney nodded with an expression of sympathy. "Here's the thing: nothing is going to work. Sochi is going to die. The sooner the better for his sake. In the absence of any supportive euthanasia laws, all I can do is try to make him comfortable and alleviate his pain. If you can make him feel loved, well, that's more than many people get."

The buzz of an electric alarm began to resonate from from Sochi's room. Eve and Finch followed Henney back to his bedside. A round of convulsions wracked Sochi's body from head to foot. Finch imagined that an invisible cord had lashed around Sochi's feet and begun to whip him through the length of his frame. As the bed shook and the alarm continued to howl, a team of four orderlies and nurses rushed into the room and strapped him to the bed rails. Finally secured, Sochi's head shifted from side to side as if the last twist of the seizure might wrench his neck from his torso. A drizzle of white foam dashed against his cheeks and beard. Suddenly the spasms ceased. A new alert sounded, a high-pitched ping. *Ping. Ping. Ping.*

"It's his heart," Henney pronounced, his voice calm and assured. "Get the paddles, Jerry. Susan, cut the alarms, please."

Seconds later a near silence filled the room, broken only by the low hum of electricity buzzing in the air. As the team hovered above Sochi's chest and prepared the defibrillator paddles, Finch scanned the wall monitors. Sochi's heart had stopped beating.

"Clear."

The team took a step back. Henney studied the heart monitor as the first shock hit Sochi's chest. A digital blip sputtered across the monitor and disappeared.

"Again." His voice conveyed the weary confidence of an air traffic controller.

"Clear."

Another blip sounded and vanished on the screen.

"And again."

"Clear."

Blip.

"Once more, please Jerry."

"Clear."

Blip.

A new hush followed as Dr. Henney turned away from the bed. "Susan, time please."

She looked at the monitor. Everyone could make out the time on the wall clock, but this aspect of the medical ritual required a sober pronouncement.

"Eleven-forty-three P.M."

"Enter it on his chart, please. I'll sign it off later." Henney blinked and looked away. Then his face brightened and he smiled. "Good effort, team. By the books. You couldn't have done any more for him. No one could."

※

During the taxi ride back to Mother Russia, Eve couldn't stop herself from shivering. She wrapped her arms around Finch, snuggled in close and shivered some more. "I'm freezing," she complained.

"No, you're just overtired. You haven't slept since the flight from Honolulu."

"Maybe." She released a final shudder and set her head on his shoulder.

When they arrived at the mansion on Nob Hill that Finch so admired, they walked up the staircase to the third floor condos, past Sochi's apartment and stood at Finch's door while he struggled to find his keys. At last he unlocked the door and swept Eve ahead of him into the living room. She stood a moment with her back to him and then burst into tears.

"My God," she whispered. "Is that Sochi's duffle bag?" Two suitcases and the duffle bag stood side by side along the wall where Finch had left them that morning. "I can't stand that this is here and he's not."

Finch tossed his jacket onto the couch and slid Sochi's bag into the closet. "That's the best I can do for now. Tomorrow I'll tell the others what happened. Maybe some of them will know what to do with his stuff." For a moment he wondered if Sochi possessed a last will and testament. He imagined that the estate would be worth millions. On the other hand, formal estate planning likely never entered Sochi's mind. Not for an instant.

"Will...." Eve set her head on his shoulder and wept helplessly. "God, I can't stop myself."

"Don't even try." He pulled her to the love seat and curled an arm around her. "Just let it all go. So much else has gone wrong. Let this go too."

His words released a flood. Seconds later she let out a loud wail and nuzzled her head against his chest.

She pulled away from his arms to wipe her face with the back of her hand. Her eyes were bloodshot, her makeup ran in streaks down her cheeks, her hair hung in damp strands over her ears. She glared at him with a look he'd never seen before. A look of desperation, hunger, fear, desire.

"This is a disaster." She managed to sit up on her own and wrapped a hand over her lips as if she needed to stop the words in her mouth.

"What's a disaster?"

"I *love* you," she said in a pleading tone.

There it was again. He waited a moment, locked his eyes on her to see ... what? What more did he want from her?

"I know." The best he could manage.

"You *know?*" She picked herself up and looked down at him. *"You know? That's it?"*

"No." He shook his head, stood up and held her again. "It just frightens me," he whispered into her ear.

"Love *frightens* you. Why does it frighten you?"

"Because every time...." He stalled, not sure how to explain his confusion. "Every time I get too close. And then someone dies."

"No. Not this time." She took his face in her hands. "This time nothing will happen. You don't know how strong I am."

"You promise?"

She shook her head, astounded that he could ask this.

"Just take me to bed, will you?" She kissed him. "And just hold me. That's all I need. Just give me that much."

CHAPTER FOURTEEN

THE NEXT MORNING Finch awoke to the sound of his phone buzzing. His arms were curled around Eve, his right hand on her stomach. The bed was warm, the pale light outside the open window filtered through a fog that had settled over the city like a sleeping cat. He tried to decide if the noise from his phone signaled a text, an email or an actual call. Then he glanced at the screen. "It's Wally," he said and set his feet on the carpet. "I need to take this."

"Okay." Eve's voice sounded bright, revived. Yesterday's despair and desperation had vanished. She kissed his shoulder and made her way to the bathroom shower stall.

"Will, I got confirmation for your interview," Wally began. "Everything's lined up for tonight."

"The interview with Senator Whitelaw?" He drew a hand over his eyes and stood up.

"Exactly. Ten P.M. eastern time in Washington. At his penthouse."

"Tonight? How'd you wrangle that?" He stood at the window and gazed into the immaculate Italianate garden below. The house gardener pulled at a tangle of buttercup weeds as he knelt on the lawn.

"Just as we planned. I sent his chief of staff a confidential note which contained the first two paragraphs from your story on Malinin. Now look. Apparently the senator's had some kind of health problem. Might even be a stroke; no one seems to know for sure. In any case, he could be dying. So I want you to write the Whitelaw profile no more than an hour after you finish the interview. Then I'm going to publish the whole story tonight. A-to-Z like we agreed. I'll take your first draft. If you need to, do a re-write on the plane back to SFO. Things are moving so fast, spit and polish doesn't matter."

"What's moving so fast?" He walked into the kitchen and pressed the Insta-Brew button on the coffee maker.

"With Fiona. As she predicted, last night the SFPD finally acknowledged the link between her abduction and Justin's suicide."

"Fantastic." He could sense the victory just ahead. Could smell it. "The whole story's going to break open."

"Except the international media are jumping all over this. So after the senator's interview I need you back here ASAP to report on Fiona's side of it. Meanwhile she's in hiding, writing all the backgrounders. But I need you to interview her about her kidnapping, confinement and escape. It's got to come out fast. If you can swing it, catch the red-eye back to town, all right?"

"What about Stutz and Wengler? I thought you recruited them when the *Post* shut down.

"They don't start until Monday."

Will thought a moment. Suddenly the workload felt overwhelming. "If you're stuck, give that kid Finkleman a shot. He's a research ninja."

"Yeah, but can he write?" He paused as if he might be considering the possibility. "Who knows? It might be smarter than pulling Bozeman from Science and Tech. Besides, he's buried with the latest skirmish in the Google-Apple-Amazon wars. Damn it, this is what happens when you try to run a news operation on a shoestring."

Finch shrugged. Why try to solve Wally's problems? He had his own job to do. "Listen, Wally, did Whitelaw know about Justin being linked to Fiona *before* he agreed to an interview."

"Yes. Look, I gotta run." His tone acquired an authoritative edge. "Okay, so Dixie's booked you on a noon flight to D.C. today and an open-end return tik when you're ready to swing back here. She emailed you the details. Get the Whitelaw story to me before we log-off here tonight. Now go."

"Wally, wait." Finch raised a hand in the air, as if he could flag down his boss and bring him to a stop. "Sochi died last night."

A pause. "He died? I thought you said he had the flu."

"No. Ricin poisoning. Looks like Malinin hit him in Honolulu just before our flight took off. Eve and I spent four hours with the FBI yesterday."

"*Ricin?* Jesus Murphy.... And Malinin killed him? Any proof of that?"

"Not yet. But all signs point in his direction."

Another pause followed as he digested the news. "So this is all part of it, right? Three murders: Toeplitz, Dean Whitelaw and now Sochi. Four if you count Gianna. Mix in the Russian oligarch, ricin poisoning and this crazy GIGcoin cartel — it's a freakin' volcano. Okay, so on your flight to Washington, write the story on Sochi and the Russian. Email it to me as soon as you touch down. Then go after Whitelaw and reel him in. Tonight's D-Day all over again. The Allies are landing on all four beaches at once."

※

After he'd showered and dressed, Finch joined Eve in the dining room. She'd made bacon and eggs and toasted two multi-grain bagels. He told her about Wally's call, the trip to Washington and the pending interview with the senator.

"So when you publish the story on Senator Whitelaw, that should wrap everything up, right?"

He laughed and began to chew on the bagel. "More like firing the starting gun. This story will run for months."

"Or until the media squeeze out the last drop of blood." She smirked and ate some of the white from her egg. "Anyway, I'll use the time when you're gone to work with Fran Bransome. She has to see me about Gianna and Toeplitz's estate probate again. Apparently the SFPD are trying to subpoena the digital files as evidence in the Whitelaw and Toeplitz murders." She waved to the email on her phone screen and set it on the table.

"I guess that was inevitable. Let the lawyers have a kick at GIGcoin now." Finch took another bite from his bagel, drew his laptop from his courier bag and began to search for Dixie's email containing his flight info. "All right," he said when he'd opened it. "Out of here at twelve-twenty. Arrive in D.C. just before nine. Cutting it pretty close."

"When do you return?"

"Dunno. Open tik. Wally wants me back on tonight's red-eye." Distracted, he sipped his coffee and scanned the scrolls of email above the note from Dixie. One in particular caught his eye. Gabe Finkleman had sent him an attachment with the title *GIGcoin patents.* He opened it and found the usual formal greeting from the intern.

Dear Mr. Finch, as you requested, please see enclosed a PDF of the patent registration for GIGcoin software. As you can see, the property is owned exclusively by Raymond Toeplitz. I've searched the federal and California corporate and property registries. From what I can see, ownership has not been transferred. Although it's unlikely, it could be registered in another country. I'll keep looking. Please let me know if there's more I can do to help on this file.

On this file. Finch chuckled to himself as he clicked on the patent registration PDF. A massive document began to download on his laptop. He scanned it for a few moments and turned to Eve. "I just received a copy of Raymond Toeplitz's patent for GIGcoin. I'll forward it to you." He tapped the "share" icon on the document and watched the process wheel spin as the file shifted through the internet.

For the next few minutes, Eve read the email from Finkleman and scanned the patent.

"Hey. You know what? This proves Toeplitz still owns the GIGcoin patent." She set her phone aside and looked at him. "He never transferred it to Whitelaw, Malinin and the rest of the consortium registered in the Caymans."

"Apparently not." Finch held her eyes as he considered the implications.

"Will … this could be it." As she leaned forward a look of astonishment slowly settled on her face. "Finally. We have a documented, indisputable motive. Raymond Toeplitz wasn't murdered because he was about to turn evidence of fraud over to the district attorney. He was killed because he refused to sell his patents."

Finch nodded. "And without them the entire international consortium running GIGcoin Bank and Exchange is nothing more than a fantasy shell company."

"So the software patents must be included in the Toeplitz estate."

"And it all belongs to you."

※

Finch's plane wheeled into the terminal of Ronald Reagan National Airport a little before nine o'clock that evening. Minutes later he settled onto a bench in the arrivals lounge and emailed the story he'd written about Sochi's death to Wally. Given the unproven allegations that the Russians were behind the murder, he closed the story with some open-ended questions. But astute readers would draw their own conclusions: Russian dirty tricks were used to kill Oscar Pocklington, a visionary leader in high tech who once saved a NASA mission when no one else could.

Next he hailed a taxi and gave the driver Senator Whitelaw's address: Washington Harbor at 3050 K Street. During the drive along the Potomac River Finch tried to orient himself. He'd only visited Washington once, in 2006, to support a briefing to the Military Intelligence command. He'd been seconded in place of his captain (who'd been wounded in a roadside attack two days earlier) for a meeting that lasted about four hours and included almost fifty senior officers. To his surprise the President attended the briefing for five or ten minutes, just enough time to shake hands with everyone before he was called away. Within a month, Finch had completed his tour in Iraq and returned to civilian life with the Distinguished Service Cross and an honorable discharge. He considered himself lucky.

The cab pulled up to the entrance to the Washington Harbor building, a condo complex perched on the river bank in the bustling Georgetown area. There'd be little seclusion available in this neighborhood, but Finch knew that the senator preferred a busy street to a quiet park. Anywhere he could be photographed jogging by small retailers, popping into restaurants and cafes, snuggling stray dogs or kissing babies — that's where the tanned senator from California wanted to be.

He walked down the brick concourse to the waterfront building. At the reception desk the concierge demanded two pieces of ID and Finch's cellphone number before he called the senator's line. With the protocols cleared, he turned to Finch.

"Mr. Peterson will be down in a minute," he said and squinted suspiciously. "He'll escort you to the senator's penthouse."

Jeb Peterson looked Texan, smelled Texan, spoke Texan. He was taller than Finch by two or three inches, heavier by twenty pounds. A two-inch scar under his lip gave his demeanor an ugly turn. But it was the aroma of the man that most impressed Finch as they entered the elevator car. It took a moment to recognize the moist, heavy bouquet of Caribbean tobacco.

"Smoke cigars, Finch?" Peterson typed a six-digit code into the elevator keypad. The doors skimmed shut.

Finch laughed. "Not any more. Gave it up after I heard about Fidel's revolution."

"Well time to come back to the tribe, pardner. Obama's fixing things for us now, isn't he?" His turn to smile.

Finch was relieved when the elevators doors slid open again. A short ride up, only seven floors.

"Mr. Finch I'm bound to tell you something most people don't know," he said in a more somber voice as he guided Will to the right and down a corridor. "Senator Whitelaw has been ... *affected* by the tragedies that have hit his family over the past few months."

"I can imagine."

"I know what your meeting is about." He stopped, turned and held Finch with a meaningful look. "He asked me to ensure that you speak to him in privacy, without me in attendance. I told him I thought that would be a mistake. But, being the kind of man he is, he insisted. In any case, if the senator needs my support in any way I'll be" — he paused as if he couldn't find the right word and simply gave up — "I'll be here when he needs me."

Peterson punched another keypad to unlock the penthouse door and waved Finch ahead of him. Then Peterson turned, stepped back into the corridor and locked the door behind him.

Will walked a few paces along the condo hallway. The floors were made from oak planks, inlaid with redwood trim set back four or five inches from the baseboards. The walls were painted mint green and adorned with at least ten photos of the senator shaking hands or embracing dignitaries and politicians. Bush one and two. Bill and Hillary Clinton. Obama, of course. Nelson Mandala. Mother Teresa. Warren Buffett. In the middle of the corridor, above a vase of fresh cut flowers, stood a framed image of the senator on his own, a TIME magazine cover of Whitelaw's ruddy, smiling face and just below his chin, his well-known motto: *"Politics is the art of asserting the People's Will"—California Senator Franklin Whitelaw.*

"Mr. Finch?"

He heard his name called from somewhere beyond the hallway.

"In the living room. On the right."

Finch continued through the miniature gallery. When he reached the end of the hall he detected more cigar smoke. Stooped next to the fireplace, propped up by a cane, the senator waved Finch forward with his free hand. He wore a black suit, charcoal golf shirt, no tie. His eyes, heavy with exhaustion, blinked once. The ever-florid tan had faded from his face, bleached into a pale gray. Compared to the incensed patriarch who'd ushered Finch out of his lodge in Cannon Beach months earlier — Senator Franklin Whitelaw now appeared to be a broken man.

❋

"Sit." He pointed to the love seat with his cane and then settled into a wing-back chair in front of the fireplace. "Let's finish this miserable business while I'm still able."

Finch considered shaking the senator's hand before they began the interview, then thought better of it. He sat opposite Whitelaw and opened his courier bag. He took out his phone, notepad, pen and a file folder and then he set up his laptop on the glass coffee table that separated the two men.

"If you don't mind, I'd like to record this." He clicked on his phone and set it on the middle of the table.

"Of course you do."

Finch tapped an icon on his audio-recorder app. "Senator Whitelaw, I'd like you to acknowledge that we're now on record for an interview to be published in the *San Francisco eXpress.*"

Whitelaw waved the hand resting on the top of his cane. "Get on with it."

Finch winced. Not quite good enough. "So you consent to this interview?"

"Yes."

"Let me begin by asking if you're familiar with something called GIGcoin."

"It's a digital currency that my step-brother, Dean, was trying to bring to market before his murder last month."

Finch glanced at him and then turned away. "I'm sorry for your loss, sir."

"Sorry? You are the *fucking cause* of my loss."

Finch blinked. Does he know that I spent a night with his daughter? That I witnessed his brother being gunned down on the top floor of a parkade? He took a moment to study the list of questions he'd compiled on his laptop.

"Senator, do you recognize this document?" He opened the file folder and passed him a copy of the GIGcoin Bank and Exchange incorporation papers.

With a dry wheeze the senator set the crook of his cane around the chair armrest and leaned forward to grasp the papers. He scanned the first page, flipped to the second and third and then set them all aside.

"No."

"No?" A surprise. "Please turn to the last page."

Whitelaw took the document up again and turned to the final sheet.

"Is that not your signature, sir?"

"No." He set it aside again. "Where do you think you're going with this Finch?"

"If it's not your signature, then whose is it?"

"It's a forgery." His body shifted in the chair and his arm shook with a brief spasm that knocked his cane to the floor. "Damn. How am I supposed to know who forged it? You're the CNN boy wonder. You tell me!" he cried with a sudden burst of emotion.

Finch narrowed his eyes. He could see that Whitelaw had entered a point in the interview that everyone reaches sooner or later: the moment when he forgets that he's on record. And that everything he says will soon be broadcast to the world.

"Senator, do you recognize any of the other signatories to the GIGcoin incorporation?"

He nodded. "Dean."

"What about Alexei Malinin?"

Whitelaw held a hand to his mouth as if he were deciding

to change his approach. For a moment Finch wondered if Whitelaw regretted his decision to talk. If Finch didn't get all the information he needed soon, the senator might bring the interview to a halt.

"All right," he said with another wheezing gasp. It seemed as if he might be about to offer a confession. "Yes, Malinin was part of it. And the others. I met them all at Dean's house in Marin County last year. It was a consortium that he and Malinin put together to exploit the software that Raymond Toeplitz developed. GIGcoin," he added.

"Toeplitz was one smart bastard," he continued in a confidential tone. "Do you know what the G-I-G stands for? *GDP In Gold*. It was the pièce de resistance." His tone was now bright, almost ebullient. "The software is designed so that once a year the currency can be adjusted to reflect global GDP, either up or down, expressed in the current price of a gold ounce. That adjustment permitted buy-in by both the Keynesians and the Neo-cons. A piece of political-economic genius. It's the keystone that bitcoin doesn't have and therefore dooms it to extinction: a mechanism to adjust the currency to population growth and the vicissitudes of economic expansion and contraction."

Finch watched the senator closely as he spoke. He seemed a different man than the shrunken figure who sat before him just minutes earlier. This was the once-youthful senator speaking now, a political visionary with an innate gift for street-fighting politics. Charisma writ large.

"But despite their efforts, the consortium never acquired the rights to the software, did they?"

The senator raised his brows. "What? Are you sure?"

Finch pushed a copy of the patent registration across the table. "According to the Patent Office, Toeplitz still owns the intellectual property rights — that is, they now belong to his estate. The document you are holding was verified as current and authentic by an arm's length, third-party attorney one day ago." He shrugged to suggest no other possibility existed.

"Christ." His hand shook again and he dropped the papers onto the table with a shrug. "Dean," he muttered dismissively as if his younger brother had fumbled the ball once again.

"I'd like to return to the forged signature on the incorporation papers."

Whitelaw shrugged and gazed into the empty hearth of the fireplace.

"It seems to me that only two people could have put your name to the corporate seal. Dean and Malinin."

He nodded, his face still turned away. His hand rattled as it rested on the chair arm. His despondent mood had returned.

"Then it would be Dean."

"You're sure? Has he forged your signature before?"

He adjusted his posture and settled his back into the chair. "We used to practice as kids. He got pretty good at it. All kinds of signatures. When he was fifteen he was good enough to bilk Dad out of fifteen hundred bucks by forging his checks."

Finch could sense a new direction ahead. Obviously there was no love lost between the step brothers. Perhaps the senator's distrust would lead to some kind of indictment of Dean Whitelaw. Maybe if Finch tried another way. "Senator, did you ever know Mark Gruman?"

215

"Who?"

"Mark Gruman, the deceased sheriff of Clallam County in Oregon."

He shrugged. "How is he relevant?"

"A case is pending in Astoria that will prove that the sheriff shot and killed Raymond Toeplitz." Finch saw the objection rising on Whitelaw's face. *"Before the bear found his corpse. He was shot in the car and left with the window rolled down. The lawyers will argue that your brother paid Gruman to kill Toeplitz after he refused to sell the GIGcoin software to your consortium."*

"Rough justice, I guess. Toeplitz died a few weeks after he declared his intention to testify against our firm in that bogus fraud charade!"

"A charade? Or a last-ditch effort to get Dean to back off?" Tit-for-tat, thought Finch. For the first time he suspected that Toeplitz's legal gambit might have been a flanking move against Dean's demands to sell the software to the cartel.

"Who knows? I couldn't keep up with it all. I have a job to do, you know." Whitelaw slumped backwards into the chair. He drew a hand over his face and moaned. His voice was full of revulsion. The sort of disgust that Finch had observed in Gianna whenever she talked about her family.

"He was a bastard. *Literally.* His mother, Martha Meyers, brought him into the family when Dad married her. When Dean was two she died of heart failure and Dad adopted him out of pity." He glanced at Finch with a look that asked, so what would you expect?

"But when we were kids — I was ten, he was seven, I

guess — he did something that I could never square. Never. Back of the lodge one summer we found a litter of kittens behind the garage." He pointed to the far wall as if the garage stood just behind Finch's shoulder. "Decent kids would take those kits home, give them some warm milk and an old blanket to nest in, and one by one give them away to friends. Not Dean. First, he never had a friend. Not one. But then he took those kittens and he tied them." Whitelaw held his hand in front of his chest as if he were tying a noose around his wrist. "Just like that. Around their necks. Then one at a time — *snap.*" He jerked his left hand as if he might be snapping it off his wrist.

Finch waited.

"That's why I didn't regret his passing. He's the only one I don't miss."

※

The senator indicated that he wanted to move onto the deck and led Finch through a set of glass doors and over to the railing. The balcony provided a view across the Potomac River onto Teddy Roosevelt Island, and beyond that, Arlington Cemetery. Finch took a moment to ensure his phone was still recording their conversation and held it in his palm as discreetly as possible.

"Tell me, Finch, what do you know about the software?" The senator had a wary look in his eye, as if he were trying to measure an intangible quality in Finch.

Sensing there might be more to learn about GIGcoin, Will decided to play along. "From the patent papers I know that your brother didn't own it. Nor did he have it in his possession."

"Go on." Whitelaw shuddered slightly, a tremor that rolled from his hand along the length of his left arm.

"I also know that a digital key is required to initialize the system."

The senator's eyes narrowed a little.

"Two keys, in fact," Finch added, to establish the extent of his knowledge.

"Mmm. You sussed out more than I gave you credit for." He leaned on his cane and let his fingers flutter on top of the crook. "And where do you imagine the software and these keys are right now?"

"With its rightful owner. "

"Rightful owner?" He chuckled at the idea.

"Eve Noon. She's the beneficiary of Gianna's estate."

Whitelaw sniffled with surprise. "Who is this Eve Noon?"

"Your daughter's best friend from Berkeley. You met her a few times." He shrugged. "At least Eve remembers you."

"Of course." Whitelaw considered this as he gazed over the river. "So Gianna must have been Raymond's beneficiary."

"Yes."

"Well, top marks. A-plus. You have done your homework." He smiled with the fawning look of a benevolent teacher. "And the two keys — where are they, do you suppose?"

"I understand that your old friend, Alexei Malinin, has one." Finch thought it better to divert this line of conversation rather than reveal that Sochi had traded it for a spiked copy of the software.

He nodded. "And the other?"

"Your brother."

"Step-brother," he corrected.

"But since his death, there's been no mention of it."

Whitelaw lapsed into a brooding silence. He studied the river front, the passing pleasure boats gliding toward the docks as the midnight darkness swallowed them.

"You know what I think, Finch. There could be ten keys, a hundred — or no key at all. It won't make a dime of difference. Why? Because money is nothing without the hypnosis of the citizens who are entranced into believing it has real substance."

Finch nodded. Despite his pale demeanor, his shudders and shakes, the senator still possessed his innate incisiveness.

"And once your story about GIGcoin emerges — along with the stories of Toeplitz's and Dean's murder, of Malinin, all of it with my name attached to the scandal — GIGcoin will be entirely discredited." He waved an imaginary wand above the patio railing. "In other words, mass hypnosis with this particular sparkling charm, *GIGcoin,* will be impossible."

"Perhaps."

"In which case this" — he drew an SD card from his pocket and held it between his trembling thumb and index finger — "has no more value to the world economy than a bent coat hanger."

He smiled at Finch again and continued.

"This is the second key. After he died, I found it in a small vault in Dean's home office."

Finch studied the chip, a Secure Digital card. The gold contact pins glittered briefly when they caught the patio lights.

"Would you like it?" He handed him the SD card, a sixty-four gigabit marvel the size of Finch's thumbnail. "You know

Mr. Finch, if you *refuse* to publish your findings — and if you possessed the first key and the software — it's likely you could salvage the entire GIGcoin project with that card. You would become a multimillionaire overnight."

Finch considered the possibilities. He and Eve would own the entire kit. But could he patch together the political partnerships that Dean and Malinin had created? He hesitated and then shook his head. "No. I think it carries more value as criminal evidence." Nonetheless, he slipped the SD card into his shirt pocket.

"Well, there you have it, then." He took his cane in one hand. "And I think that finishes our interview, Mr. Finch."

"But — "

"No." He held a hand up. "Don't fret. We have more to discuss. But off the record."

Finch put aside his disappointment. He knew the senator had much more to tell. Instead of turning off the recorder, he simply clicked off the screen. Whatever else Whitelaw said, he'd record for background purposes only. But from this moment on, Finch couldn't quote another word.

When he turned back to Whitelaw, he saw the senator gazing at the distant crosses standing on the lawns of Arlington Cemetery. Perhaps he could see the ghosts rising in the gloom. To Will it was all darkness and shadows.

"A lot of dead souls. Over four hundred thousand people are buried there," Whitelaw intoned with his signature gravitas. "I look across there and it reminds me of what I'm supposed to be doing in this town."

And what, exactly, is that? Fraud? War-mongering in Iraq?

Finch declined to pursue this line. "Senator, I know you've taken a lot of blows lately. Your daughter last month. And now — "

"You smoke, Finch?" He held out a pocket cigar humidor which held three short Cohiba Club cigars. Finch shook his head, but Whitelaw lit one for himself. "Most people don't know that I smoke. Fact is, I just took it up a few months ago. Jeb Peterson got me started." He smiled weakly and let out a jet of smoke through his lips. "Obama's initiative is bringing them back in style. What do you think?"

Finch looked down river to a finger of land sticking into the water. A narrow point called The Mole. He turned back to face Whitelaw. "I think we're running out of time, Senator."

"Indeed. We are," he said and a streak of pain seemed to grip his face, twist it and then let go. "All right. Let's get to the heart of things, shall we? You want to know about my children? About the way they died? Of course, *you* know quite a lot about that already. You and your cabal of vipers euphemistically called the media. But what you really want to know is if I conspired in their murder and suicide don't you? If I'm the *cause* of their misery!" His face turned a deep red. "You want tears, you want rage, you want fury! Well, I'm going to give it to you mister!" A horrible spasm ran up his leg as he stomped out the cigar on the deck tile and retreated back into the condo, stabbing the floor with the tip of his cane as he went.

Finch waited a moment. The heat of Whitelaw's surprise outrage sent a rush of fear along his spine. He hadn't seen this coming. But now that the senator's mood had spiked, he wondered if he should call someone. Maybe Jeb Peterson. In any case, it's time to leave, he told himself. Before Whitelaw's emotions run out of control.

When Finch stepped back into the condo, he saw Whitelaw leaning on the kitchen bar, his arms propped straight ahead, stiff-arming the counter top. The scarlet intensity of his face had ebbed but his hair was ruffled, as if he'd dragged his fist over his skull two or three times. He held his eyes on Finch without blinking. To get to the front door, Finch would have to pass directly in front of him. He tried to think of a distraction.

"Can I use your bathroom?"

The senator stared at him with a penetrating gaze. Then with a brisk jerk, he tipped his head toward the bedroom corridor.

Finch stepped down the short hallway, shut the bathroom door behind him and locked it with the finger bolt. *My God, what is going on?* He turned on the taps and let the water rush into the basin. Then he drew his phone from his pocket, found the audio file containing the senator's interview and studied it a moment.

"Yes, just in case," he murmured to himself. He clicked the share icon, typed in Wally's email address and sent the audio recording of the interview to his editor. Then another reminder of Wally entered his mind: *Stand Up 4 Justice.* The app used to record evidence of assault. He clicked on it, watched as the app spun into play. Then he turned off the sink taps and walked back into the living room with the phone in his hand.

※

The senator had moved to the center of the room where he

slumped forward and adjusted his balance on the cane. His free hand, tucked in his jacket pocket, appeared to be balled in a fist.

"I'm sorry. My behavior out there" — he nodded to the balcony — "was completely uncalled for."

Finch didn't know how to respond. He frowned and made a motion to leave.

"Wait." The senator held up a hand. "Do you know what Parkinson's Disease is?"

"Of course." Finch moved sideways. His back pressed against the bar counter next to the kitchen.

"I was diagnosed three years ago." He shrugged. "At first I thought I'd defeat the problem just like everything else that's challenged me in life. Outsmart it, out-tough it, out-spend it. But within three months I realized a war against Parkinson's is a war no one can win. Hell, I didn't even win the first skirmish." His head shook and a grimace settled on his face. "The best I could do was to keep it hidden from the public. From people like you."

"I'm sorry to hear that, sir." Finch now recognized that all the symptoms he'd seen earlier — the slumped posture, the brittle movements, the tremors and shakes in his limbs — pointed to one cause. And yet Whitelaw's mental faculties were completely intact. Another manifestation of PD.

"Then last month, after the news about Gianna's death, the disease accelerated past me, completely passed my ability to cope. Then Dean's murder. And now Justin's suicide." Whitelaw wiped a hand over his eyes, paused, and took a step toward Finch. "I felt surrounded. I realized I had no way out.

That's when I decided to hole up here. With Jeb and his cigars." He tried to grin, an effort that resulted in a bland sneer as the senator took another few steps forward. He stopped an arm's length from Finch.

"All I think about now is what lies ahead: complete loss of bodily functions. Someone to feed me. Someone to change me, wrap me in diapers and put me to bed. Aghh." He shook his head at the bleak prospect.

"I'm going to tell you something, Finch. When you reach the end of life, precious few pleasures remain. Only one, if you're lucky." He stood teetering on his cane, the right hand still bunched in his pocket. "The sense of taste. Of Cohiba Club cigars." This time his smile held, a broad grin that revealed his still beautiful teeth and his prevailing sense of irony.

"Now I'm going to give you one last gift. Here, give me your hand."

"What?"

The fragrance of Cuban tobacco wafted through Finch's nostrils as the senator leaned his cane on a side table and adjusted his weight so that he could stand on his own.

"Your hand."

Finch thought of dismissing the gesture, but from a feeling of sympathy, perhaps even a sense of duty, he shifted his phone into his left hand and held out his right. What was the senator offering? Another SD card?

Holding the flap of his jacket with his left hand, Whitelaw tugged his fist from his suit pocket and revealed a small pistol.

"What?... *What's that for?*"

"For you." He clicked off the safety, placed the gun in

Finch's palm, wrapped both his hands around Finch's fingers and pressed the snub-nose barrel against his own chest. The trembling abated. His hands felt surprisingly strong. "Now pull the trigger. Please."

"No!" As he tried to wrestle free, Finch dropped his phone on the floor. He cursed and then one at a time, he pried the senator's hands away from his own. "Christ! What are you thinking?"

"I've done some research, too. I know how your son died, Mr. Finch. I know that it broke you." Whitelaw held the gun, the barrel pressed to his heart. For a moment Finch thought, how strange, the way he holds the pistol by the very tips of his extended fingers, as if he can't bear to touch the weapon. "Then you became obsessed with me and my family. *You chose me.* Somehow you imagined that by destroying us, you could save yourself."

"What? That's crazy."

"Yes, I agree." He shrugged away the objection. "In any case, *now I've chosen you,* Mr. Finch."

"What?" Finch froze. He tried to think, tried to calculate something he could do to prevent impending disaster.

"Your fingerprints," Whitelaw whispered, his chin tipped slightly to indicate the gun.

"No!"

Whitelaw inserted his thumb through the finger guard and pressed the trigger. The pistol fired with a taut *bang* that echoed through the room and into the hall corridor. He collapsed at Finch's feet, and his body twitched in two long, rolling spasms arcing outward from his chest.

Finch kneeled at his side and inspected his face, then tried to detect a pulse in his wrist. Nothing.

Will stood and gazed at the floor. The pistol lay next to his cellphone. For the first time he could see it clearly: a Colt Cobra .38 Special. Except for the black hand grip, the revolver was identical to Eve's gun. Then he heard the pounding at the front door. The sound of Jeb Peterson about to barrel into the room and beat Finch into unconsciousness. He tried to think what to do. But there were no options. No choices to make.

Seconds later Jeb Peterson ran down the front hall. When he entered the living room he saw the senator lying on the floor, a widening pool of blood seeping under his corpse. He saw the phone. The gun.

"What the hell happened?"

"…He shot himself…."

Peterson stared at Finch. Jeb's eyes were on fire. "Like hell he did."

He clipped Finch in the face with a jab, then doubled him over with a blow to the belly. An upper-cut to the jaw dropped him to the floor. As he lay on the ground next to the senator, Finch groaned in pain. A final kick to the side of his head put him out of his misery.

※

When Finch came to, he found himself sitting on his butt, handcuffed and leaning against the kitchen wall. A medic closed the cut under his chin and taped a compress to the seeping wound above his ear. A second medic helped load the senator's corpse onto a gurney and wheel him away. As two police officers took a statement from Peterson, five or six other cops wandered through the rooms, taking photos and videos while two forensic experts made their assessments.

"Come on, Finch," a burley cop braced him under his biceps and lifted Will to his feet. "You got one long night ahead of you. Franco, you got him?" he said to his partner.

"Yeah. I got him. You lead the way, Jonny."

Supported by the two cops, Finch staggered forward and then slumped against the bar counter where Whitelaw had braced himself after his tirade on the patio. Unable to control his feet, he crashed to the floor again. Fortunately, his hands had been cuffed in front of his waist and he could brace himself for the fall.

"On your feet, man," Jonny said. "Up and at 'em."

In a moment of clarity, Finch glanced around the room. Where was his computer? His phone and courier bag? Before he could ask, the cops propped him on his feet again and frog-marched him through Whitelaw's photo gallery, into the exterior corridor and a waiting elevator car. As they descended to the main floor Finch regained his senses enough to realize the desperate situation he faced.

With his phone and computer confiscated the evidence to confirm his innocence was in jeopardy. Good thing he'd emailed the audio interview file to Wally. Had he received it yet? He tried to calculate the time in San Francisco and gave up. The main thing, he told himself, was to preserve everything that proved Senator Whitelaw had committed suicide.

Franco and Jonny marched him out of the building onto the short pedestrian mall that led up to K Street. Twenty feet along the brick road, four squad cars were parked with their lights blinking: red-blue-red-blue. Beyond them a crowd had gathered. The steady glare of two high-end video cameras illuminated the road as the gathering news teams collected raw footage of Finch's walk of shame. When Franco and Jonny guided him past a row of four concrete planters, Finch stumbled again. As he fell forward he wriggled free of the cops who held him lightly by his forearms. Sprawling on the ground, Finch turned his cuffed hands up and to his left, slipped two fingers into his shirt pocket and drew the SD card into his palm.

"Get up, Finch. You got a lot further to walk than this, man." Jonny coaxed him back onto his feet.

He was kinder than Finch expected and when he turned to thank him, he tossed the SD card behind the cop's back and into one of the planters. "Thanks," he whispered, just loud enough for both cops to appreciate his gratitude.

"All right, Jonny. Enough already. He killed a senator for God's sake." Franco tugged Finch toward the first squad car. "Let's get this creep locked up."

Taking charge now, Franco swung open the back door and pressed down on Finch's head as he shoved him onto the back seat. Before he shut the door he looked at Finch with a doubtful grin.

"You're about to start the first day of the rest of your life, asshole. Good luck."

CHAPTER FIFTEEN

EVE COULD FEEL her blood pressure rising. Sochi's horrible death from ricin poisoning had marked her and Finch for special consideration by Homeland Security and the FBI. Now they were turning up the heat.

"The FBI position is dead simple," Eve told Fran Bransome, her long-standing lawyer and friend. "Basically they said, Give us the software so we don't have to worry about you and your reporter boyfriend."

"Speaking of Will," Fran said, "where is he now?"

"In Washington interviewing Senator Whitelaw. He's due back tonight."

"Good. Given the circumstances, it might be wise not to lose sight of one another.

"All right, look," Fran continued. "I can try to block the FBI subpoena in court, but you know the story. The Feds always hold a higher trump card."

"Of course." Eve gazed through Fran's office window at the Transamerica Pyramid. Fran had represented her during the wrongful dismissal lawsuit with the SFPD. She'd been an excellent attorney then, but now she seemed more tentative and unsure of her footing. In the past Eve trusted her completely, but this time she wondered.

"Part of me," she confessed, "wants to turn everything over to them and be done with it."

Fran nodded as if to encourage her. "Definitely an option. It will relieve you of enormous legal stress."

"But unless something unforeseen happens, after Toeplitz's and Gianna's estates are cleared through probate, the software belongs to me. Right?"

"Yes. Assuming the Whitelaw family loses their claim to Gianna's estate. And neither her will, nor Toeplitz's provide much wiggle-room. Furthermore a Japanese judge in the landmark Mt. Gox case just declared that bitcoin is, quote, 'not subject to ownership.' In short, bitcoin is a liquid asset and whoever holds it, has it only for the time it's in their possession. Even though it's a foreign ruling, it adds weight to your claim to the bitcoin wallet and the GIGcoin software."

"So. I was a cop long enough to know that once material is surrendered to support an on-going investigation, chances of it being permanently confiscated, lost, eliminated, altered — or simply stolen are about five percent."

Fran shrugged again. "Sounds about right."

"The other thing is this. With GIGcoin still in my hands the Feds will keep tracking me. But once I surrender the software, all I am is a lame duck witness to Witowsky and Malinin's crimes. And frankly, Witowsky or Malinin could kill me to ensure I never testify against them."

Fran glanced away to mull over the possibilities. Eve had told her the entire saga and neither of them doubted the jeopardy she and Will Finch faced as long as Witowsky or Malinin were on the loose. And the fact that Witowsky had failed to report for duty with the SFPD was worrisome. When she turned back to Eve she tried to smile.

"All right. I'll try to block the Fed subpoena to seize the software on the grounds that ownership of GIGcoin is already subject to dispute in Gianna's estate probate. Our position will be that lawful possession must be established before it can be surrendered."

"Good."

"Looks like we can thank the Whitelaws for pursuing a rear-guard action to claim Gianna's estate," she continued. "Maybe I can delay our defense against the Whitelaws for a day or two, but if we wait longer it might actually strengthen their case that they're the rightful owners. Which we definitely have to avoid."

"Okay, do it. Two days will take us into the weekend." And with any luck, she thought, Witowsky and Malinin would be behind bars by Monday. Either that or dead.

※

Shortly after six A.M. Wally Gimbel sat at his kitchen table and sipped his coffee. He liked it black, hot and fresh, as if he'd just poured the coffee straight out of the beans. No additives, no derivatives, no nonsense. He loved this time of day and the morning rituals he'd developed over the years. His wife still slept in the room at the top of the stairs. His black lab, Carmen, dozed at his feet. The view from his apartment on Telegraph Hill looked onto the Bay Bridge and the sunrise in the distance. The day was young, so full of possibility.

He turned on his Android tablet and watched as the notifications menu cascaded down his screen. World news headlines, sports scores, stock reports, his daily meeting scheduler, the Bay area weather forecast, Word-of-the-day. And twenty-three new emails, including two from Finch. He opened the first and scanned the article about the murder of Sochi and the implied links to an unnamed Russian oligarch. A solid bit of writing, typical of Will. Then he opened the second email. No message, just an audio file of Finch's interview with Whitelaw. He listened for twenty or thirty seconds and set it aside. Unedited, no story attached, no hint of more to come. Odd.

Wally took another sip of coffee and turned his attention to the digital edition of the *New York Times*. If anyone had mastered the shift from newsprint to screen, it was the *NYT*. And the *Manchester Guardian*. To his surprise, an image of Will Finch's battered face filled the *NYT* homepage. The headline sent a shudder through his chest: "Senator Franklin Whitelaw Dead." The sub heads provided no cause for comfort: "Reporter Arrested, Small-caliber Gun Seized. Fourth Tragedy Strikes Family of Political Star."

For a moment, he froze. How could this be? More important, what could he do to save Finch from pending catastrophe? He studied Finch's picture again. The dazed reporter appeared almost unconscious as a cop led him toward the open door of a squad car. Good lord.

His phone buzzed once, twice. Finally he snapped out of his paralysis. "Gimbel here," he whispered, his voice barely stirring from his stupor.

"Wally, it's Lou Levine. I just got a call from Washington,

D.C. Have you heard? Will Finch has been arrested."

"Yeah." Wally drew a hand over his face with a sense of relief. At least the company lawyer had started to dig in. "Just reading about it now in the *Times.*"

"Well, he's in serious shit, my friend. The Feds are claiming he's an assassin, for god's sake!"

"Bullshit." Wally's voice hardened. "I sent him there to interview the senator. Can you get a lawyer to him?"

"Already on it. The firm has two criminal attorneys in D.C. But I'm going to need more than scout's honor to get him out. Have you got anything? I need tangible proof he was there on legitimate business. And that's just for starters."

"Just so happens I do." Wally studied the audio file on his tablet. "Finch sent me a copy of his interview with the senator last night. It's time-stamped at twelve-forty-two this morning."

"Fifteen minutes before the shooting. Forward it to me, Wally. I'll send it to the team in D.C. Send me anything else you come across that can build a case for him. And I mean anything. By noon the lynch mobs will be on ground zero with this."

After Wally sent the audio file to Lou he noticed the text message icon flashing in the notifications bar on his phone. A new text from Finch. He opened the message. *Stand Up 4 Justice: Will Finch has posted an urgent notice. Click this Dropbox link to download the video file related to this alert.*

Wally clicked on the video file. For the next five minutes he watched an erratic, jumping clip that could have been filmed by a monkey. When it reached the end, he watched again, then once more. After the third viewing Wally was able to make sense of the hectic scene as it unravelled. The first sequence revealed that Finch had carried the phone in his hand into a room with the senator. Next, an interval with the Senator bearing his soul in a monologue about his illness. Then he tugs a pistol from his pocket and shoves it into Finch's hand. Suddenly the phone drops to the floor, and the video portion locks on the stippled ceiling. But the audio portion continues as more dialogue follows: the tragedy of the senator's broken family and his accusations against Finch. The rant becomes increasingly muffled, almost indecipherable until it's broken by the crisp bark of the pistol firing.

Wally played the clip once more, listening for exculpatory evidence that might save Will. Then he heard it: Whitelaw begging Finch to shoot him. "Now pull the trigger. Please."

"Yes. That's it," he whispered aloud. *Now pull the trigger. Please.*

※

The morning after her meeting with Fran Bransome, Eve sat at the bay window in her condo staring across Geary Street, gazing at the Ton Kiang Restaurant. She checked her phone again. Still no word from Will. No email, no texts. He'd promised to come home last night. "I'll catch the red-eye," he'd said. But now she sat alone, worried. Wondering.

She recalled that first brunch with Will in the Ton Kiang, remembered his initial shyness as she escorted him across the street with the intention of seducing him. She'd been so hungry for him that day.

Then they'd discovered the destruction left by Toby Squire's bizarre invasion of her condo. He'd spared nothing.

She shuddered. The creep still lay in a coma. Would he ever be revived? Better if he simply rots on a bed in that locked-down hospital room, she thought. The idea made her turn away from the window in disgust. Then she nodded in mute acknowledgement of her hunger for revenge. Embrace it. *That's who you are.*

She turned on the 24-hour TV news channel and sipped her coffee. After a moment she paused. There it was bright as day: Finch handcuffed, his arms clasped by two cops as he marched toward a squad car, a black eye blooming above his bandaged cheek. A series of running headlines scrolled below the video: "Senator Franklin Whitelaw shot to death this morning. Reporter Will Finch arrested at the scene. Fourth tragic death in California's leading political family."

From a quarter-screen frame above the repeating video clip and news tracks, a reporter spoke into a field mic: "That's right, Jerry. No one has yet confirmed that Will Finch, a reporter with the *San Francisco eXpress* who was arrested in the deceased senator's Washington D.C. condo, is responsible for the senator's death. As you know, Will Finch broke the news of Raymond Toeplitz's murder in Oregon two months ago. Toeplitz was the Chief Financial Officer in the Senator's firm, Whitelaw, Whitelaw & Joss. There is growing speculation that the death of Toeplitz and the murder just last month of the senator's brother, Dean Whitelaw, may be related. This tragedy has been deepened with the recent loss of two of the senator's five children. And now Franklin Whitelaw's demise, occurring under apparently suspicious circumstances, has some commentators speculating that a conspiracy ties these crimes into a single, but very complex, story. Jerry, back to you."

"What?!" She screamed. "What happened?" She whirled back to the TV, clicked to CNN and watched Anderson Cooper confirm everything she'd just seen on the local channel.

Her heart pounded an urgent rhythm: *go, go, go.* But where? She tried to think, tried to set each word on an invisible track in her mind. *Go. To. Will.* Yes, that was the only thing that made any sense in this madness.

She grabbed her laptop, jacket, a change of clothes, toiletries and cosmetic bag and stuffed them all into a carry-on suitcase. She locked her condo door and ran down the stairs to the street and hailed a cab parked at the corner.

On the drive to SFO she booked a flight to Washington and then called Wally Gimbel at the *eXpress*. After five minutes waiting on hold, he picked up.

"Gimbel here."

"Mr. Gimbel, this is Eve Noon."

In the following pause, she thought she heard a sigh of relief.

"You don't know me," she continued, "but I know Will."

"Yes. He's told me."

"I'm on my way to D.C. to get him."

"Uhh ... I don't know if that'll be helpful. Our lawyers are already working on this."

Eve narrowed her eyes and shifted the phone to her right ear. She expected Gimbel to try to block her and she was ready for it. "Mr. Gimbel, I'm in possession of the GIGcoin software and one of two keys that will activate it. I also have Raymond Toeplitz's bitcoin wallet, the wallet that led to Gianna

Whitelaw's murder. Only Will and I can break this case open. But neither of us can do it alone." She paused to glance at her watch. "Now, my flight leaves in thirty-four minutes. I'd like to have anything Will sent to you from his last interview with the senator."

Another pause. Eve could almost hear Wally's thoughts ticking.

"Eve ... Will's interview with the senator is proprietary. If I gave you this material, he'd have my head." He let out a mock laugh, a miserable guffaw they both knew was a sham.

"And if you don't give it to me, he might not *have* a head." She took a long breath as she considered another approach. "Look. We can either be partners in this, or not. If we're partners, I guarantee that you will have access to everything I hold related to the Whitelaws. I also guarantee that I'll maintain complete confidentially with any *eXpress* materials, including everything pertaining to Will. You can send me a non-disclosure agreement and I will sign it. Immediately."

"Eve — "

"Mr. Gimbel, my taxi is pulling into the airport right now. I need Will's interview with Whitelaw before my flight departs. I don't like to be blunt, but I have no time left to explain this. If you don't send me these materials, the *eXpress* will lose all access to GIGcoin, Toeplitz's bitcoin wallet and all of my information related to this story. Furthermore, I need the contact info for Will's lawyer. Please let him know that I'll be in touch as soon as I land."

By the time she arrived in the SFO departure lounge, Eve had received the lawyer's name and cell number, Finch's audio interview with Whitelaw and the *Stand Up 4 Justice* video clip.

She would never know it, but for the first time in his forty-two year career, Wally Gimbel had breached the confidentiality of one of his reporters.

※

Eve didn't care for the view from her room in the Capitol Hill Hotel. However, it was the only decent hotel with a vacancy within driving distance to the DC Jail. But when Ornette Small met her in the hotel lobby her spirits were lifted. Ornette was a tall, heavy-set black man, built like a linebacker with the face of a choir boy. He wore a pin-striped grey suit and spoke in a hurry with a Brooklyn accent.

"Ms. Noon." He shook her hand briskly. "I just talked to Will. Considering his situation, he's holding up well."

She led him to a quiet corner where they sat on two chairs separated by a round side table. "Did they beat him?"

"Nothing he couldn't handle." He glanced away, then added, "He's fine. In a cell with another white male. A stool, I imagine. Playing tit-for-tat. He confessed to his crimes — supposedly a double homicide — to try to get Will to do the same. I cautioned him."

Eve nodded. It meant the Feds were reaching for any ploy that might incriminate him. A sign of desperation.

"I heard you were a cop with the SFPD."

"Ancient history. Did you tell him I'm here?"

"He knows."

"Can you get me in to see him?"

He shook his head. "You know how it works. But look." He leaned forward, set his thick forearms on his thighs and low-

238

ered his voice. "Against all odds, there's a good chance he won't go to trial. I might even be able to pull him out of jail."

"Really? Someone's accused of assassinating a senator and walks?" Her lips curled as if she might spit. "In this country?"

"Ain't it great? Can't accuse *me* of being a cynic." He smiled. Flawless white teeth, rosy-pink gums. Beautiful. "We've got the audio recording of Will's interview. And we have this video from *Stand Up 4 Justice*. A phone app designed for exactly this situation. I asked Wally Gimbel to publish both of them immediately. The media's all over it."

"I've heard them both." Eve guessed that after Wally emailed her the files he decided he had only one option: release the recordings to everyone. Smart. "There's one part, after he discloses he's got Parkinson's Disease when the senator says, 'Pull the trigger. Please.' That should get some airplay."

"It's the top sound bite every ten minutes. CNN won't let it go. They're pit bulls when it comes to one of their own."

"So can you spring him?"

"The firm's mounted a full-court press to get him in front of a judge for a preliminary hearing tomorrow morning." He rolled his head as if he had to work out a kink in his neck.

"And until then?"

"We'll spend every minute to prep for the judge." He stood up and glanced around the lobby, scanning for informers. "In the meantime, don't tell anyone you're in D.C. If we get him out, I want to bring him here. Did you book a room in your name?"

"No. Alice Shaw."

"Good. Once he's here, wait a day or two before you go

back to Frisco. Cover your tracks. And one more thing." His voice dropped to a whisper.

"Yes?"

"Will said you should check the second concrete flower planter outside the senator's building."

A blank look crossed her face. "The second flower planter?"

"The second one from the front door of the Washington Harbor building on K Street. And by the way, I never told you that."

※

By the time Eve stepped out of the taxi onto the brick mall leading to the Washington Harbor building, the Georgetown crowds were strolling the streets, searching out late-night diversions and entertainment. It was almost eleven o'clock but a burdensome humidity still hung in the air and the scent of decay rose from the bank of the river. Rotting fish? Seaweed stewing in the sun all day? She couldn't tell the difference.

She calculated that whatever Will had left for her in the concrete flower planter had been waiting for her for almost twenty-four hours. A sense of urgency filled her mind as she approached the four receptacles. They were perfect hemi-spheres, perhaps three feet in diameter, each one set on a flat bottom. All four brimmed with masses of mixed bedding plants: petunias, geraniums, fuchsias. She was pleased to see that they hadn't been watered for a day or two.

As she walked past each pot she scanned them for anything unusual. She lingered at the second flowerpot, hoping to dis-cover something obvious: his discarded phone or wallet, maybe a note. Nothing. After her first pass, she sat on a bench near the building entrance and studied the scene. Despite the senator's "assassination" earlier that morning, no cops were visible. Nor could she detect any sign of Witowsky or Malinin, who might have tracked her to Washington. A few tourists sauntered past on their way to the riverfront. Two couples dressed for a night at the symphony or opera returned to the building, entered their access codes on the exterior keypad and disappeared into the elegant interior. The senator would have had little to fear living here, she mused. Except for his suicidal impulses.

Assured that she wasn't being monitored, Eve approached the second receptacle again, set her bag on the ground and began to sift through the flowers spilling over the concrete lip.

"Can I help you miss?"

She glanced over her shoulder to see a uniformed man standing between her and the building entrance.

"No, thanks." She continued her search, now separating each plant from its neighbor with her hands, pressing her nose into the buds as if she might be assessing the scent of each flower.

She heard the man approach. "I'm sorry, but these planters are property of Washington Harbor."

"Are they?" She stood up and turned to face him, a puzzled expression on her face. He appeared to be about twenty or twenty-one. Most likely a college kid working his shift at a part-time job. "Are you the concierge?"

"Assistant concierge." He smiled, at ease now that they'd established a conversation. Perhaps the head man had sent him out here to see what Eve was doing and shoo her away.

"Well maybe you *can* help me." She smiled and arched her back a little and half-turned to the planter. "My sister lost a really valuable earring here last night. She thinks it must have fallen into one of these pots!" She let out a laugh, a note suggesting how absurd her sister could be. And so typical of her. "Can you look at that first one?" She pushed a hand through her hair and pointed to the planter nearest the front door.

"Happy to, ma'am. What kind of earring is it?"

"Pearl," she said. "A tiny black pearl. Size of your little toenail." She considered shaking his hand and telling him not to call her ma'am, then thought better of it and returned to her search.

A moment later the front door swung open again. Another uniformed man took a step forward. "Dirk, what're you doing out there?" His voice carried the suspicion that however Dirk might reply, his answer would be ludicrous.

"Sorry, Mr. Wayburn. This lady's sister lost a black pearl earring here last night."

"Black pearl?" He paused to consider this.

Eve glanced at Mr. Wayburn. He wore a cap over his bald skull. "Are you the concierge?"

"Yes, ma'am."

She smiled again. "Could you have a look through the third planter, over here? I know Alice will be so upset if we don't find her earring."

Wayburn stepped over to the third vessel and began to sweep the plants with his gloved hand. "Black pearl. I never heard of a black pearl."

"It's very rare," Dirk said, his nose hovering above the

flowers. "Size of your little toenail."

Partially convinced, Wayburn pointed back to the doorway and said, "Go get Pinky out here. Have him search through that last planter."

Dirk returned with another uniformed employee and together they continued the search for the missing black pearl earring.

Seconds later Eve spotted the SD card. She knew in an instant what it had to contain. She pressed it between her thumb and finger, peeked at her helpers and slipped it into her pocket.

Her next impulse was to call off the search, apologize for wasting their time and make her way back to the Capitol Hill Hotel. Instead, she decided to continue the charade for another five or ten minutes before giving up with a gasp of exasperation. Life is too short, she told herself. Enjoy the moment. After all, how often do you come across three young, uniformed men bent over to serve your whims?

CHAPTER SIXTEEN

FOUR DAYS LATER — after his appearance in court on Friday, a long wait through the weekend and a second appearance on Monday afternoon to hear the judge's "considered opinion" to conclude the preliminary hearing — Finch collected his wallet, phone, laptop and courier bag and passed through the final security screen in the DC Jail. He took a moment to look through his wallet. A pleasant surprise: every dollar accounted for. On the other side of the steel door he was joined by Ornette Small.

Will shook his lawyer's hand. "Thanks, Ornette. I can't believe I'm walking out of here."

"Nobody can." Ornette said.

"I went from 'confined without bail' to 'get out of jail free.' Who's pulling the strings?" The shock of sunlight blinded him and he held up a hand to shade his eyes.

"The Parson brothers. Must be nice to work for a company that's all heart."

Finch smiled. "I'd really like to believe that. But they know I'm more valuable to them outside a jail cell writing this story for the *eXpress.*"

"Yeah. I guess this is going to sell a truckload of ads."

As the guard turned away and left them standing on D Street, a crowd of photographers rushed toward them. Ornette held out his arm to shield Finch from the throng of reporters. "Don't say a word. I'll handle the press."

Finch smiled at the thought. As if he'd break this story to the ravenous mob. No, this one I keep for myself.

Ornette guided him to a black Lincoln waiting at the curb, opened the back door to let Finch slip onto the seat. Then he turned and faced the cameras.

"As you know William Finch has been released unconditionally. The arguments supporting his release are incontrovertible. I'll give you a brief statement but I won't answer any questions," he announced. "First, I'd like to congratulate the presiding judge, Michael Stenopolous, for having the courage to embrace the irrefutable facts presented to him in the preliminary hearing last Friday and again today. Second, based on the recorded evidence at the time of and preceding the senator's death, it's a sad but undeniable fact that Senator Franklin Whitelaw committed suicide in the presence of Mr. Finch using a weapon registered in the senator's name. And finally, this is the time for us to mourn the loss of one of our most prolific senators in recent decades. While he achieved great legislative victories, he suffered greatly, too. Not only did he suffer a string of recent tragedies in his family, but he endured the increasing debilitation of Parkinson's Disease with stoic bravery. The world would be a better place if more citizens lived his example."

Will heard the collective outcry from the reporters as Ornette declined to answer their questions. The lawyer smiled, waved a hand to the cameras, squeezed into the back seat beside Will and closed the door.

As they drove through the city, Ornette instructed the driver to employ an evasive route which led them through several bypasses and tunnels before they arrived at the Capitol Hill Hotel. When they reached C Street the car pulled up to the curb. The door lock beside Finch popped open.

"Two things, Will." Ornette clasped Finch's forearm to hold him in place. "One, don't trust your phone or laptop. These days the surveillance technology is just too good. You're better off having a pro destroy them and buying new gear. Second, hang in a day or two before you fly back to Frisco. Order room service. Watch some Netflix on the tube. Let things cool down."

"Good idea." Finch said. "Do me a favor and tell Wally that I'll be off the grid for a few days," He pressed two fingers to the swollen cheek on his bruised face. "Besides, I can use a break. And listen, I owe you big time."

"Yeah, you do." Ornette released a deep laugh. "Next time I'm out your way, you and Eve are taking me and Hennessy to dinner. Five-course meal. Ball-busting expensive."

Will laughed. Nice to know someone as hard working as Ornette had someone to love. "You got it," he said and eased out of the Lincoln.

He walked into the hotel lobby, stopped in at the florist shop for a dozen roses, picked up a box of Callebaut dark chocolate and asked the receptionist for Alice Shaw's room number. Seventy-seven. As he made his way down the corridor, he thought, wouldn't you know it. A pair of sevens. Lucky as they come.

※

"I had four days to think. For the first time since I checked out of Eden Veil, I sat back and considered where this is going." Finch pulled himself up in the bed and stirred his hand as if he could be mixing a pot of stew.

"That's where you went to dry out after Buddy died?" Eve drew the bed sheet over her breasts, leaned on an elbow, and kissed his bare shoulder.

He blinked and stared through the window. "Mostly he was all I could think about. About how I should have taken the car keys away from Bethany. If I'd done that, he'd still be alive."

"That's magical thinking, Will." She brushed a finger over the bruise on his cheek. "Go down that rabbit hole and you might never come back."

"I know." He studied her face and when she didn't turn away he looked into her eyes. She drew him in and they stayed there a moment, in a place deep and alive. Finally he glanced away.

"Whitelaw said something to me just before he shot himself."

"Yeah?"

"It's so strange, because I wondered why I didn't take the gun away from him. He stood this close to me." He held a hand in the air. "Just holding the gun. Backwards, the barrel pressed to his heart."

She drew two pillows under her head and listened to him.

"I mean, why didn't I just knock the pistol out of his

hand?" He searched her face as if she might be withholding the answer.

"So ... why?"

"Because of what he said. Just ten seconds before he did it. He said I *chose* to attack his family so I could get past what happened to Cecily and Buddy. It hit me like a brick. I froze. I couldn't do anything, let alone take his gun. Then he said *he'd chosen me*. He planned the whole thing. That's why he agreed to do the interview."

"So he could have some perverse kind of revenge."

"Yeah." He nodded. "Exactly."

He thought about revenge. Where it could take you, how it hurt you.

"You don't have to say more if you don't want to." She studied the cuts and bruises on his face. "On the other hand, you can tell me as much as you want."

He shrugged and felt an urge to have sex again. Long, deep, animal sex that would take his mind away from the precipice he'd been walking along for almost two months.

"And it doesn't have to be just now."

"What do you mean?"

"It could be tomorrow. The next day, even next year. You can tell me anything, Will. Any time."

He leaned over and kissed her mouth.

"Hold that thought," she whispered. "I'll be right back after I shower."

She let the sheet fall away, pulled herself from the bed and tip-toed into the bathroom.

Finch drifted in the haze of his confusion and memories,

his longing and exhaustion. He could easily sleep for another hour, but no, he decided, he would wait for this woman who loved him so completely and let their instincts carry them through the night, into some far-off zone of unconsciousness where he could hide for another day.

※

"Once we get home it starts all over again, you know."

"By *it* you mean Witowsky."

"And Malinin."

"Then maybe we should just stay here."

A laugh. "How many more times can you make love?"

"I don't know. A little more, I think."

They kissed.

"You won't get bored?"

"Maybe after a hundred times."

"A hundred?" Another laugh. "That's *all* it would take you?"

"It's not the loving that wears me down, darling. It's the room service."

They gazed at the stack of dinner trays piled on the desk.

"And the soap."

"The soap? Hell, it's the shampoo driving me crazy."

He nodded. She grinned.

"So. Maybe it's time to move on."

"We'd have to get dressed, first."

"Dressed? Then forget it. We're not leaving."

※

They took the bus to Philadelphia, then a taxi to the airport where they booked tickets on the next flight to San Francisco.

To avoid any digital tracking by Malinin or Witowsky, they paid their fares in cash.

"But the Feds could be on our trail as soon as we register our boarding passes," Finch said as they considered their options in the airport Starbucks outlet.

"Just as well. We'll need them at some point. The sooner the better."

But Finch wasn't convinced. Eve believed that the FBI had probably issued a warrant for her arrest by now. Her lawyer had successfully delayed the federal subpoena for the GIGcoin software and keys over the weekend but on Monday, the Feds won their court order and demanded that Eve turn over the property immediately. Fran Bransome explained to them that she'd tried and failed to contact Eve and had no idea where she might be. Indeed, Eve had removed the SIM card from her phone and turned it off. On her laptop, she read the incoming email from her lawyer, but she refused to reply to anything. Finch had also disabled his phone. While he could read the incoming messages from Wally, Fiona and Ornette Small, he set them aside, content to know that his allies were working on his behalf back home.

But moments before their departure from Philadelphia, a new message appeared from Fiona.

Will, not sure if you're rec'ing email, but hope you get this. I just got a call from the hospital. Toby Squire is out of his coma. Apparently he's coherent, but no one will say more. Cops will interview him ASAP. I put in an interview request, but told not to hold my breath. Will send more info when I get it. Take care. F.

"Another surprise," Finch said and passed his laptop to Eve so she could read the news herself.

A gaunt look fell over her face as she handed the computer back to him. "Incredible. Somehow I'd convinced myself I'd never have to deal with him again."

"Don't worry," he said as they entered the departure line-up. "You never will. Toby Squire will be locked up with the criminally insane for a very long time."

"You think so?" A shudder rippled through her shoulders.

"Count on it. Believe me: Squire is toast."

※

During the flight they tried to plan their next moves. Since only Eve possessed the functional software and keys, they knew they were vulnerable. Perhaps now more than ever. Both Malinin and Witowsky had killed to further their ambitions. Nothing suggested that Eve and Finch would be spared. As a result every possible course of action they considered seemed doomed.

"Who do you think is worse, Malinin or Witowsky?" Finch put this out as a rhetorical joke, something to lighten their mood as they soared over the Rocky Mountains on the cloudless, crystal-clear flight path.

"Depends." She shrugged. "One's a cobra, the other a weasel."

"True enough." He looked away and then turned back to her. "We do have another choice, you know."

"What?"

251

"Something else the senator said. With the software and both keys there's nothing to stop us from launching GIGcoin on our own."

"No?" A doubtful expression crossed her face. "You think that will ward off Witowsky? And Malinin?"

"No." He shrugged. "I was just checking."

"Checking what?"

"To see if you'd cross over."

She laughed, a gasp of surprise. "Really?"

"No."

"You sure?"

"Of course not."

"Good." She took his hand and set it in her lap. Then she pulled a blanket up to her shoulders and closed her eyes. Minutes later she fell into an uneasy sleep.

Will let his eyes settle on the mountains below and drifted in the weightless bubble of his imagination. He tried to envision a way forward, as if he could find a passageway that no one else could see, a hidden escape hatch that would lead him and Eve to safety. As they approached the coast he realized their current strategy was strictly defensive: wait for Witowsky and Malinin to strike them separately and fend them off one at a time until Lavigne and Sterne and a swat team of FBI black shirts rode to the rescue. A fool's fantasy.

Then a new idea struck him. He nudged Eve. She turned her head and opened her eyes.

"Why should we wait for them?"

"Malinin and Witowsky? What's the alternative?"

"We go after them."

"Cowboy Willie." She shook her head with amusement. "That Texan who smacked you toughened your cojones, huh?"

He sneered and glanced away.

"Sorry." Her voice softened. "That was uncalled for."

"Forget it."

She set a hand on his arm and drew his attention away from the window. "So. What do you propose?"

"We do it right after we land." He narrowed his eyes as he spoke. "You call Witowsky."

"What? The guy's gone AWOL and the IAD want to put him in San Quentin. You think he's going to pick up the phone and chat?"

"No. He and Malinin are doing exactly what we did for the past five days: monitoring whatever comes their way. You leave him a voice message. Tell him we'll meet him in front of the TIX booth in Union Square."

"Witowsky first?"

"Witowsky first. Then I'll call Malinin."

"You've got his number?"

"He gave it to me in Honolulu."

She took a moment to consider this. "Then what?"

"Who knows? But when you toss a cobra in a cage with a weasel, something crazy is bound to happen."

CHAPTER SEVENTEEN

UNION SQUARE BUSTLED with throngs of tourists. A troupe of French acrobats performed a series of flips and circus tricks on the north-side stage. An all-girl cheerleading squad dressed in cotton pull-overs and pleated skirts loitered in front of the Apple Store while their chaperones conducted a headcount. A crammed cable car clanged its bells as it chugged up the hill along Powell Street. A queue of twenty or thirty people stood in front of the TIX Booth to purchase half-price deals for musicals and plays. In other words, San Francisco was in full swing.

In the midst of the tumult Will and Eve settled next to the planter beside the ticket office. As he scanned the crowds, Finch couldn't detect any sign of Lavigne or Sterne or any other FBI operatives. Maybe they hadn't tracked his movements after all. And maybe they hadn't traced Eve's voice message to Witowsky.

"Looks like he's a no-show," Eve said as if she might be doubting their earlier decision to confront him.

"Give him time."

A moment later a latino boy toting a skateboard by its wheels stopped in front of Eve.

"Are you waiting for Mr. W?"

"Mr. W?" She glanced at Finch. "Yeah. I guess I am."

"He said to follow me." His voice was soft, pre-adolescent.

The boy led them across Powell along Post Street down to the First Congressional Church, a classic gothic structure wedged onto a corner in the surrounding commercial district.

"Up here." His skateboard clattered on the steps as he brought them through the arched entrance into the solitude of the nave, down a side aisle to a set of stairs that led to matched wooden doors.

"Through here." He pointed at the doors.

"Here?" Will scanned the room. He sensed they were being misdirected. "These doors lead back onto the street."

"Go through the door." He brushed a strand of hair from his forehead and pulled back a step. When Finch and Eve hesitated, he added, "He's in the white Taurus."

"What's your name?"

"Jorge."

Eve nodded as if she were sorting out a puzzle. "How much did Mr. W pay you, Jorge?"

He held up a twenty dollar bill and turned away.

"Wait." Eve called him back and waved another twenty under his chin. "Jorge, this is yours if you sneak out the front door and write Mr. W's license number on this slip of paper."

In her free hand she held a scrap of paper and a pen. The boy made a grab for the money but she quickly drew her wrist away.

"Uh-uh. License number first."

He considered the offer a moment, then took the paper and

pen and sauntered toward the front door.

"And don't let Mr. W see you," she called after him.

Moments later Jorge returned with the paper and pen in hand. She examined the note, nodded her head and passed him the twenty. "Now listen, Jorge. You buy some decent food with that. And give it to your mother. All right?"

He smirked and narrowed his eyes. "Don't got a mother." His voice cracked on the word mother. He folded the cash into his front pocket, turned and ran back through the nave. A moment later they heard the thud of the oak door as it slammed shut.

"Poor kid." Finch shrugged and turned his attention to the slip of paper. "I wonder if this's really Witowsky's number."

"Me too." She took out her cell, tapped the number Agent Sterne had entered on her phone, and waited while his message service cut in. "Agent Sterne, this is Eve Noon. This is an emergency 10-33. Will Finch and I are in the First Congressional Church on the corner of Post and Mason. We're about to join Damian Witowsky in a white Ford Taurus, license number 7MIR731. We'll stall as long as possible, but I urge you to shut this down ASAP." She clicked off her phone and narrowed her eyes. All she could see was trouble ahead.

Finch put his hand on the door knob. "Ready?"

"I guess."

They stepped out the door. At the curb sat the Taurus, the right rear window rolled down an inch or two.

"Eve does the driving," Witowsky muttered from the back seat. "Finch, you're beside her. Right in front of me."

He raised the barrel of his service pistol through the lip of the window.

"Get in or I'll kill you where you stand."

✳

As Eve walked toward the Taurus she checked the license plate. Well done, she whispered to herself, the kid got it right. She paused at the door and waited for Finch to slip into the passenger seat.

The instant she settled into the car a foul smell caught her off guard. A mix of stale tobacco and cheap whiskey swept through her nostrils. She brushed her fingers over her nose and peered over the seat at the cop.

Witowsky had shaved his head and grown a rough-cut, half-inch beard that merged with his salt-and-pepper mustache. He wore a tattered leather flight jacket and a scuffed-up pair of jeans torn at the knees. An ugly man to begin with, Eve realized that he'd managed to leverage his bad looks into something almost reptilian.

"Seat belts on," he barked.

Eve and Finch pulled the restraints over their shoulders and clicked them into place.

"So, you crossed over, Witowsky." Eve turned her head to the rear seat.

"No more bullshit, Eve. Everyone had enough of that from you for five God-damned years. Now pass me that .38 Cobra you keep next to the hankies in your purse."

"What?"

Witowsky back-handed the butt of his gun against Finch's head. He yelped in pain and tried to wrench forward out of Witowsky's reach, but the cop was too fast for him. He looped a steel cord around Will's throat and tugged him backward. Finch gasped in panic as he tried to wriggle his fingers under the wire. Witowsky crossed the ends of the garrote behind Finch's neck, then snugged the cord securely behind the head rest and locked both ends of the garrote to a stay that Eve couldn't see. Then he wedged an inch-thick wood dowel into the cable loop and gave it a turn. With his victim pinned in place he tested the tension, then let out enough slack so that Finch could breathe. Finch sat bolt-upright, wheezing for air, his neck clamped against the head rest. His face began to throb as the blood pressure in his head spiked.

"What the fuck!" Eve lashed at Witowsky's face with a backhand that didn't connect.

"Do *not* screw around with me, Eve. Otherwise I tighten the line one turn at a time." His voice had an unbalanced, angry tone. He pointed his pistol at her forehead. "Now hand me that .38."

She handed him her pistol and set her hands on the steering wheel.

He pushed her gun into his jacket pocket. "And now your cellphones."

She drew her cellphone from her purse and handed it over the seat.

"Don't forget Clark Kent."

She paused to figure out what Witowsky meant, then tugged Will's phone from his jacket and passed it to Witowsky.

"Start the car."

Eve had to try the ignition three times before the engine caught. "All right Witowsky. Your move. Where're we going?"

"To wherever you stashed Toeplitz's bitcoin wallet." He smashed the glass plate of each phone with the butt of his pistol, yanked out the SIM cards, opened his window and threw the shattered phones and cards onto the asphalt.

She shrugged and looked at Finch. His face had inflated with blood as if his head was about to explode. He gasped horribly as his fingers struggled to relieve the tension on the wire. "Take a turn off the garrote, Witowsky. My condo's in Little Russia. In this traffic, it'll take half an hour."

"Drive."

"Up yours! I'm not driving anywhere!" She cut the ignition. "I hit one pot hole with Will strung up like that and it'll kill him. Now back that thing off or you can shoot us both right now!"

Witowsky studied her face through the rearview mirror. He held the gun in one hand, the wooden dowel with his other. He bit into his lower lip.

Eve could sense his indecision. "Look, kill us now and you get nothing. But take that wire down a notch and you'll have the bitcoin wallet before noon."

She could hear Finch breathing in short, tight puffs trying to restrain the panic flooding through his body. She gasped as she considered their situation. Marat had been shot. Sochi died from ricin poison. And now came the garrote. Three ways to die. Of the three, this had to be the worst.

She turned her attention to Witowsky. "Think about it, Witowsky. How much longer can you dodge the Feds? Sure, you're clever, but not that good. Once you have Toeplitz's flash drive you can exchange the bitcoin for cash in ten minutes. You can be in Mexico for dinner. A millionaire."

"Shut up, Eve." He set his gun on the bench seat and loosened the garrote by a half rotation.

Finch gasped in relief and gulped down a lungful of air. His hands swept over his throat and he slipped his fingers under the wire on each side of his larynx. After a moment, the color in his face blanched slightly and he wheezed in wet sobs until his breathing stabilized.

"Now drive."

Eve started the Taurus again and brought the car onto Geary. The traffic bottlenecked through a construction zone between Leavenworth and Hyde Streets, a delay that she welcomed in hope that Sterne and Lavigne could catch their trail. Maybe, but she knew she couldn't count on them. Better to engage Witowsky, try to talk him out of his lunacy. After all, she'd managed to get him to loosen the garrote.

"I thought this was all about GIGcoin," she said over her shoulder. "But now you just want Toeplitz's bitcoin wallet?"

"Plan B, Eve." He snorted with disgust. "After you two shit in my drinking water."

"What?" She studied him in the mirror, wondered if he'd truly lost his mind. "I don't get that."

"No. You wouldn't." He leaned forward to inspect the garrote. Satisfied, he shifted the pistol to his right hand and continued. "After Clark Kent here shot the senator and exposed Malinin as a co-conspirator, GIGcoin became a lame duck. Instant poison. GIGcoin only had value when it was in mint condition. But with the media storm he caused" — he thumped the back of Finch's seat — "GIGcoin is dead."

She glanced at Finch. The color in his bruised face seemed to ebb between various hues of red. His breathing had stabilized but he still held his fingers under the wire at the front of his throat. When he saw her looking at him, he blinked with both eyes. *Go on.*

"So your first idea was what? To secure the GIGcoin software and sell it back to the cartel? Or maybe just one of the keys. That's all it would take, right?"

Witowsky snorted as if he couldn't believe it himself. "Why not? They had the play all lined up. High-profile politicians, oligarchs, the international bank, the technical know-how, the name, the patent. Everything but the software itself. And the keys, of course."

"So you were going to run a money swap. Trade one of the keys for cash."

He mulled this over as if he was considering how much to reveal. "All right. Yeah, that was the play. Came to me when I started an investigation of Toeplitz's estate. You know, dug into the digital side. I got one of our tech geeks to case all of Toeplitz's files. Incredible what that guy did."

"Toeplitz?" Eve guided the car into the right lane and coasted behind a bus. She had to keep him talking. The longer, the better. "Yeah. Everyone says he was some kind of Einstein."

"He built GIGcoin based on the bitcoin system with a few sexy layers added for the banker set." He raked his fingernails over the scrap of his beard and studied the stalled traffic. "Then I recalled the bitcoin ripoff in February 2014."

"I know. It was huge." She glanced at Finch, who'd settled into a trance-like daze, his fingers still curled under the front of the wire.

"Huge? Try four-hundred and fifty million dollars worth of huge. It's only worth a third of that now. But still...." He exhaled with a snort of amazement. "Think about it. Who is the one person with the savvy to pull that off and get away without leaving a trace?"

"You think Toeplitz?"

"Tell me something, Eve. Have you even opened his bit-coin wallet?"

She tried to think where this could go. Did Witowsky know the flash drive was password protected? That Sochi had spent days cracking the code? More important, that the password was written on a sticky note she'd stashed in Will's apartment back in Russian Hill. She realized that he had no more chance of opening the bitcoin wallet on his own than surviving a month in San Quentin.

"You know, I haven't," she confessed. "It's true. No joke."

Another snort of surprise. "Well then, you're even dumber than your tits, Eve. And God knows, they fooled a lot of guys over the years."

Eve set her jaw and tightened her grip on the wheel as a string of tourist busses heading west of Divisadero blocked their lane. Once again Witowsky had managed to slither under her skin. The sooner she brought this to an end, the better. Still, she knew she had to continue drawing him out of this madness.

"So why'd you cross over?"

He waited a moment, as if he wasn't sure how to explain his motivation. "Just like you I guess. No future in the SFPD."

"Sure, I get that. But what was the trigger?" She studied

him in the mirror. "I heard rumors that IAD is investigating you."

He ignored this.

"Maybe when they discovered that you were playing Justin Whitelaw for a piece of GIGcoin. You know the forensics lab found your prints on a brandy snifter in Justin's walk-up in Claude Lane. Were you there before or after he kidnapped Fiona Paige?"

When Witowsky didn't respond Eve decided to keep the pressure on.

"Or was it when IAD realized you shot Marat in Honolulu — was that it?"

"That Russian geek? You're dreaming in three-D."

"Am I?" She knew she had him. Now to set the hook with a small white lie. "Did you know a kid from Punahou School filmed the whole thing on his phone? Did you know that?"

He growled with a low snarl.

"Let me tell you what happened. The whole thing. When you realized that Justin kidnapped that reporter, you decided to step in. In exchange for getting the second GIGcoin key from his father, you promised to protect Justin from the kidnapping charges. That's why you stalled the investigation. Why you took a week to interview Will."

"Pfff." He spit into the footwell behind Eve.

"But when Justin dove in front of the subway train, the game changed completely. You knew there'd be no way to shut down the press. Fiona was standing in front of him when Justin killed himself. And with Justin gone you lost your leverage to get the senator's key. Suddenly your game plan collapsed."

"You are so far out of touch you've gone psychotic, Eve."

"Am I?" She tightened her grip on the steering wheel and pressed on. "So instead of working your way to the software through Justin, now you had to make an end run and grab the software and keys on your own. When you discovered I was meeting Malinin, you saw your opportunity."

Witowsky let out a burp. "You are one cute bitch. You know that?"

"I still wonder how long it took you to realize that the copy of GIGcoin software on Malinin's computer was spiked." She glanced in the rearview mirror to study his face before she continued. "But whenever the truth hit you, it was too late to cross back, wasn't it? IAD had your number and all you could do was move into the shadows. Then you thought of Toeplitz's bitcoin wallet." She paused again. "What makes you think it isn't spiked, too?"

"Enough! *Not another word, bitch!*"

He smacked the barrel of his pistol into Finch's ear. Finch yelped as he pulled his left hand away from the garrote and held it to the side of his head.

"All right!" she screamed. "Lay off!"

She pulled the Taurus into a parking slot in front of her condo.

"We're here for God's sake. Now let Will go and tell me your next move, Witowsky."

※

Eve led the way up the staircase from the street landing to her condo. Finch followed, his neck still cinched in the garrote which Witowsky held by the dowel in his fist. In his right hand he carried his SIG Sauer P228. He kept the gun pointed at Eve's back, and when she slipped the key into the door lock, Witowsky stepped past Finch and held the gun to her throat.

"Slowly, now. I'd hate to trip and have this thing go off by mistake."

As she eased the door open it squeaked with the familiar whine that had set her nerves on edge for months. She glanced at the open window. The curtain fluttered in the on-shore breeze.

In the big armchair next to the bookcase sat Alexei Malinin. His face rose from an open book as if he might have been sitting here for hours, distracting himself with a crime novel while he waited for Eve to arrive. He held a pistol in his lap and when he heard the murmuring behind Eve, he raised the gun and pointed it in her direction without taking precise aim.

Witowsky pushed into the room behind her and tugged Finch along by the arm. "Who the hell are you?"

"An invited guest. Which I think is more than I can say for you."

Witowsky narrowed his eyes as he glanced at Eve. "Is this some kind of setup?"

When no one replied, he pushed Finch a step forward and wrapped the fingers of his left hand around the dowel. He leveled his gun at Malinin. He studied the Russian for a moment, then a shock of recognition passed over his face. "Alexei Malinin. A lot of people are looking for you."

"And you are?"

"Damian Witowsky," Eve announced and took a step to one side.

"Ah, yes." Malinin let out a long sigh. "I believe some people are seeking you, too." A frown turned his mouth in a grimace. "With regards to my nephew."

Witowsky glanced around the room as if he were being pranked. "Who?"

"My brother's son. Marat Malinin."

Eve took another step toward the bathroom door. She glanced inside and saw a shadow move in the darkness. An arm slipped forward. A hand poised in the air. Was it Kirill?

"I should shoot you now," Witowsky hissed at Malinin.

"If you did, you'd regret it," he said with equanimity. "Kirill, please."

The big Russian stepped out of the bathroom past Eve, a forty-four caliber Magnum stuck in his fist and pointed at Witowsky's head.

The cop glanced at Kirill, swung his pistol around and fixed Eve in his sights. "Try anything and the girl goes. Then you never get the software."

For the first time Malinin hesitated. Witowsky's gambit seemed to have some merit. "That would be a shame," he conceded, "but at least Marat would be avenged."

Dots of perspiration oozed from Witowsky's forehead. He turned his gun toward Kirill and at the same time he released his hold on Finch. Finch took a step toward Eve, stumbled and collapsed on the floor wheezing as his hands struggled to untie the garrote from the back of his neck.

Witowsky stood about six feet from Kirill. Both men had their arms raised, the guns poised to fire point-blank at one another. Eve took a step toward Finch, then hesitated. Will finally unknotted the garrote and threw the wire across the carpet with a loud gasp. Malinin, meanwhile, sat in the easy chair, his pistol leveled at Witowsky, the book now closed in his lap. Since he and Kirill had Witowsky aligned in a cross fire, his mood brightened. His face radiated a calm glow.

"Detective Witowsky. Yes, I've done my homework, as you Americans like to say. What still puzzles me, and what I'd like to know, is why you shot Marat. Surely you could have simply put your pistol in his face and stolen his laptop. He would never resist. He was a skinny kid, ill with cirrhosis of the liver. I always told him: 'Don't resist. Just give the perps what they want and live another day.' "

Witowsky tightened his grip on his P228 and stared into Kirill's eyes as if he were trying to solve a problem whose answer lay behind Kirill's inscrutable gaze.

"Please enlighten me," Malinin continued. "What kind of man does this?"

"Shut the fuck up," Witowsky whispered. The glow on his face had broken into a dewy sweat. He wiped the back of his free hand over his eyes and blinked.

"Is he a man or — "

The room exploded with the crack of both pistols. Kirill slumped backwards against the bathroom door jam, rolled to the side and buckled at Eve's feet where she could see the clean, surgical perforation through the Russian's forehead. The shock sent her sideways and she slumped along the wall and fell parallel to Finch. Witowsky, driven backwards by the immense force of the Magnum, flew to the near side of the sofa. He bounced backwards and fell face-up beside Finch's legs, his pistol dangling from his fingers.

"Blyad!" Malinin gripped his left hand. The bullet from the Magnum had ricochetted and sliced across his ring finger. He pulled himself up from the chair, tugged a handkerchief from his pocket and wrapped it around the wound. His face winced in pain as he stood above Witowsky. He studied the gaping gash in Witowsky's throat and watched his blood pulse onto the floor. Satisfied that the cop was helpless, Malinin kicked Witowsky's gun away with the toe of his shoe. Then he held his pistol two feet from Witowsky's head and fired a single bullet through his temple.

"Now we know what kind of man you are." He spat on Witowsky's face. "A dead one."

He walked over to Kirill and carefully inspected the circular wound above his left eye. It oozed a trickle of dark blood across his cheek. Malinin shook his head with a look of weary regret.

"Do svidaniya staryy drug," he murmured and turned to Eve.

She pulled herself up from the floor and braced herself against the wall.

"Now dear girl, I believe you have something I want." He clamped his wounded finger in the ball of his fist to ease the pain.

Unable to speak, she nodded. She glanced at Finch, hoping he might still be conscious.

"Let's be smart, Miss Noon. There's no need for any more of this." He waved his pistol at the two corpses on the floor behind him. "I want the original software from Toeplitz, the one which Sochi did not spike. And I want the key which you acquired from Whitelaw."

"The key from Whitelaw?"

"Do not toy with me, girl. I am an old hunter. You would not have set up this elaborate trap without sufficient bait." He pointed the gun at her and clenched his jaw.

She nodded. What was it Malinin had told Marat? Do not resist. Live for another day.

"In the heat of battle it's easy to become impetuous," he continued. "But the battle is now over. Simply give me the software and the second key and I will depart. In one minute this will be over."

Eve drew a hand over her face and nodded again. "I have the second key here." She pulled the SD card from her pocket.

"And the other?"

She stumbled to the far side of the living room, to the air vent on the floor and swung her hand toward the metal grill. "The flash drive is in a box."

He tightened the bloodstained handkerchief on his injured hand. "Good. A good place for it. Now pass them to me."

Eve gave him the SD card and then knelt at the vent and pried at one edge with her fingers. She remembered the tight fit, the metal-on-metal friction. "I need a knife from the drawer." She tipped her head toward the kitchen.

Malinin shook his head doubtfully. "A small one."

She considered her odds and didn't like them at all. *Do not resist.* She selected a butter knife and returned to the vent.

As she crossed the floor she saw Finch blink. His eyes followed her. His head turned. His hand flexed.

A moment later Eve pulled the small box from the vent. Squatting on the floor, she looked up at Malinin. For the first time he revealed something that might resemble an emotion. Anticipation.

"Open it and give the flash drive to me." He made a sideways gesture with his gun.

Behind Malinin, Finch stirred. His hand crept over Witowsky's flight jacket, patted the blood-soaked leather with his hand.

Eve passed the thumb drive to Malinin.

When the Russian held the card and the flash drive together in his palm, he let out a light gasp of surprise. Perhaps he felt some long-cherished goal was now at hand and the victory was more pleasant than he'd ever imagined.

"I think, Miss Noon, that you have no idea what this is." As he held the drive between his thumb and index finger a dot of blood escaped from the handkerchief. With a light moan he carefully set the SD card and flash drive into his jacket pocket.

She knelt below him. Something told her not to stand up. Not to distract him. Better if he would just turn around and disappear down the stairs. A rabbit down the rabbit hole.

He closed, then opened his eyes, a slow-motion gesture of regret. "I'm sorry that this isn't as simple as I suggested."

She shrugged. "What?"

"No witnesses." He leveled his pistol at her forehead.

A shot rang out, then another. Malinin crashed against the window and pulled the curtain away from the wall as he fell to the floor. Finch hoisted himself up to his knees and fired a third shot into Malinin's back. Then he stood and staggered over to the Russian. Malinin's eyes fluttered. He gazed at Finch standing above him and his face registered a look of shock. Finch fired the pistol again and then once more. Two shots through the heart. The Russian choked with a loud gasp and set his eyes on the far wall. He didn't move again.

Eve stood up and peeled her gun from Finch's fingers. She realized that somehow he'd dug her .38 from Witowsky's pocket, the pistol he'd confiscated in the Taurus when the first step of their simple plan had gone so wrong.

Finch managed to walk over to the sofa and set himself onto the cushions with a loud gasp. His fingers clutched at his throat as if the garrote had finally choked him into complete submission.

"Eve," he whispered, but his larynx was so badly scarred that he couldn't utter another word.

CHAPTER EIGHTEEN

Two weeks later Will sat in his condo at the dining room table staring into the blank screen of his laptop. He was completely lost and he knew it. Rarely did he fail to answer the single question that precedes every story: where to begin? He massaged the tender scar that encircled his neck and then rubbed the clipped tip of his earlobe. The story had taken a piece of him, but at least he was still around to tell the tale. As Wally said, "Get over it. You're bent, not broken."

For a while it seemed hard to tell the difference. But when the forensic and ballistic evidence proved that Finch and Eve had acted in self defense, they were released with a warning from the SPFD Chief to give up their "self-righteous vigilantism." And after they emerged from the rounds of interrogations with Homeland Security and the FBI, the consultations with the corporate lawyers and District Attorney, Finch thought, yeah, definitely bent. Only partially broken.

A little later, Will sat down with Wally and Fiona for the now-routine debriefing that laid out a plan to tell the separate and combined stories that had gripped them since Finch drove up to Oregon to report on Toeplitz's death. It seemed like a lifetime ago.

Only one thing appeared certain. The *eXpress* would have enough exclusive material to publish right through the summer and into the early fall. Wally abandoned his earlier plan — the A to Z strategy — to flood the market and issue everything at once. His new approach called for a series of single articles that would wrap the Whitelaw chronicles into a coherent whole. Furthermore, the slow-drip approach would keep the nation waiting — "salivating," he insisted — for the next installment and build their readership into hundreds of millions.

"The sort of thing Woodward and Bernstein did with the Watergate scandal," he suggested. "One day at a time. It made their careers."

True enough, Finch thought, but Wally's analogy was imperfect. Woodward and Bernstein reported the daily unravelling of the US Presidency as it ticked forward through the excruciating process of legal inquisition. In Finch's case, he'd endured something closer to a personal war and the farther back in time he reached to retrieve the details, the more his reporting resembled a memoir. But he wasn't in the mood for an argument, much less a discussion, so he agreed to Wally's plan. As did Fiona.

Over the next three days the two reporters made a series of appearances on the national TV outlets, just enough to whet the public appetite for details.

"Teasers," Fiona called them. Now that she was a veteran news hand, everyone allowed her enough slack to handle the interviews any way she saw fit. She never took a false step.

Despite the fawning attention from the media Will had no

idea how to begin his narrative. As he sat at the table considering the possibilities for the tenth — the twentieth — time, the door swung open and Eve tossed her jacket onto the sofa.

"So. That was *not* a good meeting."

"No?" Finch closed the story file. Maybe later.

"No. Fran Bransome did her best, I'll give her that. But the FBI just confiscated the GIGcoin software and the two keys. The feds did *not* use the terms 'borrow,' 'share,' or 'lease.' It's all gone."

"The originals — or copies that Sochi cooked up?"

She sat beside him. "No, the good stuff. And by the way, no more games for me. I've decided to live my life without deceit from now on."

He laughed. She had a way of kidding herself that almost sounded convincing. "What about the estate? Can Fran prove you're the rightful owner?"

"Maybe when I'm dead." She laughed, too. "Then you can try to claim everything."

He turned his head. Had she put him in her will? Bad time to ask. "What about the bitcoin wallet?"

"That, my darling, is a different story. I still have it." She took his hand in her fingers and smiled again.

Apparently her meeting wasn't *all* bad, he thought. "You mean nobody's asked for it?"

"Not yet. Fran said that we'll have to conform with section 485 of the California Penal Code. Which means she has to publish notice that the wallet has been found. Anyone has one hundred and twenty days to claim the wallet and its contents — *if* they can identify the bitcoin value, the time of the transaction when they lost their funds and how many transactions were involved. If they can't, then according to the grants made in Gianna's and Toeplitz's estates, and the rules governing 'found money' in section 485 — any unclaimed bitcoins belong to me."

Finch chuckled. It all felt like a school yard game. "Which is how much?"

"Dunno."

"I thought you and Fran were going to open the wallet."

"Not yet. That's the next step. So. Go get the password." She lifted the flash drive in her fingers and slipped it into the USB slot on Finch's laptop.

"Which is where?"

"A place I knew I wouldn't forget." She smiled again, very pleased with her clever game. "Guess."

He shrugged.

"Bottom of your underwear drawer, Darling."

Her mood was infectious and Finch broke into an easy laughter. He went into the bedroom and retrieved the yellow sticky which Sochi had so carefully inscribed with the thirty-two character password.

"The guy had nice handwriting. A twelfth-century monk couldn't have done this," she said as she typed the code into the password box on the screen.

"There was a lot to like about Sochi."

"Yeah. There was." She waited a moment.

Finch wondered what she was thinking. He knew she'd liked Sochi well enough. They both had.

"All right, see if it works."

She tapped the enter button. A message appeared on the screen: *Enter the six-digit code from your authorized device.* Below this message the cursor blinked in the first of six blank spaces.

Eve stared at the screen. "What does this mean?"

"Hell, who knows?"

"Damn it, I can't bear any more of Toeplitz's scavenger hunts." She pushed the laptop aside and dropped her face into her hands.

Finch walked behind her to the French doors and stared into the gardens. A memory of the senator standing on his balcony, staring across the Potomac River, entered his mind. He'd been fixated by the gravestones, over four hundred thousand of them, he said. Perhaps he'd been thinking of his daughter. Then again, he didn't talk much about Gianna. Perhaps Finch missed her more than her own father. Gianna was —

He turned back to Eve. "Gianna."

She looked into his face. "What about her?"

"Her phone. Toeplitz's email to her. Remember? He said her phone 'was part of it.' He must have set up a two-step verification for the bitcoin wallet."

She raised her hands, palms up. "What?"

"The same process we used to get into Gianna's email."

"Yes. Of course."

"Where's her phone?"

She glanced around the room. "In my bag, I think."

Finch rolled his shoulders in a gesture of impatience.

"Next to the door," she said and skipped across the carpet and grabbed her purse from the chair. She opened it, clawed through the bag with one hand. "Here. I've got it."

She brandished the phone in her hand but when she clicked it, her broad smile sunk into a frown. "Shit. Dead ... just like everything else."

"Okay. None of that, all right." Will tried to infuse a tone of composure into his voice. He smiled, then beckoned with his open hand.

Eve passed the phone to him. He plugged the phone into the charger next to the radio. A moment later a ping sounded. He entered the password into her phone: g-i-a-n-n-a. A text appeared. *Enter this code to authorize your access: 545649.* He passed the phone back to Eve. "Okay. Go ahead."

She entered the digits into the verification box on the computer. The screen went blank and then filled with a cascading series of numbers aligned in three columns: Debit, Credit, Balance.

"Look at this," he whispered. "It looks like a bank account statement."

Eve stared at the screen with a growing sense of awe. "Like something Sochi might have devised. What does it all mean?"

"Check the bottom line."

Eve scrolled down to the end of the file. Current balance: 350,628 bitcoins. "Will ... how much is that in dollars?"

"Let me see." Finch took over the keyboard and googled a currency exchange program. He read aloud from the screen: "Today's exchange rate is one bitcoin equals three hundred and eighty-four dollars and ninety-two cents." He typed in the bitcoin balance from the wallet and clicked the US Dollar converter.

He blinked. Eve gasped. *Impossible.*
$134,963,729.76.

※

Finch checked the clock as he padded from the bathroom into the kitchen. 4:27. Looked like he'd slept longer than most nights, he figured. Since Kirill, Witowsky and Malinin had been shot he was lucky to snatch more than an hour of sleep at a time. Usually he'd drift off sometime after midnight, then wake up in a shock. Dead awake, he called it. The words described his condition exactly.

The rest of the night he'd either lie sleepless beside Eve, move to the living room to read (Nietzsche's *Human, All Too Human*) or sit at the table and try to write. But no matter how he distracted himself his mind always turned back to the shootings. Malinin wasn't the first man he'd killed. There'd been two others in Baghdad, during an attack that he never spoke of. Considering what he'd seen in Iraq, Malinin's death paled in comparison. But the fact that he actually knew Malinin changed things. War was one thing. Killing your personal enemy, quite another.

From that bleak realization his mind inevitably turned to Buddy. Maybe Whitelaw was right. Finch had pursued Whitelaw in order to purge his own misery over his son's death. Could it be? Was he that bent out of shape?

Maybe he should take the two-month leave that Wally proposed. Go down to Mexico. Live cheap. Write a draft of his book, find an agent who could ignite a bidding war for his story. Eve thought it made sense. But what, exactly, is "sense"? Even Nietzsche didn't seem to know.

On his way back to bed he saw the message light blink on his new phone. He waited for a second blink, picked up the Samsung and entered his password.

A text from Fiona appeared on the screen: *Around 3.45 this morning Toby Squire escaped from the SF General Hospital. SFPD aren't revealing details. I'll follow up. You may want to let Eve know. Hang in there. All the best, Fiona.*

The message jarred him out of his sleepy fog. How could Toby Squire escape? And furthermore, what was Fiona doing up at this hour? He ignored the questions and read the text a second time.

"The idiots," he whispered and turned his phone face down on the night table.

He pulled the cover from the bed and slid next to Eve's inviting body. As she rolled into his arms he could smell the aroma of their love and passion still warm on her skin. Maybe this was all the sense he needed. Maybe it was the only sense that anyone could ever find.

"What's up, Darling?" Her eyes remained closed, heavy with sleep.

"Nothing. Go back to Neverland." He kissed her cheek and pressed his nose into the length of hair falling past her shoulder and inhaled the fragrance of his new life.

"I'll tell you tomorrow," he murmured. Until then, he told himself, you're safe right here.

READ THE COMPLETE WILL FINCH TRILOGY

Bone Maker — A death in the wilderness. A woman mourns alone. A reporter works a single lead. Can Will Finch break the story of murder and massive financial fraud? Or will he become the Bone Maker's next victim?

Stone Eater — A reporter on the rebound. An ex-cop with nothing to lose. A murder they can only solve together. Sparks fly when Will Finch agrees to work with Eve Noon to uncover a murder plot. But can they unmask the Stone Eater before he destroys them both?

Lone Hunter — One billion dollars. Two killers. Three ways to die. Will Finch and Eve Noon bait the trap. But could their clever ploy trigger catastrophe when two killers battle for a billion dollar prize? Or can Will and Eve defeat their most cunning adversary yet?

ENJOY THESE OTHER NOVELS BY D. F. BAILEY

Fire Eyes — a W.H. Smith First Novel Award finalist
"Fire Eyes is a taut psychological thriller with literary overtones, a very contemporary terrorist romance."
— Globe and Mail

Healing the Dead
"You start reading Healing the Dead with a gasp and never get a proper chance to exhale."
— Globe and Mail

The Good Lie
"A tale that looks at a universal theme...that readers are going to love."
— Boulevard Magazine

Exit from America
"Another great story of moral revelation, despair and redemption by a contemporary master."
— Lawrence Russell, culturecourt.com

Made in the USA
Las Vegas, NV
08 January 2023

65251466R00166